HOW TO CON

a Crime Boss

New York Times & *USA Today* Bestselling Author

CYNTHIA EDEN

This book is a work of fiction. Any similarities to real people, places, or events are not intentional and are purely the result of coincidence. The characters, places, and events in this story are fictional.

Published by Hocus Pocus Publishing, Inc.

Copyright ©2023 by Cindy Roussos

All rights reserved. This publication may not be reproduced, distributed, or transmitted in any form without the express written consent of the author except for the use of small quotes or excerpts used in book reviews.

Copy-editing by: J. R. T. Editing

Ed. 2

CHAPTER ONE

*Step One: Appearances are everything when
you're taking a walk on the wild side.*

*People believe what they see—so be sure to give
them one hell of a show.*

"*I'm a badass.* Want to say those words with
me? You know, say them until you believe them,
and they sink into your very soul."

Seth Wellington blinked and realized that
he'd been staring into the crystal whiskey glass in
his hand for far too long. The limo cruised along,
sliding down the rain-slickened streets, and the
faint hint of seductive perfume teased the air
around him. *Her* perfume. Smelled like freaking
lilies or roses or just something beautiful. His gaze
drifted from the whiskey he hadn't tasted and
over to her.

Harley Adaire sat across from him in the limo.
One foot—adorned in a spiky, black, high heel—
swung lazily. His stare started on that foot, then
drifted slowly up the tempting expanse of her
legs—tanned, toned legs—then toward the lower
edge of the black dress that skimmed her thighs.

His breath rushed out.

Up, up, his gaze went, past the middle of the
dress that dipped at her waist, then higher as the

dark material stretched over what he suspected were truly spectacular breasts. Then, higher still, his focus shifted to the long, thick tresses of hair that spilled over her shoulders. Hair that looked completely dark now, but in the sunlight, faint red highlights could catch fire within that darkness. As he continued his perusal, Seth took in her face. The face that had been slipping into his mind far too much lately.

Right, like images of her body don't slip into my head practically nonstop.

A curving jaw. A delicate nose. Wide eyes. Not brown, not gold, either. Somewhere in the middle. Deep and so bold. When those eyes locked on you, a man felt it to his soul.

Seth sure felt her stare seeming to sink through him. While he'd been looking at her, beautiful Harley had been taking her time studying him, too. And he could clearly hear the disappointment in the sigh she expelled.

"They are going to eat you up and spit you out." A dire warning.

Seth blinked. "No, please, tell me what you really think." Talk about insulting. Way to rip into a man's ego and shred it on the pavement.

"*I* think you're GQ perfect." She waved an annoyed hand his way. "Which, honestly, you look *fine.*"

"Thanks. Your compliments are killer. Not sure if anyone has ever told you that, so just in case, do let me be the first."

"It's the attitude that is way off." She leaned forward. The top of the dress dipped. "It will be what sinks us."

His jaw locked. *Do not look at the top of her dipping dress.* "Attitude?"

"I am a badass."

"So you keep telling me." He cleared his throat and put down the whiskey. He'd originally thought a drink might help to settle his nerves, but now he realized he didn't want to go into this meeting with anything less than a completely clear head. *After all this time, I am finally so close to my goal.*

"Not me. The line isn't for me. *You.* You are the badass. You are the one who is supposed to be projecting this devil-may-care, I-can-take-on-the-world-and-burn-it-down-if-I'm-bored vibe." She made a tsk-tsk sound. Actual *tsk-tsk*. "Instead, I look at you, and the vibe I get is prep-school grad."

His shoulders stiffened.

"Ivy League player."

Seth's hand shoved through his hair.

"Bored rich kid turned equally bored—and somewhat jaded—man."

The hand that had just shoved through his hair flattened on the leather seat next to him.

"Again, they will eat you up and spit you out." She huffed out a breath. "God, you are so lucky to have me right now."

Only, he didn't have her. Not really. What he had—

"With me as your bodyguard," Harley plowed on, "you at least have a chance of coming out alive. But you *seriously* have got to listen to me. Do everything I say in there, or some very, very dangerous people—real badasses, not pretend ones like you—will realize that you are trying to scam them. Then they will dump your body in a place where it will never be found." Her lips pursed. "Actually, this *is* Louisiana. I suppose they could just drop you in a swamp. Bloody you up a bit, and then let the gators take care of everything else."

"You are an absolute ray of sunshine." He stared straight into her eyes. "And I am grateful every day for the moment we met."

Her smile came, immediately lighting her eyes to a more golden hue even as she stretched her full lips and let the dimple on the right side of her face wink teasingly at him. "You mean that poignant first moment when I tased you? Our electric initial meeting."

Yep. That moment. The one that was burned into his memory. Because the woman sitting so casually across from him—telling him that he might very well wind up as gator bait—had originally met him when she pumped who the hell knew how many volts of electricity into his body.

"In my defense," she murmured, clearly fighting her smile...as if the memory of him shuddering brought her pleasure, "I did think you were a bad guy who was running away. I believed you were a murderer. And, seriously, pro tip, innocent men shouldn't run."

He rolled back his shoulders. "They do if they are being framed."

Her fingers snapped together. "That's the whole vibe we need to recapture," Harley exclaimed. Her normally sultry voice had ramped up with excitement. "Channel the bad guy vibe you used to have."

The woman was making him crazy.

Harley gave two encouraging nods. "We want the people that we are about to meet to believe you're a murderer. And not a pampered rich kid playing at undercover work."

A muscle jerked along his jaw. "I'm not playing at anything." He was also far, far from a kid.

"Oh." She leaned forward more. Her top dipped more, too.

Dammit. He'd looked. Fuck. Fuck. Fuck.

Her tongue swiped over her plump lower lip. "Did I strike a nerve?"

Lots and lots of them. "You're working for *me*, Harley. I'm the one who gives the orders." At the time, hiring her had seemed like such a brilliant plan. The woman clearly knew how to take care of herself. After all, she worked for Wilde, the *best* security agency in the country. Or, at least, that was what Eric Wilde, the owner of the place, claimed. The company catered to the rich and famous. If you wanted discrete protection, Wilde was your go-to for service.

Because of the rather unusual situation in which Seth found himself, he'd needed some discrete protection. The kind of protection that would fly right under the radar. He was currently in a mess way, way over his head, and having a bodyguard at the ready in case things went to hell?

Excellent notion.

But the longer he was with Harley, the more he started to doubt the sheer brilliance of his plan. Instead of brilliance, he felt like it edged more and more toward madness. "Maybe I should have hired someone else."

"Why?" Her foot swung lazily. "You have the best."

"I have the one with the biggest ego, clearly." He turned his head to peer through the window. They were almost to the Garden District and their destination. "You were convenient."

Her laughter filled the back of the limo. Warm, husky, and utterly amused. "I assure you, you are the first man who has ever used that word to describe me."

"I *knew* you when I made the job offer," he continued through gritted teeth. *Harley is definitely not convenient.* A miscalculation. He'd learned that fast. "I'd seen you in action." He had. The woman could handle herself well when danger unfolded. She didn't hesitate to go after targets twice her size, and she kept an arctic cool about herself. And... "I didn't want my enemies to know I had a bodyguard at my side. I needed a confidant who could help balance the scales so they'd be caught off guard." Once more, his gaze slid back to her. "You look defenseless as hell." She could definitely catch people off guard.

Her full lips tugged down into a pout. "Now you're hurting my feelings. Is this because I said you were a pampered, rich boy? Want me to take it back?"

"You know my words are a compliment." *Unlike yours.* "You *want* to look defenseless and seductive." He waved his hand toward her. "It's all part of your vibe. You like to catch people by surprise so they underestimate you. That's what I needed. Someone my enemies would underestimate. They won't think you're a threat, and that can help me in a pinch, but..." His words kind of drifted away.

She waited.

Shit. He was going to have to finish talking. "There's having something in theory," he muttered. "And then having to deal with it in actual practice." Fear slid through him. Not for himself, but for her. Who the hell would have thought that he'd ever be *worried* about his bodyguard's safety? But here he was. Here they were. "If my targets find out I'm lying, you'll be just as much gator bait as I will be. Because I pulled you into this mess, we'll die together."

She kept waiting. No hint of fear showed on her face. No hesitation at all. *I am a badass.* Right, that was pure Harley Adaire.

As the tension stretched between them, Harley finally said, "Death is a risk on every job that I take from Wilde. Your case isn't anything special."

"Uh, I think it is. You're usually watching bored celebrities or keeping crazed fans away from rock stars. You're not—" He broke off and glanced toward the front of the limo. The privacy shield was in place, blocking them from the view of the driver, a driver who wasn't really his employee. Instead, the man taking them to this late-night meet-up with plenty of shady characters was an FBI agent. Seth's life seemed to suddenly be filled with Feds.

Mostly because it was the FBI pulling the strings on his current nightmare world. When it turned out that your father was a murdering mob boss with more ties to the criminal underworld than anyone else…there was a penalty to be paid. You didn't just get to go skipping off into the sunset.

You got a swift trip right into the middle of hell. Courtesy of dear old dad's contacts.

"I'm not—what?" Harley asked, and Seth realized he'd just left the words hanging in the air. Before he could think of something to say, she added, "I'm not currently watching some billionaire with a death wish as he decides to infiltrate a criminal underworld for shits and giggles?" She slid from her seat and came to sit right beside him. Her leg brushed against his even as her enchanting scent wrapped around him. *Was* that perfume? Or was that just pure Harley? And why was he practically gulping in her scent like some kind of obsessed stalker?

Then her words registered, and Seth stiffened. "I'm not doing this for shits and giggles." Not even close. His plans had been in motion for a long time.

"No?" Careful doubt. "Then is it because the Feds are *making* you do this? You haven't quite been clear with me. Another issue I have with our partnership. You can't communicate worth a damn."

It was hard to communicate when you were keeping so many secrets. "Things are on a, uh, need-to-know basis."

"Bullshit." The word slid from her lips like a caress.

That word should *not* have been sexy. In no universe was *bullshit* a sexy word. The problem was that Harley was sexy.

And she wasn't done. Her measuring gaze seemed to look for cracks in his armor. "You hired me because you said you wanted someone you could trust at your side." Her body pressed a little closer to him. "Well, here I am. Right at your side."

He swallowed. "You are very close right now." Wonderfully close. Nope. Not an option. *Get back on track, man.*

"Your details on this operation have been scant. I get that you're working with the Feds. My own dives and intel pulls showed me that. Only I don't understand quite why you're doing it. You have a fortune at your fingertips. Houses all over the world. You could jet off on a plane tomorrow and never look back." Her head tilted to the right. "Instead, you're in bed with the Feds and you're about to risk your life by walking into the devil's den."

"I'm not *in* bed with the Feds." He wasn't in bed with anyone. And if he was...*let it be Harley*. Dammit. This attraction was getting out of hand. "I'm working the cases with them, I'm *here* now because someone has to clean up all the blood my father left behind." Gruff and truthful. His father had killed so many people. He'd lied. He'd betrayed. And...*he wanted me to be just like him.* Plenty of people—the wrong people—thought that Seth was, in fact, just like his father. Edward Wellington. Also known as Big Eddie Wells. And there had been plenty of other aliases. When it came down to the bitter truth, his father had been a murdering monster. *Like father, like son?*

Most in the underworld believed that to be the case, and that was why the Feds were trying to use him.

Flying away? Never looking back? Not an option. The Feds wanted to use him, and he, in turn, intended to use them. A symbiotic relationship. Of sorts.

"You want to clean up the bloodshed your father left. That sounds almost badassy." A nod from her. "Excellent first step for your new persona."

"Harley—" He'd been doing this persona just fine for quite a while without her. He wasn't completely inept. Now he was just getting insulted.

"You picked the right bodyguard, Seth." Her stare didn't waver. "I do slide under the radar. Story of my life, always being underestimated. That happens when you're five-foot-three and have crazy doe eyes that make people think you need protecting."

He would not describe them as doe eyes. Maybe when she'd been a kid, but now they were intense. Deep. Filled with passion.

"One day I realized that instead of letting that make me angry, I'd just use other people's low expectations against them." A shrug that just had her brushing against him even more. "It works for me. I can make it work for you, too. But you have to listen to me. You have to trust me. Just as I have to trust you."

He did trust her. Wasn't that why she was in the limo with him? He trusted her more than he did the Feds. The Feds were working their own agenda. Harley was...his.

His, um, bodyguard. His confidant.

"I've been around the type of people you will find waiting for us. They are people that can smell blood in the water and come in faster than any shark. Leave your manners at the door. If someone gives you shit, then you shove it right back in their faces."

His mouth opened. Closed. Maybe he should take her advice.

"Act like you can kill someone in a second if they piss you off. Act like you are the one with the power and nothing else matters. You don't have fear. You see what you want, and you take it. Done. They aren't going to respect you if you have nice manners, Seth. They don't care if you went to etiquette classes when you were a kid and you know which fork to pick up at a fancy dinner. They're only going to respect you if they think you can kick all of their asses."

Hell. "This is supposed to be a business meeting. Not a fight."

"The business is death and murder. Accept that and things will go much easier." Her hand rose and patted his cheek.

Patted. Like he was a baby or a puppy or some such annoying BS.

"Everything in your new world is a fight," she informed him. "It just might not look that way on the surface, but it is. Elegance is a lie. Beauty is a trick. And civilized behavior? That's the greatest scam they can play on you."

His father had certainly been a master at that scam. *And he thought I would be just like him.* Her hand started to slide away, but Seth's fingers rose to curl around her wrist. "Maybe I'm not as civilized as you think."

Her smile came again, making that distracting dimple wink. "I hope you're not. I hope you're completely savage under your cold veneer."

"I can be whatever the situation needs me to be." Harley didn't know it yet, but one of the reasons the Feds had been so eager to use him? He could be a chameleon. A trait that had been honed to knife-point sharpness over the years. Information about him that most wouldn't know? If he needed to be savage, he could be the most brutal bastard in the room. *Thanks for the life lessons, Dad.* If he needed to be the polished businessman, he could play that part in his sleep.

Evil. Good. Everything in between—he could be that. And so much more. The Feds had been damn gleeful the first time they'd seen him in action. He'd been in action several times over the last few months. He'd already nabbed more than his share of criminals in stings that the bad guys had never seen coming. *And can't tie back to me.*

Harley might think he was playing some amateur-hour show, but she was about to see that he could bluff his way through just about anything. "Have a little faith. I'm more than you expect." A delicate pause. "I *have* managed several operations just fine without you."

"Well, if you had bothered to fully *explain* things to me, then I wouldn't be so worried. And I wouldn't feel like I needed to lecture you on stuff. I hate being the lecturing one."

They hadn't exactly had time for long chats where he revealed all his secrets. Not that he was big on revealing his secrets to anyone. He'd basically gotten Harley's agreement to come on board as his bodyguard, he'd signed contracts with Wilde, and then he'd received the news that they had to haul ass to the Big Easy. And off they'd flown. "I told you to trust me. I'm not going to crash and burn. I can handle myself."

"I hope so." A slightly disgruntled mutter from her. "Just how many operations have you done solo?"

He couldn't answer that, not without getting a whole lot of federal agents pissed at him. So he stared at her and realized he still held her wrist. Whoops. He should let her go. He didn't. After all, part of the big masterplan was that he was supposed to pretend she was his girlfriend. That way, no one would know just how lethal she could be. A beautiful, bombshell girlfriend was something to be admired, not feared. They wouldn't know to fear her until it was too late. "Are you armed?" Seth suddenly asked her. They were close to their destination, and he didn't think they would let her in the door if she had any weapons on her. After they'd gotten settled at the hotel, he'd received the message about this little meet and greet, and he'd been told explicitly...

No weapons. Not from anyone attending this exclusive gathering.

It was supposed to be a neutral meeting zone. No weapons meant nobody died. Hopefully. He was so new at this freaking thing. Working with a partner was a completely different undertaking for him. *Mental note—you do have to start sharing more with Harley.* Not everything, of course. Just...more.

"Why don't you frisk me and find out?" she dared.

Heat immediately pooled in his eager dick. Another major problem that he hadn't anticipated when he first proposed their partnership—just how much he would want Harley. Okay, fine, he *had* known that he wanted her. It would be pretty much impossible not to want her because she constantly oozed this whole blend of sexiness and temptation. Sultry. That was what she was with her curves and sensual lips and bedroom eyes and—

"I am armed. I'd never let you go into any meeting without being able to protect your back."

Her words yanked him out of the haze that should *not* have consumed him. "They'll find the weapon. The game will be over before it starts. They said *no* weapons." He was sure he'd told her that before they left their hotel suite. But things had been pretty frantic, so maybe he hadn't.

Her face leaned closer to his. "They won't find anything on me. At least, not if you get into the role you're supposed to play. Stop being so good.

Stop following rules. Try making the rules instead. People do what you order or you tell them to screw off."

The limo slowed once more. Only this time, it wasn't slowing to turn. They'd reached their destination. It was showtime, whether he wanted it to be or not.

She's got a weapon on her. It will be found. Someone will hurt her. His hand jerked from hers and flew down to her thigh. He heard her swift inhalation as his fingers touched the silk of her skin and then—

"We're here, Mr. Wellington." The limo driver—and undercover FBI agent—had opened the limo's door for them. Brent Marchello leaned inside, and his expression didn't change even a little when he saw Seth's hand curled around Harley's thigh. An intimate position. Considering that Seth's mouth was also inches from Harley's, it would definitely look as if they'd been interrupted at an untimely moment. "Sorry to interrupt," Brent added, voice carrying quite clearly in the air.

"We weren't finished." Harley's husky voice. "Too bad. Guess we can conclude later, hmm, Seth?"

No, they could not because she would be searched, the charade would be over, and they'd both be potential gator bait. But, before he could say any of those things, she'd already slipped gracefully from the limo, and he had no choice but to follow her.

Seth climbed from the car and automatically swept his gaze to the mansion that waited behind the high, wrought iron gate. Nestled in the heart of the New Orleans Garden District, the mansion was a massive, stone-covered beast that rose from the shadows of giant oaks.

Harley nestled her body close to his. Even with her heels, he still had to bend his head toward her as she murmured, "Private and gated street. Got guards about every fifteen feet. Cameras strategically positioned to catch every movement. Security here is top notch." She sent him a teasing smile. To onlookers, it would probably appear as if she was whispering something sweet and seductive to him. In Harley speak, maybe she was. She continued, "The guys near the front door both have holsters under the suit coats. So much for no weapons. Or was that a rule that only applied to invited guests?"

They were so screwed. His fault. He should have made certain the woman didn't have a weapon on her. *I was distracted. Too close to my end goal. Not thinking clearly.*

Now what to do?

If they jumped back into the limo and sped away, what then? All of his plans would go up in smoke and he'd probably find a price on his head—and Harley's head. No, he had to do this. At least try to do it. Squaring his shoulders, he offered his arm to her. She took the offering, laughing lightly as if she was having the time of her life—hell, maybe she was—and they headed up the stone walkway as the limo driver slammed the door shut behind them.

"If I had to guess..." Harley's voice drifted lightly on the wind. "I'd say this house was built around 1915. It's all in the architecture, you know. Truly, a magnificent home. Three stories. And would you look at that courtyard…"

He was just looking at the goons who'd opened the gate that guarded the house. Harley had been right before. The street had been private and gated, but a second gate led to the home, as well. The two men in suits opened the gate without a word, and Seth nodded curtly toward them because that seemed to be the thing to do.

He advanced toward the front of the house, knowing his quarry waited inside. *So close.* But the men at the door—men Harley had tagged as being armed before—shifted their positions. He saw the bulge of their holsters, too. Damn. Instead of waiting to the side, the men were now blocking the entrance to the house.

"Mr. Wellington," one greeted, voice pleasant. Well, pleasant enough. "I'm sure you understand that we need to frisk you. That's a rule for attending the private party tonight."

Right. Because this wasn't a one-on-one meeting. He could hear the faint hum of music coming from inside the sprawling mansion. Other limos would have dropped off guests during the night, too. Standard procedure for an event like this.

"No one gets in without being searched," the man on the right said. He was smaller and stockier than his partner, with dark hair while the other guy had bright, blond hair. "Orders from our boss."

Seth let go of Harley and raised his hands. "Knock yourself out." He was impressed by his own bored tone. *Have one hell of a good time. You won't find a weapon on me.*

They immediately patted him down. Fast and thorough. "Yeah, that's my dick," Seth said when the blond got a little too close. "Though I have been told it's quite the impressive weapon on more than one occasion."

The blond rolled his eyes and backed away.

Had that sounded badass? Or douchey? Did it matter? The search was over. Seth reached for Harley's arm.

"She has to be searched, too." From the blond. "Like I said, no one gets in without being searched."

Seth tensed.

"Oh, darling, it's fine." Harley laughed. "What do I have to hide?" She put her hands in the air and did a little twirl. "Where would I even hide it?"

The blond reached for her.

Seth tensed. This was about to go south.

The man's hands slid over her hips.

What the fuck? Rage built inside of Seth. Rage and jealousy, and Seth got one hell of an idea.

Then the blond bastard put his hands on her thighs and began to lift up her skirt—

Seth launched at him before he could second guess the plan bursting in his head. His body slammed into the blond's as Seth shoved him aside. "You don't put your fucking fingers on her." He caught Harley's hand. Pulled her behind him. Then both of his hands clenched into powerful fists. "*No one* touches her but me. Ever. Understand? If I say my lady doesn't have a weapon, she doesn't have a weapon. And if you want to call me a fucking liar, then do it. Then I'll break your face, and I'll leave this house, and *you* can tell your boss how you screwed up the meeting he requested." The words hurled out in rapid-fire succession as his shoulders heaved. Shit, that had just kind of erupted. He cleared his throat. "Cool?" No, there was nothing cool about this scene.

Harley's fingers pressed to the base of his back. "He didn't find a weapon, darling. He knows I'm clear."

"Fuck what he knows." Seth didn't take his eyes off the other man. "You don't put your hands on her. I break the hands that try to touch what belongs to me."

The blond wet his lips. "She's clear. You can both go inside."

His partner yanked open the door for Seth.

Seth rolled back his shoulders. "That's what I thought." His hand reached back, and his fingers twined with Harley's as he pulled her to his side. As they crossed over the threshold that would take them into the house, he leaned close to her. His lips brushed over the shell of her ear as he whispered, for her alone, "Was that badass enough for you?"

He could have sworn that he felt her shiver in response.

"Maybe I was holding back a little with you." A careful breath to her. "Guess you're not the only one who has been underestimated?"

Her head turned. Her eyes were wide. *Impressed.* "I won't make that mistake again." Husky and low. For him alone.

He was glad as hell that she approved, but the truth was—as they crossed into the foyer and the door shut behind them—Seth knew he was in way over his head. This wasn't some small op like the ones he'd handled in the past. Those had been the little fish.

Now he was stepping out of the pond and into a swirling ocean. *Big league time.*

They'd gotten past the first obstacle. But that had just been the beginning.

Let's see if we manage to survive the rest of the night. He exhaled.

I am a badass.

CHAPTER TWO

Step Two: He held out on me. Tricky bastard. No, that's not a real step, and I don't care. Actually, wait, let's make it a step—don't hold out on your partner. Ever. Your partner can't do her job if you're lying to her.

Color her impressed.

Seth had been holding back on her. The man had layers and layers that she'd never expected, plus, one heck of an acting ability. For a moment there, she'd actually believed he'd gotten all rage-filled and jealous when the guard had been frisking her. Wow. She would not underestimate him again.

But, if he'd bothered to actually *explain fully* to her before they'd rushed to the scene, she might have been better prepared. On the way there, she'd been rattling off all kinds of advice because she'd been worried about her client.

Turned out, he had a secret badass side. Rather hot.

No, stop. You are not to think that Seth Wellington is hot. Even if he very much was.

He'd been quiet and cold in the limo ride, and she'd believed nerves were getting to her new boss. She'd been wrong. He'd just handled the scene at the entranceway like a true pro. Or, well, like one seriously jealous and potentially unstable lover.

Just what you'd expect from a crime boss.

Not that Seth was a crime boss. He wasn't. She'd discovered the truth about him while working a previous case. That was one of her talents. She looked beneath the layers, and she saw what others wanted to hide. When it came to Seth, there was plenty he wanted to keep hidden.

Seth's father had been a crime lord who hid beneath the guise of being a law-abiding, community-loving, family man. In public, he'd been all good deeds and charity donations. In private, he'd been brutal, terrifying.

Edward Wellington had been one incredible actor. He'd shown people exactly what he wanted them to see. She'd just realized that Seth had his father's chameleon abilities. Actually, he might even be a better actor than Edward had been. Time would tell.

Edward's death had been as violent as his life, but Seth hadn't learned the truth about his old man until the very end. Up until that point, he'd thought his dad was an upstanding member of society. A loving father. A real *nice* guy who put family first.

Mostly, he was a guy who put his enemies in the ground.

Now Seth thought he was cleaning up the mess that his dear old dad had left behind. That was rather noble. And hot. Not that she'd tell Seth that bit of info. What she would tell him…

Her gaze raked the scene they'd just walked into. "This looks more like an orgy than a high-stakes meeting."

His head whipped toward her.

She shrugged. "Call them like I see them." What she *saw* was lots of bodies gyrating together in one very elegant home. Music beat from the dimly lit den. Men and women in expensive clothing rubbed against each other. Some couples were kissing. Others drinking. Some probably getting high. Expensive jewelry dripped from the hands and throats of the ladies. A true jewel thief's wet dream. Drunk people plus expensive jewelry always equaled easy pickings.

Or, ah, so she'd been told.

"Who are you meeting?" Harley asked. Another piece of info her new boss hadn't given her. *This shit will be changing.* Getting to New Orleans and then rushing to the meeting had been like a whirlwind. Seth had told her to grab her sexiest dress and to get ready to cover his back.

Here she was. Ready to cover. But they couldn't stand in the foyer all night. Shouldn't some host be greeting them?

"I didn't like his hands on you." Gritted from Seth. "Sorry that happened."

Her brows rose, and her head swung toward him. "I thought that was you acting." Giving a performance that should get the guy one of those big, golden awards.

His lips pressed together. Lips that could occasionally look a bit cruel, but dammit, cruel worked for him. Which was one incredibly weird thing to think, but there you were. She'd never intended to find Seth Wellington attractive. When they'd first met, she truly had thought he was a bad guy. But...

Appearances could deceive.

Seth Wellington was tall, elegant, and sexy. Yes, *sexy*. His features were hard, a little too sharp to be perfectly handsome, but there was something about the man that just worked. Maybe it was his eyes. Hazel. A mix of blue, green, and gold that swirled and burned with his emotions. When his stare locked on her, she felt as if he often looked *into* her. His hair was thick and dark, and it had a tendency to tumble a bit over his forehead. The man's shoulders were broad, his body powerful, and she bet that when his fancy suit came off...

Muscles for days.

Not that his suit had come off anywhere around her. Not that she intended for it to come off anytime soon, either. He was, after all, her boss. And she had never, ever mixed business with pleasure on a case before. She didn't intend to start now.

But that didn't mean a woman didn't notice certain things. When it came to Seth, there was no way not to notice that hot, barely restrained sexuality of his. The man seemed to always be clamping down on his control, and that just made her wonder...

What will it be like when you lose it? All that tightly wrapped tension. Seeing it explode could be a thing of beauty. Or it could be an utter disaster.

"If he'd found your weapon..."

Oh, wait, was he still worried about that business? She sent him a breezy smile, and her hand rose to reassuringly pat his cheek. "He would not have found—"

His hand flew up and caught hers. "I'm not a fucking puppy."

Um. What?

His hold tightened. "I'm also not a kid. Don't *pet* me unless you want to see—"

"Seth Wellington." A rumble of laughter followed the pronouncement. "Right here in New Orleans. You actually showed."

Her head swung toward the spiral staircase and toward the man who was casually sauntering down those stairs, one hand trailing over the gleaming banister, the other hand holding a martini.

Okay, so, who was this guy? She took stock of him even as she kept a polite mask on her face. Tall, dressed in an expensive black suit. His brown hair had been shoved away from his forehead, and his dark gaze focused completely on Seth. He didn't seem to see her at all, and that was more than fine with Harley. It gave her a chance to size him up before—

His gaze cut her way.

She sucked in a swift breath.

In that one instant, before he blinked, she knew she'd seen *hate* in his eyes. A hatred that she knew must be for Seth. Not good. So not good.

Yep, we need to get the hell out of here. Abort, abort. This mission is going to hell. Because your host was not supposed to look at you as if he wanted to put a bullet in your brain.

As the mystery man hit the landing, a waiter appeared, as if by magic, and spirited away his martini. The dark-haired man's focus remained on Harley. "I do not believe you were on my guest list." He crossed toward them. His hand extended toward her. "You are…"

"With me," Seth informed him. He also tugged Harley back so she couldn't take the other man's offered hand. "What's up with the party? I thought I was here for business. I hate having my time wasted." Just the right edge of impatience darkened his tone, and Harley realized that she had definitely underestimated Seth's acting skills.

She didn't like to make mistakes, so she'd be sure not to underestimate him again.

A faint tightness came and went around the other man's mouth. "Don't you know that the best place to do business is at a party? Most people are too drunk to even realize what's happening right under their noses."

"Easy pickings," she breathed.

The man's head tilted just a little. "Yes, so I've always believed." He smiled at her. "I must have your name."

"I don't think I caught yours," she demurred. *Because Seth didn't tell me. He's been keeping me in the dark, and I can't work blindly without getting us both killed.*

This was some BS as far as she was concerned. Why didn't he just tie her hands behind her back and make her more useless? Info was power, and Seth should know that.

"On the way here, he didn't tell me who our host was going to be." She put a bright smile on, working her dimple. She'd been told before that it was disarming.

"He can't tell what he didn't know."

What in the heck was that supposed to mean? Hold up. Was he saying *Seth* didn't know him? Well, that would explain Seth's lack of sharing info on the car ride. Her mind grasped for something to fill the silence before it grew uncomfortable. "You have a lovely home. Early nineteenth century?"

"You have a definite eye, Ms....?"

"Harley. Just call me Harley. All my friends do, and I'm sure we will be great friends." She was one hundred percent sure they would not be. In no universe would they be friends.

Seth wrapped his arm around her waist and pulled her up against him. "Harley and I aren't here to dance, and we're not here to drink." A loud moan came from upstairs. Seth and Harley both glanced upward. "And we're not here to fuck," Seth finished, voice curt. "I thought we had business, but if we don't, I'll leave now."

Their mysterious host crossed his arms over his chest. A faint smile tilted up his lips. No cruelty in his lips. Warmth seemed to pour from him. If she hadn't seen the hatred flashing so brilliantly earlier, she might have believed his lie.

Oh, who am I kidding? This man gives me the creeps. She had goose bumps on her arms.

"We definitely have business to discuss." Their host inclined his head toward the stairs. "How about we go up, get away from the crowd, and we can talk, privately?"

"Absolutely." Seth urged her forward.

But the host stepped into his path. No, into her path.

His smile flickered toward her. "The lovely Harley will need to stay here. If you want to find out exactly what I know...exactly what I can offer...and exactly *who* I really am, then this meeting is just for the two of us."

Seth looked over at her. With her gaze, she tried very, very hard to convey one message. *Absolutely not. Package deal, Wellington. We are a package deal.* It would be exceedingly hard for her to watch his ass if he was, oh, say a whole flight of stairs above her. A bodyguard couldn't guard a body unless that body was within actual sight. And actual touching distance. Separating them would be the worst mistake imaginable.

Seth smiled at her.

Great. He'd gotten the message. She felt a sigh of relief slip from her lips.

His hand lifted and...patted her cheek.

Oh, hell. He hadn't gotten the message. At all. Or if he had, the man had clearly chosen to ignore it. Damn him.

"Get a drink, darling," Seth urged her. "Don't dance with anyone but me. You know how jealous I get."

Her eyes narrowed. "I didn't come to a party so that I could be alone." *Get a clue, Seth. You don't leave your bodyguard.* That was like, Protection 101.

"You won't be alone for long. I'll be back before you know it." Seth's head bent toward her, and before she fully grasped his intent, his lips brushed over hers.

A fast, fleeting kiss. One that shouldn't have sent fire skittering along her nerve endings because it was so brief. And meaningless. Clearly, it was meaningless. But…

The fire skittered.

He sidled away and followed their mystery host up the stairs, leaving her.

Oh, no, he had *not.*

She took a step after him, only to find a guy materialize in her path. Big, way over six foot—probably clocking in closer to six-foot-five—and the man was a wall of muscle as he positioned himself at the base of the stairs.

"Sorry, ma'am," he told her in a soft voice at odds with his size, "but only the boss and his very special guests get to go upstairs."

She caught another moan floating from somewhere on the second floor. Harley's lips twisted. "Definitely not in that 'special' category."

He motioned toward the crowd dancing in the nearby room. "You can dance there. You can get drinks in the library. Food is in the dining room and solarium."

Great. So she was basically in a giant house that resembled the one from the old board game, Clue. Talk about a crazy night. *And if I find out that my boss gets hit with a candlestick while he's screwing around in the billiard room, I will not be happy.* "A drink sounds grand. Which way to the wine?"

He pointed. "Solarium has a whole setup waiting."

"Fabulous." Her gaze lifted. Seth was nowhere in sight. Jaw locking, she turned and headed down the narrow corridor to the right. Harley knew the drill. She should try to keep a low profile. Blend in. Pick up as much information as she could while she mixed and mingled. And that was certainly on her agenda but—

But when she passed a closed door on the right, Harley was pretty sure that she caught the sound of a muffled sob. She stopped. The thick carpeting had swallowed the sounds of her steps— and made her heels sink a wee bit—so she didn't think the occupants of that room had heard her approach.

And maybe she was wrong about the sob. A moment before, she'd caught pleasure-filled moans reverberating through the place. So maybe this was just—

The sob came again, only this time, it was quickly cut off. But it *had* been a sob. Now she turned fully toward the door.

Her client was upstairs. Protecting him was the priority. Except he'd had the foolish plan of heading up on his own.

She was supposed to be keeping a low profile. If she blew her cover, Seth would be pissed.

Her hand reached for the doorknob. There were no sounds at all coming from that room any longer. She could just turn away and keep walking. Go pick up that intel for Seth.

Or...

Or she could just let herself into that room. Her fingers curled around the doorknob. It twisted easily within her grasp, and she shoved open the door. As she took in the scene before her, rage filled Harley's body. A woman—thin, small, with curly, red hair—stood against the far wall. A man had his hand wrapped around her neck, and his face loomed next to hers. His head whipped toward Harley, and he snapped, "Get the fuck out!"

Absolutely not. "Is this the solarium?" She tottered forward into the little room. "I was looking for a drink."

"*Help,*" the redhead mouthed. Tears stained her cheeks and dripped mascara down her face.

Just what kind of hell had Seth brought her to?

The woman wore black pants and a white top, and Harley realized it was the same attire she'd seen the waiter wearing earlier. The hulking jerk, on the other hand, was dressed in a poorly fitting suit that stretched across his belly and shoulders. They were in what looked like a small storage room. Linens filled the shelves on the walls.

The bruiser snarled, "No damn drink here! Get *out!*"

Because she was just going to walk out in the middle of an assault? Undercover mission or no undercover mission, that wasn't how she operated. "I don't think so." Harley pointed at the redhead as she took another step forward. No soft carpeting in this little room, just a hard stone floor. *How the hell do I get the redhead out of here?* Maybe by playing the drunk bitch? "*She's* going to take me to get a drink. She's a waitress. That's her job."

"She's busy!" he snapped at Harley.

Busy what? Getting choked out? Stomping her right foot, Harley demanded, "I want her to take me to get a—"

He came barreling at Harley. Finally, he'd released the other woman. As he surged at Harley, she caught the powerful cloud of booze that clung to him. Jeez, she could probably get drunk from the smell alone. His meaty hands flew toward her. Harley shook her head and felt she had to warn him, "My boyfriend is going to be so pissed at you."

He didn't seem to care. His hands grabbed for her.

Harley ducked. A beautiful advantage of being so small against a giant jerk like him. She ducked and he missed her and his hands just grasped air. Meanwhile, she brought up her right heel in a powerful kick. One that she aimed right at his groin. Hello, fabulous spike heels.

He opened his mouth in what she feared would be a scream that would bring everyone running. Only instead of screaming, he sucked in air and made a croaking sound. He grabbed his balls—and probably his little dick—and stumbled back. His feet seemed to lose purchase beneath him in a drunken tangle, and the SOB lost his balance. He fell backwards, and his head slammed into the floor.

The smack was loud.

He didn't get up. His body immediately went slack.

"OhmyGod." From the redhead. "Did you kill him?"

That would certainly be inconvenient. "Let's find out," Harley said. She crouched and put her fingers to his throat.

CHAPTER THREE

Step Three: When you walk into the devil's den, prepare to get burned. In other words, your ass is going to be in trouble. That's why you need a fabulous bodyguard at your side. So don't do anything stupid like, say, separate from said fabulous bodyguard.

"I'm not one for games." Seth propped a hip on the edge of the pool table and raised his brows. "So how about we cut the cloak and dagger BS? I was told by an…acquaintance that we should meet. Now I'm second guessing his advice." That acquaintance had been one of the lower-level thugs Seth had already taken down via his undercover activities with the Feds. And that particular message had been conveyed before the fellow wound up in a cell. He'd verified to the power hitters that Seth was, indeed, taking over where Edward Wellington had left off.

The family business is in play once again.

The man had gotten his job done. He'd hooked Seth up with the next level of power. *And now I'm here for the meet and greet.*

The host shut the door and slowly approached Seth. "We have quite a few friends in common, don't we? Isn't that how our world works? You know people…those people give you connections to others. Some of those connections are beneficial." He stopped at the edge of the table. "Some aren't. You have to eliminate those unbeneficial connections. Get rid of the waste, if you will."

Okay, was that a threat? It sounded like one. To give himself a moment to think, Seth glanced down at his watch.

"Nice Rolex. Let me guess, a gift from dear old dad?"

The thunder of his heartbeat filled Seth's ears. "No. Something I earned myself." His head lifted. "Who the fuck are you?" He wanted a name. Unfortunately, names were often BS in this world. Mostly because so many had different names. Hadn't that been the case with Seth's own father? But a name would be a starting point. It would tell him if the tip he'd received as he fought his way through the darkness had been right. If *this* man could be the key to Seth's hunt.

"Our fathers were acquainted. Like yours, my dad is dead, too. Want to know who killed him?"

Fuck, fuck, fuck. Seth didn't move from his relaxed position. Suddenly, this felt a whole lot less like a lead...and more of a setup. "Let me guess, would it have been *my* father?"

No response.

Wonderful. Fabulous. "Is this meeting about business or do you just want revenge?" He straightened from his position and walked toward the pool cues that were hung on the nearby wall. He reached for one with a gleaming, black handle and a curving snake engraved on the end. "Because if you're looking for revenge..." His hold tightened around the pool cue. It was better than no weapon at all. Seth turned toward his new enemy. "I'm afraid you're going to be shit out of luck."

***

The pulse beat beneath her fingers. "He's alive." She could hear the relief in her own voice. But, seriously, awesome. Having to explain a dead body would have been one major pain in her ass. Harley straightened and smoothed down the skirt of her dress. "Now you have a choice. Are we calling the cops?"

"Cops don't belong in this place," the redhead breathed. "You trying to get me dumped in the Mississippi?"

"Definitely not. Let's both avoid a swim, shall we?" Her head cocked as she assessed the other woman. "You're going to have bruises on your throat."

The redhead's hand flew to touch her neck. "He—he came at me. Followed me inside. I knew working tonight was a risk, but the pay—it's insane. I couldn't turn down the cash. I was just coming to get more tablecloths, and I turned around and he..." She licked her lips. "Some guys think they can do anything."

She'd come across the type. "He can't."

"You don't know who he is." The redhead edged closer to Harley. "He'll be furious when he wakes up. We need to get away from here."

Harley considered the situation. "He's drunk off his ass. He may not remember anything at all when he wakes up. And if he does…" She shrugged. "I'm the one who put him down. He can come after me." She'd gladly take him on. She'd never liked bullies and men who thought they could hurt women? *Worst kind of scum.* "But I would strongly suggest you take your leave from the party before he wakes up."

"Yeah, yeah, I love that suggestion." The woman shot for the door.

Harley's hand flew out and curled around her arm. "You sure you don't want to call the cops?"

"That's one of Fabian Butler's men. In the inner circle. I don't care what song I give the cops, he'd never serve a day in jail. Then he'd just hunt me down." A ragged breath. "I'm getting out of here. Think it might be time for me to head back to Biloxi and visit my mom."

Fabian Butler. Harley filed away the name because it meant nothing to her. *Nothing now, but I think it will mean a whole lot soon.* "This is Fabian's house?"

"One of many. The man rules New Orleans."

"I've never heard of him."

"Then you must not be running in the right circles." A grimace. "Or maybe just not the wrong ones."

Probably. "I am new in town."

"You don't want Fabian for an enemy. And you *don't* want his men coming for you." She tugged free of Harley's grip. "Look, lady, I know you really wanted a drink and all—"

Harley frowned at her. Oh, right. The drink. Her excuse to get in the little room.

"But I want to get the hell out of here. This is way, way over my head, and even for a grand, I'm not staying here any longer."

"Totally understandable."

"Thanks for the help." She hesitated. "You weren't thirsty, were you?" A sudden question. "You didn't care about a drink, did you?"

Harley shrugged.

"I owe you," the redhead told her. "Thank you."

The woman was going to disappear. Considering that an asshole had just tried to *choke* her, disappearing seemed like a great plan. But first... "Want to pay back that debt real fast?"

Her shoulders stiffened as she paused near the door. "How?"

"Oh, super easy. Just tell me how I can get upstairs without alerting the hulking guy who looks like he eats steroids for breakfast."

The redhead glanced back at her, a frown pulling at her brow.

"He's the one standing at the bottom of the staircase," Harley elaborated. "Soft voice, scary big size. I need to get to the second level, but I wasn't a 'special' guest so he wasn't letting me sashay up there."

A nervous lick of her tongue over her bottom lip, then... "There's a staff staircase on the other side of the kitchen. The door is red. Open the red door and you'll go up a narrow flight of stairs. There's a guard stationed at the bottom, though."

Dammit.

"But he's been letting pretty women go up all night without questioning them."

Harley arched a brow. *Has he now?* Good thing she'd worn her sexiest dress.

"There's, um, a lot of action going on upstairs." A delicate clearing of her throat. "The ladies on that floor are getting way more than a grand. So just be very, very sure you want to go up there. I mean, I stayed on the ground floor..." Her gaze shot to the unconscious man. "Look what happened to me."

"I'll be good. Don't worry. I have a friend up there who'll look after me." *Technically, I'm supposed to be looking after him.* "You should go." Before this whole deal went way more south than it already had.

The other woman needed no additional urging. She darted out and didn't look back. A ball of lead seemed to settle in Harley's stomach. She looked at the fallen attacker and decided a quick search wouldn't be the worst thing in the world to do. A pat-down revealed he had three knives on him. Big, sharp knives. So obviously, that no-weapons rule was BS. She decided to hide those knives, ditching them under some linens because when he woke up, she didn't exactly want him to quickly reach for a knife. She also couldn't just hide those big-ass knives on her person, so stowing them away seemed like a good option.

When she was sure they wouldn't be found— at least not without some serious hunting effort— Harley snagged the downed man's wallet to take a look at his ID.

Justin Florent.

The man's phone was also just *there,* hanging from his pocket, so she plucked it out. She used his finger and a carefully positioned shot of his head—she *did* have to lift his eyelids—to unlock the phone, and then Harley helped herself to a quick scroll through his recent texts and—

A picture of Seth stopped her. About an hour ago, Justin had received a text that included a pic of Seth and the instructions...

He doesn't get to leave.

She thought about the three big knives she'd just hidden. The super sharp knives. And the way that Justin had been choking a helpless woman. Physical violence was obviously his forte. Her eyes lifted to the ceiling. Seth was somewhere on that second floor.

And he needed her.

Time to get her ass to that red door.

***

"I want your name." Seth kept the pool cue gripped in his right hand.

"Fabian Butler."

The name rang a loud bell but Seth didn't change his expression because he knew not to let his excitement show. *Finally. A major player has entered the field.* "Are you looking for revenge or for a business deal?"

"What makes you think I'm the type to punish the son for the sins of the father?" Fabian strolled over and picked up a pool cue, too. "Thought you weren't one for games."

How did you say...*Oh, I'm not. Just grabbed this cue because I thought it might make for a good weapon.* Simple. You *didn't* say that. "Maybe I changed my mind."

"Um." Fabian tested the weight of his cue. "I never said your father killed mine. Your father's exploits are certainly legendary, at least in certain circles." He cast a questioning look back at Seth. "Tell me, were you always aware that your father was the monster that everyone else feared? The big beast in the dark?"

"You're wearing a wire." *Bluff this shit out.* "We're done here." Still gripping the cue, he strode for the door.

Fabian sidestepped and extended his cue like it was some kind of sword, blocking Seth's path. "I was wondering the same thing about you. I hear these stories...you're the true blue one. Eddie's *good* son. The one who is above reproach."

Seth snorted.

"And then...then I start hearing rumors that *you* killed your own father because you wanted to take over his business."

"Not true." There had been plenty of rumors. Still were. "My father was killed by a dirty cop. Maybe my dad should have been a bit more careful about the people he let into *his* circle." A circle of blood and death and betrayal.

"You're trying to rebuild his empire."

That was certainly what the Feds wanted people to think. Seth used his cue to knock Fabian's out of his way. "You don't have to rebuild what's already there. Rebuilding isn't necessary. Growing, evolving, *consuming* the competition— that's what I'm about."

"You think you'll consume me?"

"I think we have mutual interests." That bell that had chimed at the mention of Fabian's name peeled again. *Fabian Butler.* A shadowy figure in the gambling underworld. Not like the man had a giant social media page where he posted all of his vacation photos—or murder shots, considering his business. He was secrets and darkness, and Seth figured Fabian probably had a dozen other names that he went by.

The bell had also chimed in Seth's head because when the Feds had first approached him to take on this crazy task, Fabian had been one of the targets mentioned. A long shot because the guy was so powerful and insulated. Like Seth's own father, Fabian was a target the Feds had tried to take down for years, but so far, they'd had no success. Mostly because you couldn't capture a ghost.

Except that ghost is standing in front of me right now.

"You're not your father," Fabian said.

Seth took the other man's measure. Fabian looked to be close to his own age. Maybe a few years older. Seth had zero clue about what might have happened to Fabian's family or what ties they might have shared. But typically, when people brought up Seth's dad, the experience had *not* been good. "I'm not. Though we do share certain similarities."

"Is it the eyes?" A drawl. "Do tell me more about how you are like your bastard of a father—"

"Punish the betrayer." A line his dad had given him at the end. "Never forget your killer instinct."

A muscle flexed along Fabian's jaw.

"I'm in New Orleans because I am looking for new opportunities." Truth. "My business is start-ups. Investments. I got a...tip about a potential business here. Something that might benefit from my talents. So I flew down. If there was a serious investment opportunity here, a real chance for growth, then I wanted to learn about it. Got here and was sent a message to come to this party." He assessed Fabian. "But maybe I was misled and there's nothing here for me. Think I'll go find my lady and get the hell out." He sauntered for the door. "Thought the southern hospitality would be a whole lot better down here. I hate disappointment." His shoulders tensed as he walked forward because Seth half expected Fabian to swing with that pool cue at his back and—

A shrill cry—no, a shrill *ring*—cut through the silence behind him. Seth spun around.

The ring came again.

Swearing, Fabian tossed his pool stick onto the table and yanked out his phone. He swiped his fingers over the screen before he put the device to his ear and blasted, "There had better be a damn fire—"

A knock sounded at the door. Automatically, Seth whirled toward it. He felt like a freaking spinning top. Two steps forward, and he reached out to haul open the door.

Harley stood on the other side. With her hands behind her back and her eyes wide. "Found you." That teasing smile of hers spread over her lips.

A smile that was like a punch straight to his gut. "Harley—"

Her smile flickered. Died. "Something happened." Her voice pitched lower, but not too low. He was aware of the silence behind him. Fabian wasn't talking on his phone any longer, and Seth knew Harley's voice would reach him. "I want to leave."

Every alarm bell possible blasted in Seth's head. "We're done." He strode over the threshold. He didn't like the look in her eyes. *What in the hell happened?* Savage urgency flooded through him as he extended his hand toward her. With only the slightest hesitation, she twined her fingers with his, and then they were striding toward the stairs. Not double-timing it. He didn't want to look too eager. Not like he was running away.

More...*I'm done here.* That was probably the air he was supposed to project.

"Seth?" Fabian called after him. "We aren't finished."

They were at the top of the stairs. Seth glanced back. "I am. Unless you have a real opportunity that you want to talk about." A pause. "Next time, I pick the location. You can rest assured, it won't be a damn party." With that, he and Harley headed down the stairs. As they descended, he saw what had to be a guard at the bottom. The man was linebacker huge, and a furrow appeared between his brows as he glanced up at Harley.

"Surprise," she murmured.

Seth had no idea what she meant by that.

They were almost at the bottom. Fabian tailed them. The bruiser at the base of the stairs kept frowning, but Seth ignored him. So did Harley. They climbed off the last step. The front doorway was in sight. Seth knew he should send a text to the driver so the limo would be ready. A getaway car felt like a necessity right then. But even as his left hand shoved into the pocket of his suit coat so he could pull out the phone, Seth heard—

"Already contacted him. The car is waiting. Keep walking." A rushed whisper from Harley as she pushed her body closer to his. "Let's go. *Now*."

Her sense of urgency fueled his own. He grabbed for the front door and yanked it open. The two bouncers were still there, and they turned to him, eyes wide. They didn't speak, though. They just backed the hell up and got out of his way.

His right hand stayed tightly twined with Harley's. He was probably squeezing her fingers too hard, but he couldn't stop himself. He felt like he had to hold tightly to her.

The limo waited just beyond the wrought iron gate. The driver stood at the back, near the open limo door. His arms were loose at his sides, and his gaze was directed straight at Seth.

"Good job." Another careful whisper from Harley. "About fifteen feet to go. Whatever happens, do not stop until we are in the limo."

Then, the woman dropped back a bit so that she was behind him. And he realized she was protecting his back. Seth automatically stiffened and turned to—

"Don't stop!" Harley snapped at him, voice still low and hopefully carrying only to him. "Seth—"

A roar. That was the only way to describe the sound that burst through the night. Seth whipped around and saw that the sound had come from a man who was charging out of the mansion. Bigger than the two guards who stood outside, this fellow's stomach and shoulder width strained his suit. His tousled hair shot up in several directions, and his lips curled in a snarl as his furious stare locked on Harley.

Something happened. Her words rang through Seth's head. Automatically, he stopped because she was between him and this charging bastard.

"No." Her sharp cry. She grabbed Seth and tried to heave him forward. "I said *don't* stop!"

Screw that. This prick was *running* after her. His hands were outstretched like he'd grab Harley, and that wasn't happening. Oh, hell, no, it wasn't—

"Gun," the limo driver barked.

Seth's head whipped toward him and damn if the fellow didn't *throw* a gun at him. Seth's hands flew out automatically because when someone throws a gun at you, grabbing it seemed natural or maybe crazy, he didn't know which. He only knew that he caught it and then Seth whirled with that gun in his hand. "Down!" he snarled at Harley.

She dropped.

He had the gun aimed at the charging SOB who'd bounded off the porch. "Freeze or die."

The prick had the good sense to freeze.

In fact, everyone seemed to freeze. Seth was highly conscious of the pounding of his heart. Each beat slammed into his chest with the force of a hammer. *Boom. Boom. Boom.* And his hand was sweaty as it gripped the gun. His whole body was sweaty. Beneath the suit, he could feel sweat trickling down his back.

"No weapons in the house," Seth said, forcing a cold smile when he felt anything but cold. "Good thing I'm not in the house anymore, hmm?"

The big bastard in the too tight suit jerked up his chin.

Harley pressed her fingers to Seth's arm. He realized she'd sidled around him. "What part..." Harley murmured, "of 'don't stop until you are in the limo' did you miss?"

He hadn't missed any part. "Get in the car," he ordered her. A loud order that would carry. The other guards near the house hadn't reached for their weapons yet. A good thing. Because if they both drew their guns, this scene would turn into a blood bath.

"Seth," she began.

"Limo. *Now.*"

Behind the frozen bastard, he saw Fabian appear. The flickering gaslight lanterns on either side of the entranceway clearly revealed the fury on Fabian's face.

"Not the way to treat your guests," Seth called as he backed up a step. Then another. He kept his eyes and his whole body toward the threats as he walked backwards toward the limo. "I will remember this."

He was pretty sure everyone there would remember him, too. He could see other people peeking from behind Fabian. So much for a smooth night. Flawless execution? Not so much.

But he'd finally reached the limo. The driver was still there, and Seth realized he had a gun out and aimed at the group on the porch, too. Okay, that was good. Two guns being better than one and all that. "Get in the driver's seat," Seth directed him. "Now."

Fabian shoved his way off the porch. "There's been a mistake. We can make a deal."

Could they? "It had better be one damn fine deal." The driver had gotten into the car. Excellent. Time to go. "A very, very fine one. Because like I said before, so far, your hospitality has been shit." With that, he ducked into the car and yanked the door shut behind him.

The driver floored it, and the limo flew forward with a lurch.

CHAPTER FOUR

Step Four: Pivot when necessary. Better to run and live another day...than to get your client killed so that you both die, you know...right then and there. Blood and death are so messy.

"Give me the gun," Harley ordered.

Seth was staring through the window, his gaze on the house that they were fleeing.

She craned around to try and see what waited in front of them. They'd come through gates earlier, when they first entered the posh neighborhood, and she sure hoped that the driver knew if the gates were closed...*Floor it and go through them.*

But she couldn't get a good glimpse of the gates from her position. So Harley surged forward and pressed the button to lower the privacy shield. "Don't even think of stopping," she blasted at the driver-slash-Fed. Brent Marchello. Special Agent Brent Marchello.

He didn't look her way. "Wouldn't dream of it."

Excellent. She turned back to Seth. "Gun." She opened her hand. "Now."

He blinked and peered down at the gun in his hand, as if surprised he held it. Since he wasn't handing it over, her breath huffed out and she just grabbed it from him even as her rage exploded on the driver. "Dammit! I can't believe you *threw* a loaded weapon at him, Brent! That's such BS! He is not Jason Statham, and he's not—"

"Not loaded," Brent grunted. "I don't normally throw loaded guns into the air. If he'd missed it, the gun could have hit the ground and gone off. You could have gotten shot. He could have."

"What? Not loaded?" She focused on that part and not the whole "you could have gotten shot" bit. But, yes, she could feel the weight of the weapon and—

"Kinda busy. Talk later?" The limo careened to the right as Brent took a hard turn. The gate had been open. Thank goodness. Now they were off the private street and hauling ass. And, yes, talking with him later sounded like a plan. Especially since she needed to have one major talk with Seth at that moment.

"It wasn't loaded," Seth said.

She slammed her left fist into the button to raise the privacy screen even as her right hand dropped the gun onto the seat. "You didn't know that." *I didn't know that.*

He leaned back against the seat. "I think the important thing is that the bad guys didn't know that."

The bad guys. The ones who were probably following them. "Tell me you got some major information that you can use in this crazy con with the Feds."

His gaze cut away from her.

She took that cutting gaze as a no. Wonderful. Not. She bounded toward him. "He wanted you dead." Adrenaline spiked in her blood.

Seth's gaze flew back to her. "What?"

"The big goon who chased us out of the fancy mansion? I took his phone."

"How did you—"

She waved that away because they had bigger issues at the moment. "I accessed his last text. Saw a message that had been sent about you. Your picture. Instructions that *you were not to leave.*" Her breath heaved out as remembered fear and rage thundered through her blood mixing with the adrenaline in a fiery brew of a cocktail that left Harley feeling as if she might jump from her skin at any moment. "Do you get what I'm telling you?"

He didn't even blink.

Ahem. She realized that when she'd bounded toward him, she had *seriously* bounded forward and onto him. One of her hands gripped the seat behind him, while her knee shoved into the seat near his hip. She was practically straddling him. A very unnecessary pose, and she should back up.

Now.

She should back up now.

She began to inch back.

His hands flew out and curled around her hips. His touch seemed to burn right through her dress. Whenever he touched her, she could have sworn the man scorched her. Sometimes, she could ignore the scorch. This was not one of those times.

"It was a setup, Seth." That was why she'd been so desperate to get him out of that place.

"You went in with no weapons so you'd be a sitting duck. That wasn't about a deal. It was just about you being dead."

His eyes widened. A faint glow of light came from the limo's bar, so she could see his expression. The problem was understanding his expression because he had just gone totally unreadable on her. And where did he get those skills? Where did the guy who'd grown up with a silver spoon in his mouth get the ability to control his emotions and be such a chameleon in high-stress situations?

He'd been impressive in there. A totally different person.

She suspected his control ran bone deep, and, yes, that made her jealous. No, envious. Control had always been an issue for her. Just ask her brothers.

"Why would Fabian want me dead?" Seth asked. "Tonight was our first meeting."

Fabian. That name again. And there had been something about Seth's tone. *He's holding back on me.* "I don't know why he wants you in the ground. Let me just take a stab or two in the dark." She was good at stabbing. "Maybe your dad killed someone he cared about? Or screwed him over in business? Or maybe Fabian discovered that you're faking this whole crime boss persona because you have some deal going with the Feds?"

His fingers flexed against her.

Still straddling him, check. Technically, though, it was a partial straddle, not the full-on thing. For the full-on straddle, she'd need to put both of her knees on the seat and bring her hips in even closer. Maybe grab his shoulders for balance with her hands and—

What am I even doing?

"Answers," she bit out. "I want them all, now. I took this job and came with you on a whirlwind because you said you needed me immediately. I felt bad for tasing you at our first meeting, so I agreed to the contract." A signed, sealed, and delivered contract with Wilde. She'd agreed to be Seth's bodyguard, twenty-four, seven, and he'd paid a more than hefty sum for her services. She did not come cheap.

"Didn't realize you regretted tasing me. Can't say I recall you apologizing."

He was focusing on that, now? "I didn't apologize. And I won't." For the record. "You were running. You seemed guilty. I did my job." Her nostrils flared and damn if she didn't pull in his oddly intoxicating scent. Seth did not use cologne. It was just—his scent. Masculine. Crisp. Sexy. "Get your hands off me." This nonsense—this weird need that was flaring so hotly inside of her—had to stop. Immediately.

He looked down, as if surprised to see that his hands were, indeed, on her person. He swallowed. "You going to get off me if I do?"

"I didn't mean to get on you in the first place. It was the heat of the moment. I, um, I'm riding adrenaline."

His gaze lifted. Held hers. Heated. "Sweetheart, I'm pretty sure you're riding me."

She wasn't the type to blush, thank goodness. If she had been, her cheeks would have been on fire in that moment. But that wasn't her. She was the kind of woman who took a challenge and tossed it right back at her opponent. Her head leaned closer to his. "Sweetheart," she purred, "when I ride you, you'll know."

Primitive hunger flashed on his face, breaking through his mask. A hunger so startling, so strong, that her breath caught.

Harley realized that she might have made a tactical mistake. Because his hands were pulling her closer, not letting her go, and a big, traitorous part of her wanted to rub against him. Straddle him fully. And put her mouth on his as she tried to find out if he'd kiss her with the same wild hunger that she could see blazing in his eyes.

Nope. Bad idea. Bad. Her hands flew down and curled around his wrists. He was so warm, dang the man. Sucking in a deep breath, she pulled his hands off her and put them on the seat, positioning them on either side of Seth's body. Then she moved back. Slowly. The feel of her body sliding away from his sent an odd shiver darting down her spine.

Too much adrenaline. That was the problem. She was going to have a serious crash that night. For the moment though, there was business to handle. Harley settled back in the seat opposite Seth. She rolled back her shoulders and crossed her legs. Her fingers even plucked a microscopic bit of string from her skirt, just to give her another moment to compose herself. Then... "Let's focus on business."

His hands had flattened on either side of his body, pressing hard to the seat. "Right. Business."

"The business of keeping you alive," she clarified.

"I happen to think that's a very important business."

"So do I. That's why I'm here." *And not to straddle you. Not to see how you kiss when it's not for show.* A slow exhale. "I'm not working in the dark any longer."

He stared at her.

"Full disclosure or I walk."

His body jerked. "What?"

She'd learned to bluff when she was thirteen, and she'd joined her brother Wade's poker game. He'd been playing with some of the new recruits, and she just hadn't been able to help herself. By the end of the night, she'd cleaned those guys out. "You heard me." Her tone was careless.

"We have a contract."

"Yes, but you should have read the fine print better. If an agent at Wilde feels that the client is engaging in 'deceptive practices' with the firm, then the agent may dissolve the relationship with cause." Every Wilde agent was told this bit of info because you never knew when you might need to use it in a pinch as leverage against said client.

"You're going to leave me?"

An odd note had entered his voice. She couldn't quite figure out that note, but then again, she couldn't quite figure him out, either. "I'm going to do my job. The proper way. And the way to do that? Get answers from you. Real answers, not some BS where you tell me that you're 'not at liberty to say' because of some deal you're working with the Feds."

When he didn't respond, she glanced out of the window. They were almost back at their hotel. She hoped Brent had used some of his FBI training to make sure they weren't tailed. But then again, not like the limo was ideal for blending. Talk about sticking out and not exactly being able to fly from the scene.

When we get into the hotel, we should be safe. Seth had booked them a suite at a posh place right on the river that gave incredible views of the Big Easy while also offering top notch security. He'd gotten them the Royal Suite at the hotel, and that meant top floor, key card access only. There were two bedrooms, so not like she'd have to bunk on the couch. *Or with him.* Not that bunking with Seth was an option.

Her breath slid out. "How long have you been working with the Feds?"

Silence.

Dammit, Seth, just answer—

"Since the night my father took a bullet to the brain."

She flinched.

"Shortly before his death, he'd revealed the truth about himself to me. And by shortly before, I mean that very night. Everything I knew in that moment was ripped away. My dad had plans for me. Big plans. He was dying of cancer, and he intended for me to take over the empire he'd built. When I didn't exactly jump with joy at joining a criminal underworld, he threatened to end my life and told me I was useless." Emotionless words. "Great father-son chat. The stuff of dreams."

"More like nightmares." She'd truly planned to stay on *her* side of the limo. But suddenly she was reaching over and putting her hand on his knee. "I'm sorry." She'd known the story already, but hearing the words from him just hit different in that moment.

He looked down at her hand.

"Sorry that your father died in such a violent manner. Sorry that he said those things to you. Sorry that he hurt you." She couldn't imagine a father being so cruel, but, when it came to Edward Wellington, cruelty had been a way of life for him. At least, according to all of his many, many enemies.

"I don't need pity." Sharp.

She pulled her hand back. Shrugged. "Good. I wasn't giving it. That was empathy. Or at least, my attempt at empathy because I have no idea how painful that night must have been for you." Seth's mother had died when he was seven years old, and he'd grown up just with his father, no other siblings. "He was the person closest to you in the world, so I would imagine learning that he'd lied and deceived..." *And killed. Killed lots of people.* "I imagine that's the kind of thing that would rip your world apart, and, oh, say, make you suddenly begin some massive path of atonement for sins that aren't even yours as you team up with Feds who are all too eager to use you for their own gain."

His left hand moved and settled over his knee, in the same position she'd touched him just moments before. His hand pushed down, then lifted, returning to the seat. "My father was a cold bastard even on his good days. Turned out, there were just fewer of those than I thought." Seth cleared his throat. "He was freaking citizen of the year in our town. For three years in a row. Got the key to the city. Everyone loved him."

Not the people he killed. Her lips pressed together. Now was not the time for her flippant statements. They just tended to come out, but she was *trying* to hold them back. Her brother Wade had told her once—after he got his PhD and thought he was all fancy—that she used her flippancy as a form of defense. When things got too emotional or if they hit too close for her, she tossed out sarcasm or a joke.

She would never admit to Wade that he might be right.

"Growing up, my father attended every one of my ball games. He showed up at every school function. He was the picture of the proud and doting dad. The man was absolutely amazing at keeping up appearances." A shake of Seth's head. "Edward Wellington was a world-class actor, and I guess I inherited more of his talent than I realized."

She couldn't argue on that point. "You were really good at acting tonight."

His chin jerked.

Yep. She should have held that one back, too. Obviously, it was not a compliment he wanted. But, since she'd already started... "You played the possessive lover perfectly. Totally didn't expect that from you. You sank straight into character. Kudos to you."

"I didn't want the fucker putting his hands all over you." Another hard shake of Seth's head. "He would have found your weapon, then we both would have been screwed."

She sighed. And hiked up the edges of her skirt, letting it rise higher on her thighs. A little more—

"What are you doing?" Growled.

Showing him. "No weapon." She had nothing strapped to her thighs. No cool knife tucked into a garter or anything like that. "And I certainly don't have anything shoved up my ah—well, I think you get the picture."

"Picture gotten."

She tugged down the skirt and lifted one heel. One incredibly spiky heel. "In a pinch, these are the weapons I need."

He swallowed. His gaze slid over the length of her leg and lingered on the extended heel. "You have a blade hidden in there?"

"Okay, first, someone is watching way too many spy movies. That someone is you. No, I do *not* have a knife hidden in the heel of my shoe." She rolled her eyes. "Are you looking at this thing? Do you know how much damage I could do with both of these spiky heels? Then just think of the shame my victim will feel. He'll have to tell all of his friends that he lost an eye or got a severe puncture in his thigh and nearly bled out all because a petite woman with heels took him down." She shook her head. "Sad. So sad."

"You're joking. Trying to lighten the tension, aren't you?"

Her shoulders straightened. "I'm being one hundred percent serious with you."

"The only *weapon* you had when we went in that place was your heels?" Seth seemed to strangle a bit on those words. "You're supposed to be some super bodyguard! You didn't even have your taser?"

"Again, where exactly would you have me *put* the taser?" Harley grimaced at the options. "I didn't take a handbag with me, and I'm certainly not putting a taser in my—"

"*No.*" Horror flashed on his face. "Do not dare put it—"

A sigh. "Seth, you are far too concerned with what is or is not in my—"

"*Just stop.*" His hand flew up and pressed to his eyes. "I need a drink."

She didn't point out that the bar was right next to him. They'd seriously gotten off track. And just when he'd started giving her actual, usable intel. "I am quite capable of defending myself with or without traditional weapons. And defending you, too. I have been trained, quite extensively, in fact. If you'd like, I'm happy to supply you with a resume. I've studied judo, krav maga," her brother Ford had *insisted* on that, "as well as aikido and—"

"Doesn't matter when your attacker has a gun, does it? When it comes to martial arts fighting versus a gun, I'm pretty sure the gun wins every time."

Not necessarily. Harley sniffed. "A gun means you have to get quite creative."

"And your long list of skills doesn't really matter when the guy is twice your size."

What was he talking about? She'd been taking down opponents twice her size since she hit puberty.

"Fuck. This was a bad idea. I should not have—"

"I didn't have any trouble taking out Justin Florent." Now Seth had annoyed her and insulted her. "I'm sure you've heard before that you shouldn't judge someone or something based on size. Aren't men often the ones saying how it's not the size of the boat that matters? But the, I believe the saying is, 'motion of the ocean' that gets the job done? I've got great ocean motion, and I can get the job done."

He coughed. Choked. Coughed again. Then, "I have *never* had a problem with my size, for the record."

She shrugged. "For the record, I've never had a problem with my size, either. Like I said, I had no problem taking out Justin."

"Who. The. Fuck. Is. Justin?" He pinched the bridge of his nose. "I think you're trying to give me an aneurysm. Tell me we are at the hotel."

"No, I'm not trying to give you an aneurysm. I am trying to keep you quite healthy and alive." That was, after all, a bodyguard's job. "Justin Florent was the big bruiser who chased after us when we were leaving the mansion. The one who'd gotten orders that you weren't to leave the house. But I got you out because I'm awesome."

His hand dropped back to his side. "You stole his phone."

"Um, hmmm." That was a yes in her book. "Then I ever-so-cleverly called the number back that had sent the text about you. A name wasn't included with the number, and I needed to know the identity of the person who'd given that order."

His body jolted to attention just as they pulled to a stop. "Fabian's phone rang right before you entered the room."

"A billiard room," she muttered still disbelieving on that point. "Such a living game of Clue that I almost couldn't believe it when I walked in and saw the big table."

"It was a pool table. A billiard table doesn't have pockets."

Huh. "Interesting." And totally something that she would expect a rich boy who'd grown up in a mansion of his own to know. The limo had stopped and when she craned her head, she could see the hotel lights through the window. "We're here. Let's haul ass up to the suite." *Where I know you are protected.* "Then you can spill every secret you have to me."

The driver had pulled them right up to the entrance. She saw one of the doormen begin to rush toward the limo.

She reached for the door.

Seth reached for her. His fingers curled around her wrist. "How did you get his phone?"

"I got it when I patted him down. Found his wallet first, that's how I learned his name, then I helped myself to his phone." She tugged free. Reached for the door again.

And, again, his fingers curled around her wrist.

Why did she get that odd jittery rush every time he touched her? A mix of heat and nerves. Crazy. "We need to exit the vehicle, Seth. We can talk inside." The doorman would be pulling open the limo door in about five seconds.

"Why did you pat him down?"

"Uh, because I was looking for weapons?" Obviously? "He had three. But don't worry, I hid the knives."

"Jesus."

"Couldn't very well have him coming after you with them when he woke up." A pause. "He could have come after me, too. I wasn't sure how much he would remember before the fall."

"The *fall?*"

She turned her head. They were so very, very close. "Size doesn't matter," she whispered to him. "I took Justin down just fine." Though in the interest of complete honesty... "After one of my heels hit him in the groin, he tripped over his own two feet. He was drunk off his ass, then he fell on his ass...and his head. The crack of his head against the tile is what knocked him out."

The limo door swung open. Seth stared at her, with his mouth open, so she lifted her hand and gently pushed up his strong jaw, closing his mouth in what should look like a tender caress to the doorman. "Time to go, darling," she cooed to Seth before climbing from the limo.

CHAPTER FIVE

Step Five: Some clients need...guidance. They're scared and uncertain. A good agent makes them feel safe. Remember that. Make the client feel safe.

She was making him feel crazy. Absolutely, certifiably insane. Seth jumped from the limo and immediately grabbed for Harley because he had the feeling that if he didn't keep her close she might do something like...oh, say attack a man who was easily twice—almost three times—her size and then *hide knives*.

He locked his arm around her shoulders and hauled her against his side.

The limo driver quirked a brow. Brent had been standing near the doorman.

"We need to talk," Seth gritted to the driver. "ASAP."

Brent dipped his head forward.

Seth palmed a twenty to the doorman and headed into the hotel with Harley snugly under his arm. They went straight for the elevator, and he ignored the glittering and pricey decorations around him. A celebrity ducked out of the elevator, a man he recognized from a vampire show that was filming in the city, and Seth barely glanced his way. All of his focus was on Harley.

She fought that prick at the house?

He used his keycard, and the elevator doors closed. With his index finger, he jabbed the button for their floor. A moment later, the elevator flew upward.

Harley pulled away. Since he didn't exactly have a reason to keep her close when they were literally behind closed doors—closed elevator doors, anyway—he let her go. Then he exploded, "What the fuck were you thinking?"

Her incredibly long and incredibly dark eyelashes fluttered. "Excuse me?"

"Oh, you heard me." She'd backed away, moving to the rear of the elevator. He stalked closer to her. Towered over her. Rage and fear twisted inside of him. "What the *fuck* were you thinking?"

Her eyes narrowed. Iced. "Don't like the tone, Seth."

"And I don't like that you were going up against a guy who probably outweighs you by two hundred pounds."

She scoffed. "Hardly that much. And like I said, it's not size that—"

His hands flew out and flattened on the elevator wall behind her. "Were you in danger? Yes or no."

Her tongue snaked along her lower lip. "Yes. But it was danger I could handle."

His temples throbbed, and he tried to stop looking at her lips.

"I don't see the problem here." Impatience simmered in her words. "You *do* understand how being a bodyguard works, yes?"

His gaze snapped up to meet hers. "I know how it works. You are supposed to stay beside me."

"Right. And I would have, only you're the one who went scampering up the stairs without me—"

The elevator dinged. They were on the top floor. The doors slid open.

She sent him an angelic smile.

He snapped his teeth together and took her arm. They walked out of that elevator cuddling close, looking like lovers to anyone who might be watching. After all, there were other suites on that floor, along with plenty of security cameras. It only took a few moments, though, and they were opening the door to their suite. Going inside. He shut the door, flipped the extra lock on top, and turned to face Harley.

She kicked off her shoes and immediately appeared even more delicate and *breakable*.

As he glared, she picked up the shoes and pointed one spiky heel at him. "You're the one who sashayed up the stairs even though it's incredibly difficult for a bodyguard to *guard* a body that is a whole floor away! Talk about making my job extra challenging."

He marched toward her. Glared at the shoes. "These are all you had to defend yourself?"

"They worked great. Trust me, Justin is going to remember the pain I gave him for quite a while."

"That means he is going to remember *you*."

She shrugged. "Yep, that is a possibility. Knew it at the time. But I did what had to be done when he charged at me."

Fuck. Fuck. Fuck. "Why did he charge at you?"

"Because he's an asshole who likes hurting women? Because I looked weak and defenseless and he thought it would be fun to attack?" Her lips pursed. "I don't know. I can't read the minds of jackasses. I *did* tell him that you would be pissed when he first tried to grab me, so you can't say I didn't warn him."

He was more than pissed. Seth was enraged. A fury he'd never felt before swamped him as he imagined that big bastard grabbing at Harley. The man could have broken her. "This was a mistake."

She sighed. "Here we go."

"I shouldn't have hired you." What the hell had he been thinking? Yes, she'd taken him down with a taser, and yes, she handled herself well in stressful situations, but this was far beyond *stressful.* She was too small. The threats were too staggering.

Harley tossed her high heels onto the couch. Then she crept close and put her hands on his shoulders.

"I'm putting you in danger," he continued gruffly.

"You are."

No argument. Not even a half-hearted one to make him feel better. His brows snapped together.

She exhaled. "If I knew *exactly* what game you were playing and *exactly* who we are facing, I'd be way better prepared."

His head shook. Her scent wrapped around him and made thinking hard. No, fuck it, she just made him hard. Another problem. Another reason why this was a mistake. He wasn't reacting normally to her. Not at all. The thought that she might have been hurt, that the bastard at the mansion could have put his hands on her, that—

"You asked for this," she whispered, tilting her head up.

And his head was already lowering toward hers. His mouth suddenly going right for hers. No, he hadn't asked for a kiss, but he sure wanted her mouth. Had wanted that smart, sexy mouth from the very first even when she'd—

Her leg slid against his. A sensual move he hadn't expected, but he could feel her foot inching up his calf. She rubbed her upper body against his, leaning into him, and he wrapped his arms around her as she...*pushed him back*. A sudden, fast push, and he realized that her leg had lowered and was behind him and he fell smack on his ass.

But he also pulled her down with him. She landed on top of him, straddling him, and oh, hell, but this had to be the stuff both dreams and nightmares were made of because she *smiled* at him.

"I took you down with no problem." Her hands pressed against his chest as she levered herself up a bit. Her lower body pressed harder against his, and there was no way the woman could miss the giant bulge shoving against her sex.

Her lashes flickered, and he knew, nope, she had not missed it.

But she didn't immediately jump up and put distance between them. Instead, she tilted her head and studied him from her position. That insane, make-him-beg position. "Is that what this is really about?" Harley asked.

"You should...get up."

"Make me."

"What?"

"You suddenly have this whole Harley-can't-get-shit-done vibe going on, and it's infuriating me. You want me to move, then make me. Because I just took your big, bad ass down with barely any effort. Just like I took down Justin."

Just like I took down Justin. Something exploded in him, and he didn't even know what it was. But he twisted her and rolled, and had Harley beneath him three seconds later. "You almost *kissed* the bastard?"

Something tapped against his chest. Not tapped, poked.

His head whipped down, and he found a small knife with a wicked blade pressed against his chest. Now he was absolutely stunned. "Where the hell did you get that?"

"Remember when I said I didn't have a knife strapped to my thigh?"

His gaze found hers once more.

Her lips curled. "It wasn't hooked to my thigh. It was hidden in the back of my dress. I'm always armed, in many ways." She gave that *tsk, tsk* sound of hers. "You should really stop underestimating me. It's annoying as hell. The story of my life, yes, but annoying, and I truly expected more from you."

"From me? Why?"

A little furrow appeared between her brows. "I don't know." Her words were uncertain, as if she, in fact, didn't know.

In that instant, Seth realized that he was between her legs, that her dress had hiked up, and that the woman still held a small knife over his heart. And he also realized he had never wanted anyone more in his life.

I am so screwed up.

"Just so that you are fully aware of what went down, I didn't nearly kiss Justin Florent. The man is not exactly my type. My turn-ons do not include men who get off on choking women."

His eyes widened. "He choked you?" *Dead. The bastard was—*

"I caught him with his hand around the throat of a woman working as one of the waitstaff tonight. She was scared and crying, and I wasn't just going to stand there while he hurt her."

Of course, that wasn't Harley.

"Someone needed to stop him. So I did." Casual. "He came barreling at me, so I took him down. Then I took his knives. I took his phone. And I rushed to the rescue before anyone could hurt you. I actually consider that a job well done. I should get a gold star. Or two."

"Harley…"

"I'm capable of protecting myself. I'm capable of protecting *you.* I'm also capable of taking out threats that come our way. You need me. Don't let the fact that you want to fuck me ruin everything. I'd sure hate for you to die because you want me so badly."

He did want her. Badly. And he did need her. Because there was a whole lot happening in his life, and Seth wasn't sure exactly who he could trust. "What do you want?" Seth heard himself ask.

Those long lashes flickered again. The gold of her eyes deepened.

And a fist pounded against the door.

That pounding fist was like cold water pouring over him. "What the hell am I doing?" he asked. He let her go and jumped to his feet.

Harley sat up, slowly, and shoved the hair out of her eyes. "Interesting. A knife to the heart doesn't scare you, but a knock at the door does. I'll remember that for future encounters."

"I'm not scared." He extended a hand and hauled Harley to her feet. "Just didn't want Marchello to burst in and see me...ah...see us...I just don't want him seeing you that way, okay?" He blinked, and the knife had vanished from her hand.

Okay. That had been fast.

She sat down on the couch, next to her discarded shoes, crossed her legs, and folded her hands in her lap. "You should answer the door."

Another fierce round of knocks followed her words. He rushed for the door.

"But check first, to make sure it's Brent Marchello and not one of the many people I now think want you dead."

He was already checking, dammit. His eye pressed to the peephole, and he saw Brent glaring back at him.

"And how about you keep your doubts about my ability to do the job just between us for now, hmm? Let's not air our dirty laundry in front of the FBI agent that neither one of us completely trusts."

He spun to stare at her.

She gave him a wide-eyed blink. "Oh, what? Like that was a secret? If you were one hundred percent on team FBI, I wouldn't be here. Isn't your lack of trust the whole reason you brought me on board in the first place?"

She had an excellent point. No, he didn't trust the Feds. Mostly because his father had been working with far too many dirty cops and federal agents. When it came to people that he trusted, the list was very short.

And...Harley was on the list. In the top two, actually. The other spot belonged to his best friend, Cooper Fairmont. But since Cooper knew jack and shit about handling dangerous situations...

Harley gets to move into spot number one.

Brent pounded again. Talk about impatient. Seth whirled for the door once more. He flipped the locks, jerked open the door, and hauled the agent inside. And as soon as Seth shut the door behind the FBI Agent...

"Tonight sure as hell went to shit," Brent drawled. "Which one of you is responsible for that clusterfuck?" His gaze darted to the couch. Lingered on Harley. "My money is on the Wilde agent. Told you there was no point in bringing in someone from the outside. You should have just gone with a Fed who could have taken care of business without any fuss."

Seth moved to the side, putting himself between Brent and Harley. "She was perfect. She saved my ass."

"You did notice," Harley murmured from behind him. "That's touching."

He didn't look back at her. "Harley thinks the meeting tonight was a setup."

"Oh, is that what Harley thinks?" Brent sauntered around the room, poking and prodding various things.

"Yes," Harley said clearly. "That's what I think. That's also what Seth just said. I believe the whole intent of the meeting was to draw Seth out and eliminate him."

Brent frowned as he stopped poking at a vase of flowers. "Seriously? Why the hell would you think that?"

"Oh, probably because I found a text with that intent on the phone of the man who chased us from the house."

"Where's the phone now?" Brent demanded. "Let me see it."

Seth would like to see that phone, too.

"It's back at the house," Harley said as she continued sitting in her casual pose on the couch. "Seeing as how it would look suspicious as hell if I took the thing with me and it was traced back to this suite, I thought it prudent to drop the phone on my way out. I'm hoping Justin just thinks he lost it during all that fierce huffing and puffing he was doing at the entranceway to the old mansion as we left."

Now Seth was the one to frown. "But won't he find it suspicious that you kicked his ass?"

"*Tell me she didn't.*" An order from Brent. "Because if she did, she blew our cover to hell and back."

Harley shrugged her delicate shoulders. "I'm not one hundred percent sure Justin remembers those events. Time will tell. Taking the phone and having it traced to us would have certainly tipped the scales in a negative manner, so I figured I'd leave it behind and we'd just see how things played out."

"*Bringing her on was a major mistake.*" Brent's face had reddened. "I warned you. Told you that she'd get in the way. We have trained professionals for this type of case!"

"Yes, but you're not using them." She rose. Pointed to Seth. "You're using a civilian to work what I think might be one of the most dangerous undercover ops I've ever heard of. So when you're running a case like this one, rules need to be bent. I'm great when it comes to bending rules."

"Shocking," Brent muttered, sarcasm dripping from his voice. "Never saw that coming."

Seth knew he had to take control of the situation. "Is my cover blown or not?" Seth fired out. "Because I've been working my ass off for months to try and look the damn part, just like the Feds ordered me to do. Like *you* ordered. I thought I was moving in with the big players, finally establishing myself with this meeting tonight, but if all they are doing is drawing me out to kill me...then what in the hell is the point of all this?"

Brent helped himself to some chocolates that had been left by the hotel staff. He unwrapped one slowly. "We all know plenty of people were gunning for your father. Not like he made a ton of friends in the underworld. You don't typically *have* friends there. You have enemies who are just waiting to take you down and take over your business."

Great. Like he didn't get that the whole deal was like jumping into the ocean with a swarm of hungry sharks who'd had chum dumped near them.

"Do they know he's working with the Feds?" Harley asked. "Can you be certain there is no leak from your agents?"

Brent balled up the chocolate wrapper. "Only a select few know what we're doing. And, no, the people on my team *aren't* criminals."

She didn't look convinced.

"What did this message say, exactly?" Brent pushed.

"It said that Seth wasn't to leave the house."

"That's it?" Brent's stare flickered to Seth. "Doesn't really sound like a death threat to me."

"No?" Harley strolled around and snagged a piece of chocolate for herself. "What about the giant goon who rushed out after us with blood in his eyes? Did that look like a threat?"

"He could have been coming because of *you*."

She put down the chocolate without eating it. "Seth was in danger. Seth *is* in danger as long as he's doing this work. The man is in way over his head and—"

Brent's laughter cut her off.

Her head angled toward Seth. "Did I make a joke?" A brief pause as her nose wrinkled. "Because I don't remember making a joke."

"He's not some helpless baby." A snicker from Brent. "Seth knows how to watch after himself."

Her eyes narrowed.

"His dear old dad might have kept secrets about his business," Brent continued, "but do you really think he let his kid grow up with zero training? Especially with Seth's mom being murdered when he was a kid? Seth has experienced training more brutal and thorough than freaking Navy SEALs."

Seth saw the shock flash in her eyes. "That's enough, Brent." The FBI agent needed to stop, now.

But Brent kept right on rolling. "After his wife's murder, Eddie Wells was a man on a mission. He trained his kid in every marital arts possible, had him at the gun range, sent him to survival trainings, enrolled him in military school instead of boarding school for several years and then he—"

"*Enough.*" The Fed had such a big mouth.

"Well, well." Her gaze slowly trekked down Seth's body. "Aren't you full of surprises? How come this didn't come up when I did my search on you?"

"Because the FBI is in charge of his background right now." A smooth reply from Brent. "We control what gets seen and what doesn't."

"In other words…" She strolled toward Seth. Slow, silent steps on her bare feet. Cute feet. Toes with soft pink polish.

Why am I looking at her toes?

Her hand pressed to his chest. "In other words, you wanted your enemies to think you were weak prey. Easy pickings. So you had the Feds make a BS life story for you."

"I don't like the word 'easy' or 'prey' when we're talking about me," he groused.

Her mouth curved in a half-smile. One that didn't reach her eyes. He realized that while she was smiling, Harley was actually quite pissed. The gold of her gaze dimmed as the brown blazed. "You kept more secrets from me."

He had. He kept secrets from pretty much everyone, though, so it was hardly anything personal.

"He's trained," Brent said from behind her before Seth could figure out how to respond to her accusing words. "I'm not sending some clueless civilian into a war zone. I'm not that much of an asshole."

"Aren't you?"

Seth's jaw hardened at her soft words.

Brent didn't seem to have heard her taunting question. "Seth can handle himself if things go to shit. Another reason why he doesn't need you," Brent pointed out. "So, now that it's clear you messed up our meeting, how about you pack your things and go so we can try to save what's left of this operation?"

Harley sucked in a breath. Her gaze never wavered from Seth's. "Do you want me to go?"

He'd thought they weren't supposed to air dirty laundry in front of the federal agent.

"Your services just aren't needed." Brent's voice was smooth. "I'm sure Seth can get someone to cut you a check so your time will be compensated, but we truly can't afford any additional screw ups. Lives are on the line."

Harley nodded. "Yes." Her voice was soft. "Your life is on the line, Seth."

Her hand still pressed to his chest. Soft and delicate. But the delicacy was only on the surface. Shouldn't he know plenty about how surfaces could deceive?

"We need to try and make up lost ground with Fabian." Brent began to pace. "Couldn't believe it when I saw that SOB peeking out from the house. I'd only seen one or two surveillance photos of him—and they were grainy because the guy has *tight* security—but I recognized him. *Fabian Butler*. Big fish, man. Big, freaking fish. You'll need to contact him. Apologize. You can tell him that your girlfriend went crazy or something and you dumped her ass."

Her jaw jerked up. "No."

"Yes, Seth. Yes. You don't take orders from her. Jeez. Listen to me. You'll need to reach out to Fabian. Give him some BS story about your crazy girlfriend—"

Her eyes blazed. "*He's a dick*," she mouthed.

"And then you'll ask him for a second chance," Brent continued. He ambled toward the window and peered out at the city. "If we're lucky, he'll give you one."

Her hand pressed harder to Seth's chest. "Don't do a thing that idiot tells you. You go apologize, and you'll look weak. If the Fabian guy is just waiting to kill you, well, an apology makes you look weak and like a dumbass. A double mistake."

"I'm not a dumbass," Seth growled. He was really getting tired of the agent's bullshit. And if Brent said the "crazy girlfriend" line one more time...

"Excellent, so glad to hear that," Harley praised him. "Because not being a dumbass should be like, step one, for all Wilde clients. I'll make an addendum and have that included in future contracts."

"This is absurd!" Brent snarled as he spun toward them. "Don't listen to her. Maybe the hard-on you have for Harley is making you incapable of good decisions. You know, because all of the blood is flowing down to your dick instead of your head. Let me help you out. She doesn't belong here. She is going to royally screw this mission."

His head whipped toward Brent. "What the hell did you just say?"

Whatever Brent saw on Seth's face had the agent swallowing. "What I meant was..."

Seth's phone dinged. A message had just come through. Normally, he would have ignored that message because he had some extremely pressing issues right in front of him.

"I'll bet you a pound of chocolate that's going to be Fabian," Harley said. "He'll be the one apologizing and asking for a meeting."

"Intermediaries set up the meeting tonight. It's doubtful he'd be able to contact me personally so fast. Not like he has my number."

She gave a little sigh as his phone beeped again. "He's got your contact info. That's going to be him. And you're going to owe me chocolate."

Seth pulled out the phone. He didn't recognize the number, but Harley craned closer.

"Yep, that's him."

His head lifted.

"Same number that was on Justin's phone."

Well, well. Seth swiped his finger over the screen and read the text.

My apologies to you.

Okay, first, points for Harley.

I learned my associate acted inappropriately to your lady. That behavior is not tolerated in my house. I assure you, he's been handled.

What did "handled" mean? Because Seth thought that might be another word for "killed" in Fabian's book.

The text continued...*I would like another meeting with you. A meeting, not a party. This time, you pick the location. I will be there.*

"What does he want?" Brent asked.

"A meeting." Seth exhaled slowly.

"*Agree,*" Brent urged. "Agree right away. Meet ASAP. Wait, not ASAP. I need to get other agents in place. We'll want to be sure we can monitor everything that's said at the meeting. Fabian is a prime target. Prime, I tell you. So major that I almost shit myself when I caught a glimpse of him peeking out from that house in the Garden."

"What a lovely visual," Harley demurred. "Thank you for sharing it with us all."

Brent grunted. "That man has just as many illegal ties as your bastard of a father, Seth. We need to take him down. This is the kind of collar we have been building up for. Everyone else was small-time. Fabian is what we want. He's got real power."

Seth's back teeth ground together.

"His fingers are reportedly in every illegal pie you can imagine." Brent gave a low whistle. "But he stays behind the scenes. Rarely seen in public, but with a pull that stretches far and wide. Agents have been wanting to nail him for years, ever since he took over *his* family's business. Kid was just eighteen then, but already one serious sonofabitch."

Harley's head turned toward the agent. "Hate to tell you your business, but you're starting to sound like a fan boy."

He flipped her off.

"My, my, agent, that is hurtful."

Seth ignored their byplay. He got that Fabian was a big deal. In Brent's mind, taking out Fabian would probably be like cutting off the head of a snake.

Provided, of course, that the snake didn't bite Seth first.

He tapped out a quick response to Fabian's text.

Harley laughed softly as she once again craned closer. "Good choice." Her scent surrounded him.

"What?" Brent bounded forward.

Harley backed away.

"What are you saying to him?" Anxious words from the agent. "Are you setting up a meeting? Are you telling him that you want to deal?"

He sent the text. Then told the FBI agent, "Fuck off."

Brent's eyes widened. "Excuse me?"

"I told Fabian to fuck off for now. When I'm ready to talk, I'll let him know."

Brent's jaw dropped so far it almost hit the floor. "Are you crazy?"

"No, quite sane." *Despite Harley's current attempts to push me over the edge.* "Thanks for asking, though. Appreciate your concern."

Brent's face went from red to a pale purple. Had to be unhealthy. "You just blew months of work! He is never going to want to talk to you again—"

"Yes, he will." Harley's confidence filled her voice. "The fact that Seth doesn't seem too eager makes him look less like a plant. And are you just *forgetting* that Fabian tried to put a hit on Seth tonight? Fabian is trying to figure out how much Seth knows. He's hoping like hell that Seth is in the dark.'"

"You don't know that." A sharp, negative shake of Brent's head. "You have no clue what Fabian is thinking. You're not psychic."

Another ding as a new text arrived.

Seth read it. Nodded.

Brent tried to see it, but Seth just shoved the phone into his pocket.

"What did it say?" Brent glared at Seth.

So Seth told him, "*I'll send you a gift by way of apology. Perhaps then you won't make me wait too long.*"

Brent jerked back. "A gift? What the hell kind of gift is he going to be sending to you?"

"I don't know, but something tells me it is *not* going to be a gift I want." Not at all. Then again, what about this mess had he wanted?

"Answers," Harley snapped. "We want them right now, Brent. You tell us what we need to know, and only then will Seth schedule that meeting with your target."

"Uh, lady, you're overstepping. This is the part where Seth fires you and kicks your pretty ass out of the door." Brent pointed to said door. "Then he and I get to work, and we can put some very bad people behind bars."

Seth tossed his phone onto the couch. It landed near Harley's shoes. "Don't talk about her ass again."

"Excuse me?" Brent peered at him as if fearing Seth had lost his mind.

Hadn't he just told the agent he wasn't crazy? He hated repeating himself. "She's not going anywhere. I've got a signed contract with her. Until this case is closed, she's watching *my* ass."

"I don't know that I would call *your* ass pretty," Harley said as she peered around Seth. "But it is nice. Looks all firm and muscled."

He shook his head. That woman...

"You're *keeping* her?" Brent choked out.

Seth's eyes held Harley's. "Yes, I do believe I am."

CHAPTER SIX

Step Six: Don't be a dumbass.

*(This should have been said earlier. My bad.
Let's make it step one.)*

"She's not cleared for classified intel." Brent crossed his arms over his chest. "We've been over this before, Seth. I told you when you first announced you were bringing her on that she'd have to work in the dark if you insisted on this BS plan."

Brent didn't like her. Check. Message received and returned. "I can assure you that I will pass any background check you run on me. There's not so much as a traffic ticket associated with my name." Mostly because she was really, really good at talking her way out of tickets.

Brent growled. Then glowered.

She sent him her full-wattage smile.

"Get her clearance," Seth ordered. "And then get your crew to find out if Fabian has a real hit on me or if he was just trying to play hardball."

She opened her mouth to tell him that people didn't typically play hardball quite that way, but then stopped. Brent had been right on one point. The order on the phone she'd seen hadn't been specifically for a kill. Though, not like you could just straight out order a kill, either. You always had to be careful so that hits couldn't be traced back to you.

Fabian would be smart enough to know how to phrase his texts so nothing would come back to bite him in the ass. Not like the man would casually order a hit that could be tied to him and used in a court of law.

Oh, no, Fabian would know how to phrase things just right. Like that bit about "handling" Justin and sending Seth some kind of "gift" as atonement? Lots of red flags flew for her when she thought about those words.

"Fine. If she's some kind of deal breaker for you—"

"She is," Seth replied.

Those words made her go all warm and tingly. "So sweet."

Seth cut her a glare.

"It is sweet," she maintained.

"If she's a deal breaker," Brent huffed, "then I will see about clearance. But it's gonna take time. I'll also see what my people can find out about the potential hit." Brent rolled back his shoulders. "Promise me that you're in for the night. You're not going to stage some late-night sneak out and meet up with Fabian? You won't do anything reckless?"

"Do I look reckless?" Seth asked.

That wasn't exactly an answer.

"She does." Brent pointed her way.

She looked behind her because the man certainly was not talking about her.

"Yep, gorgeous, talking about you."

Her head swung back toward him. Had she imagined it or had the annoying agent just called her gorgeous?

"*No*," Seth said flatly.

Brent seemed to relax. "Good. Glad I have your word on that."

"No, you don't fucking flirt with her right in front of me."

Brent's thick eyebrows raised. "Excuse me?"

"I didn't think of it as flirting," Harley felt duty bound to point out that fact. "More like him just being annoying."

But Seth had closed in on the agent. "I don't like your attitude toward her."

"Uh, say again?"

"Why? You heard me the first time. You've been against her from the beginning. You're either insulting her or hitting on her, and that shit is stopping. You aren't talking about her ass again. You aren't talking about how gorgeous she is. You're being professional. Or *you're* the one who is out. Got me? Consider it another deal breaker."

Brent's mouth opened.

"I can do it." Seth delivered the vow in a smooth voice. "I'm the one most needed, right? The civilian who had to be pulled in because I had the perfect cover ready to go. If I bail, this whole operation goes to shit."

Brent's mouth snapped closed. "If you *bail*, then what happens to your business and all of those employees you have? Or the potential pending charges against you? Did you forget all of that?"

Ah. So Seth was being blackmailed into this con. She'd suspected as much. From her experience, the Feds didn't always play nicely with others.

"I've forgotten nothing." Seth didn't seem particularly intimidated. Points for him. "You shouldn't forget, either. Without me, there is no operation."

"And you'd blow it all because you don't like the way I'm talking to her?" The words seemed to choke him. "That's some bullshit!"

Seth just waited.

"Fuck. Fine. *Sorry,* Harley." Brent threw her a fuming glare.

She didn't point out that his apology hardly seemed sincere, especially in light of the glare that accompanied his words.

"Anything else?" Brent choked out.

"The clearance," Seth reminded him. "Get it for her, ASAP. Run every background check necessary."

A gleam of intent filled Brent's eyes. "Oh, I will," he promised. "I will run every possible check, don't you worry about that."

And she knew he was going to try and dig up dirt on her. The man wanted her out of the way so badly.

Unfortunately for him, she didn't plan on going anywhere.

Brent marched for the door. "I'll be in contact first thing tomorrow, and we can figure out a secure meeting location for you and Fabian. The Feds can have the place staked out before you arrive, and if we're lucky, we'll get the SOB to make a confession that we can use against him."

A moment later, the door swung shut behind Brent. Seth immediately advanced and flipped the extra lock. He stood there a moment, with his back to her and his shoulders tense.

A whole lot had been dropped in that little conversation, and Harley tried to figure out exactly where she should start on the unwrapping of it all.

"You should go to bed."

Bed wasn't where she wanted to start. Her mind flew back over their conversation and stuck on one point. "I am very sorry about your mother."

His broad shoulders tensed even more. "Not tonight."

She stepped toward him. Her feet sank in the thick carpet. "Do you know who murdered her?" *Was it your dad?* She'd read about his mother's death, and as far as she was aware, the case had never been solved. But maybe there were details that had been left out of the public reports.

A negative shake of his head. "Too much adrenaline. Too much fury still running through me." He turned toward her. "Not tonight," he said again.

"You have fury pumping through you?" Now she was the one impressed. "I got that you were annoyed with Brent—he annoys me plenty, too, totally understand the reaction—but I didn't get a white-hot-fury vibe from you. That control of yours is quite something."

His head tilted, just an inch or so to the right. Then he began to stalk toward her.

She almost retreated, and she was so very not the retreating type. Instead, she straightened her spine and looked up at him as he stopped right in front of her. "Hi." A nervous response. Dammit.

The faint lines near his mouth tightened. "My father taught me that control was the most important thing a man can have in this world."

Oh, jeez. A life lesson from a monster. She was afraid to ask just how his father had instilled that particular lesson. "The same dad who made sure you had all sorts of martial arts training? Training you didn't bother to tell your bodyguard you possessed? So many secrets you keep."

"If I couldn't handle myself in a dangerous situation, I never would have agreed to the deal with the Feds. I don't have a death wish."

"Are you sure?" Damn. The question just blurted out.

But there it was. Hanging in the air between them. Too late to take back.

"That what you think this is about?" He edged closer, and he'd already been plenty close. "I have a death wish so I'm taking a dive on the dark side of life? You think that's who I am? What I'm doing?"

"I can't quite figure you out." The more she learned, the more of a puzzle he seemed. "Are you a good man pretending to be someone bad?" That was what it would seem like, to some. But she'd learned tonight that he was very, very good at pretending. "Or a bad man pretending to be someone good?"

"Why would I pretend to be good?"

Why, indeed? "So you can get a deal with the Feds and walk away scot-free when this is all over?"

His stare held hers. "Go to bed, Harley."

"You're jealous."

His jaw hardened.

"You didn't like it when Brent called me gorgeous. You didn't like it when he commented on my ass."

"Also didn't like it when he said I had a hard-on for you and that it was clouding my judgment. Brent can be a total prick."

She wet her lips. "You do have a hard-on for me."

No denial. Just a shrug. "Want me to apologize for that?"

A shake of her head. "No, because I want you, too." Finally, *finally,* she caught him by surprise. She heard the surprise in his sharp inhale.

"Be careful what you say," Seth warned her, voice roughening and hazel eyes glittering.

"Why? If you're the *good* guy at your core, it won't matter. You'll stick to some magical code of conduct that you're following. The code that is making you be some martyr who risks everything he has because he's trying to atone for the sins of his father. Not *your* sins. His."

"I have plenty of my own sins."

"Right. Because if you're the secret *bad* guy of the piece, you'll be hiding those sins. And me saying I want you? Well, that will push that dark, dangerous part of you into action. You'll say to hell with any rules, and you'll take what we both want."

His hands lifted as if he'd touch her, but then he caught himself. His hands fisted. "This is a test?"

"No, this is me saying I want you. I don't know if that want is good or bad, just like I don't know if you are. I know I have a contract that says I will protect you. I know that you just protected me in front of the Fed. We have an alliance, you and I."

His fisted hands fell back to his sides. "Go to bed."

She could see the desire in his eyes. That desire just fed the fuel simmering in her own blood. "I've never fucked a client before."

"Bed. And good to fucking know."

"It is important to know because that's not who I am. I'm not casual about sex. Never have been. I guarded a rock star for three months once. We were together twenty-four, seven. I kept hearing how he was this incredible sex god."

His face could not get harder. The vein at his temple seemed close to bursting. That couldn't be good. And his gaze? The hazel was on fire.

"There it is again," Harley noted, her voice soft. "Jealousy. You don't need to be jealous. I'm telling you I didn't sleep with him. I'm telling you that I haven't been tempted. Until you. Because there is something about you that pulls me close, and I'm not quite sure what to do about that attraction. To be honest, I'm a little afraid of the way you make me feel." She was confused. And tired. And, yes, deep down, scared. So much about this case—and about Seth—scared her.

Normally, Wilde agents always went out with backup. A requirement of the job. But because of the nature of this particular case, there was no backup from Wilde. Brent was supposed to be filling that role. *And that doesn't make me feel reassured.*

"You're afraid of me?"

"I said I was afraid of how you made me feel. Not that I was afraid of you."

"Isn't that the same thing?"

No, it wasn't. "You need to remember something about me." Was she leaning up toward him? Why, yes, she was.

"What's that?"

"I'm the bodyguard. Me. I don't care what kind of super special training your mob boss of a father gave you, when danger is calling, I'm the one who is supposed to take the risks."

"And what if I don't want you taking risks?" Was his head dipping closer to hers?

Why, yes, she believed it was. But what had he just asked? Something about her not taking risks? Ah, well, if that was what he wanted... "Then you have the wrong bodyguard." She pulled in a deep breath and got ready to take one very big risk. "How unfortunate for you." Her toes shoved down against the carpet. Her body thrust up. Her hands flew to curve around his shoulders, and she hauled him down toward her. Their mouths crashed together in a firestorm of need.

His mouth was open. So was hers. Open and eager, and his tongue swept into her mouth as if he'd been dying to taste her.

Sometimes, passion didn't live up to the hype. Sometimes, you thought you wanted something, but that desire led you astray. A kiss could be nothing. It could show you how wrong two people were when they got together.

Or it could show you just how smoking right they were going to be.

The kiss wasn't cold. It wasn't fleeting. It was burn-you-alive intense, and she felt lust explode in every cell of her body. When she'd been on the floor beneath him, yes, even with her knife pressed to his heart, need had surged through her. The attraction between them was undeniable.

A kiss could tell you so much…

This kiss told her that if their clothes weren't in the way, he'd be fucking her. Because Seth kissed with a single-minded, consuming focus. His lips. His tongue. This was no amateur hour. He devoured, and she loved every single second of his kiss.

Loved it so much that she knew he was going to be extra dangerous to her.

His hands slid down to her hips. Curled around her ass, and he brought her closer against him. No missing the bulge of his arousal. Brent the Bastard had been right on that point. Seth very much had a hard-on for her.

Only fair, considering how wet she was getting for him.

Stop it. Pull back. Red alert. Red. Alert.

Her fingers dug into his shoulders. Her mouth pulled from his. Pulled, then, dammit, darted back, and she kissed him once more.

No, no, no. She jerked back a second time. Harley might have even taken a wee tumble if his hands hadn't steadied her. But he did steady her, and he stared down at her with a gaze that swirled with his emotions and glinted with his lust.

"Bed," Seth growled.

"Is that an invitation or...?" She stopped. Okay. Words were often her weapon. Her best defense growing up with so many brothers had been a flippant tongue designed to drive them crazy. But this wasn't a situation where crazy would work. She needed some space because her whole body felt like it could overheat at any moment. "Going to bed. Alone." That was for the best.

They had some trust issues to work through. She didn't take a man to bed without trusting him completely. Seth had proved tonight that he was holding back on her. He was a closet badass disguised as a mild-mannered rich boy. She would *not* find that sexy.

Dammit. She did. Chalk that up to her Clark Kent issues. She loved a good secret identity that housed a badass. Turning sharply on her heel, Harley headed for her room. Hers, not his. But just as she neared the open doorway, she stopped. Her hands flew out and curled around the doorframe. "I'm very sorry about your mother." Yes, she'd just gone back to that. Because it mattered.

"It was a long time ago."

Sure, it was. Agreed. She looked over her shoulder. "There are some things we never forget."

"Yes." His voice had gentled, but the desire on his face and in his eyes hadn't lessened.

"And some things we never forgive?" A deliberate question.

Bingo. She saw the hit in his eyes and knew that her suspicion had been right. So much more was at play with Seth than he let on. Yes, he might be working with the Feds to bring down criminals who'd been on their watchlist for years. But she also believed, with every fiber of her being, that Seth was working his own agenda.

Some things were never forgotten or forgiven. Like the murder of your mother.

"Good night, Seth," she whispered.

He gave a slow shake of his head. "There's been nothing good in my world for a very long time."

***

It was the faint click of a door shutting that caught her attention an hour and a half later. If she'd been asleep, she would never have heard the sound. Too soft. But sleep had eluded her, and she'd been in the dark, staring up at the ceiling and running through her conversation—and the damn kiss—with Seth over and over again.

At that click, she whipped to attention. Her hand flew into the nightstand and drew out the gun she'd hidden there earlier. Wearing jogging shorts and a tank top, she tiptoed to her own door. She'd left it open, an inch or so, before bed. The open door allowed her to peek into the exterior area without making any noises, the reason she'd left the door open in the first place.

Darkness waited outside of her room. She was sure that had been a door *closing,* and that meant someone had snuck into their suite—or someone had just left. Since she didn't plan to give any would-be intruder time to off her boss, she rushed out of her room on silent steps and went straight for Seth's bedroom. Luckily, her eyes had adjusted quickly to the darkness. She darted into his room and as the faint light from the nearby buildings spilled through the blinds, she realized that the bed was empty.

A chill skated down her spine even as she whirled and ran back to the sitting area. A quick scan showed no intruders and that meant that Seth had been the one clicking the door closed. *On his way out.*

"I don't think so," she whispered. You didn't ditch your bodyguard. Certainly not twice in one night. Had the man not learned his lesson? Well, he was *about* to learn it. But she would seriously have to haul ass. He had a lead on her.

Luckily, she had a few tricks up her sleeve.

In one frantic minute, she was dressed. Jeans. Long sleeved shirt. Tennis shoes. And a loose raincoat to better hide the gun she'd holstered at her side and because she knew more rain had been predicted for the night. After flying from the suite, she pounded the button for the elevator and tapped her foot as she waited and waited...

He could be going out for a breath of fresh air. He could have been unable to sleep.

Or he could be off for a secret meeting without me.

Because now that she *thought* about it, she'd only actually seen the first text that Seth had received from Fabian. He'd *recited* the second text to her and Brent. She'd never seen the words. For all she knew, he'd lied about the message that he'd received.

If he'd lied, so well and completely, then that was certainly very, very naughty of him.

She strode out of the elevator the instant it hit the ground floor. The lobby was deserted at this time of night, and it felt eerily like a tomb because the silence was so complete. Seth wasn't hanging anywhere nearby, so she double-timed it for the doors that led outside and for the security guard who lounged in the chair, scanning his phone, right beside those doors.

"You don't get the money," she said as she approached him, "unless you can tell me exactly where he went."

He looked up with a quick grin. "How'd you know the guy would run in the middle of the night?"

It wasn't running. It was...ditching her. And she didn't like it. In fact, she found it downright insulting. You didn't kiss a woman like your life depended on it one moment and then sneak away when you thought she was sleeping. Not cool. "I don't have time to waste." She also liked to plan ahead, and that was why she'd made the secret deal with the night guard.

"Your man left on foot about two minutes ago."

"Already know that."

"He was wearing a black hoodie and jeans. Had the hood pulled up. Obviously, the guy was trying to keep a low profile."

"Where, James?" She took out a hundred-dollar bill.

He tapped the screen of his phone, then put the device to his ear. "Got eyes on him?"

James had told her that he had plenty of friends in the city who would be willing to keep watch. The guards all along the riverfront and Canal Street knew each other.

"Uh, huh. Thanks." He lowered the phone. "Your man is heading to Bourbon. That's where most folks go this time of night." His nimble fingers took the money. "Better watch yourself out there. Things can get wild."

"So I've heard." She wasn't interested in watching herself so much, though. She had a client who needed protecting. Even if he seemed hell-bent on ignoring his bodyguard and her orders.

His mistake. He was about to find out that she wasn't the type of woman he could ever ignore.

CHAPTER SEVEN

Step Seven: When you're pulling a con, you can find yourself in some unexpected places. That's when you really need to blend in. Blend, don't stick out. That's the goal.

She ducked outside and made a beeline for Bourbon. This wasn't her first time in the city. Far from it. She knew her way around and had, in fact, spent far too much time on Bourbon back in the day. Those parties had been helluva fun for a college girl, especially one who had been way too sheltered her whole life by five extremely overprotective, older brothers.

Her steps quickened over the rain-slick streets. A little drizzle fell onto her, but she ignored the weather. She had her coat, after all, and she'd pulled up the hood just as she left the shelter of the hotel. A dark coat, perfect for blending into the night. Her steps were fast and certain, and in minutes, as she closed in on Bourbon, she saw...him. Or rather, his black hoodie.

The black hoodie turned right.

So did she.

Like she wouldn't recognize those shoulders anywhere. Those shoulders, that broad back, that fine ass, and that impatient, powerful walk that was all pure Seth.

Where are we going tonight, Seth? To a bar, to blow off some steam? While she could certainly understand the urge, it wasn't safe for the man to go prancing around alone. Didn't matter what training he had, they were supposed to stick together.

She stayed about fifteen feet back, wanting to keep him in sight, but not wanting to risk him giving her the slip.

"Hey, pretty lady!" A man with a giant hurricane drink in his hand stumbled toward her. "You looking for company—"

"Never gonna happen." She didn't even glance his way and her steps never slowed. "I am full-up on company."

"But, baby, I can—"

"Nope. You can't." The bright lights from the bars illuminated the street. Sign after sign. Bar after bar. The faint drizzle wasn't slowing down the party. She could see people up on the second-floor balconies, with drinks in hand. Even though it was far from the Mardi Gras season, many of the people—tourists—had beaded necklaces around their necks. They were dancing and singing and seeming to have one hell of a time.

People walked in seemingly every direction. Those glowing signs above the bars promised cheap drinks, they promised dancers, they promised a night that would not be forgotten.

Yet Seth walked straight ahead, not even glancing toward them. Then he turned on

Bienville, heading away from the bustle and the cries of the party street.

Where are you going? Her steps quickened once more because he wasn't going to ditch her. Well, not again, anyway. Bienville was a whole lot quieter than Bourbon, and it took only moments on that stretch to feel as if you were in another world. A darker world. Where the businesses were all closed down. Where every now and then, she caught a shadowy figure moving in a doorway. One that didn't speak. Just watched.

Seth didn't look back. Not even once. Either the man had zero situational awareness—something she doubted—or he just didn't care if someone decided to jump him and attack. At this point, she was starting to think he wanted an attack.

Her breath shuddered out when he took another turn. It felt like they'd been on the streets forever, but a glance at her phone showed her that she'd only been out there for about fifteen minutes. When he took the turn on Basin, her stomach knotted. She knew what waited on that street, and there was no good reason for anyone to be visiting that particular location in the middle of the night.

Not unless you were looking for death.

She couldn't see him because he'd turned that corner so quickly. Her steps rushed forward. Harley took the turn, too, and—

He grabbed her. Seth's hands flew out, curled around her, and yanked her against his body. Her back flattened to his rock-hard stomach. "Why the hell are you following me?" he snarled. His hold was just slight of bruising. Promising pain.

"Because that's what you pay me to do." She kicked back at his shin even as she drove her elbow toward his ribs.

Her elbow didn't make contact because he'd spun her around. His hold had changed in a blink. Not promising pain anymore, but still tight. Determined. "Harley?"

Her hood had fallen off. His hadn't. She knew that, even in the dark, he could see the tumble of her hair and her features because the corner location happened to be close to a flickering gaslight. "Who else did you expect?" A murmur. "Oh, wait, could it have been one of the many *bad guys* you are playing your dangerous game with? Perhaps the man who chased you from the mansion earlier? Or just some thief in New Orleans who decided you were easy prey?"

"I'm not easy."

Yeah, figured that out.

"Why are you here?" he gritted. He didn't let go.

She didn't fight his hold because, well, why? If she wanted out, she'd get out. At the moment, what she wanted to get were answers. Apparently, he wanted answers, too, so she'd be the bigger person and get things rolling. "I'm here because you hired me to stick close to you, remember?" A sugary-sweet response. "Hard to do when you're out galivanting through the Big Easy while I'm tucked all snug and warm in bed at the hotel."

"You were sleeping."

"No, I was thinking." *About you and that crazy kiss.* Ridiculous. She should not be mooning over the client. So amateur hour. "I was making plans. Formulating scenarios." *Uh, huh.* "Then I heard you leave, and I followed." She didn't mention her bribe to the downstairs security guard. If Seth decided to go for more strolls, she wanted her little network to still be in position to help her out. "Newsflash, hotshot, we stick together. You can't go off on little side jobs when the mood strikes you. That's not how we are going to work."

His fingers flexed against her. "This isn't a side job."

"No?" She nodded. "Right. You're just taking a post-midnight tour of a cemetery because you—wait, let me guess...you're into the paranormal, that it?" He had to be going to the cemetery. The St. Louis Cemetery was the main attraction on that street. A perfect place for all sorts of criminal undertakings. After all, who was going to complain about the dark deeds going down? The dead? Her eyes narrowed on him. "You got the urge to sneak out because you were just dying to see if you could stir up the dead?" *Dying* was really the operative word. If Seth didn't start following her orders, she was very much afraid he would be dying. In a most brutal fashion.

He let her go.

Without his touch sending her blood to a high burn, the night suddenly felt colder. Since he hadn't answered her, Harley pushed, "No? Playing with the paranormal isn't your passion? Too bad. Those New Orleans haunted tours are helluva fun. Of course, you have to do them during the day when the cemetery is actually open as opposed to coming in the *dead* of night. People who come in the dead of night usually have other agendas." Such darker agendas. "They're working drug deals. They're looking for trouble. They're having meetings with dangerous people. You know, typically doing things they should not be doing."

"Go back to the hotel."

Her hands flew to her hips. Fisted. "Don't be an ass. Where you go, I go."

"I'm not in any danger. Go back to the hotel." He took two steps away from her.

So cute, the way he thought he could walk away. "What did the last text say?"

Seth hesitated. His gaze cut away from her, seemingly searching the darkness around them.

They really should move away from the gaslight. So she did. A few quick sidesteps. "I didn't actually *see* that text. Saw the first one. Didn't see the second one. I can't quite remember the full message on that one. Me and my faulty memory. Can you tell me once more, what, exactly, it said?"

He looked over at her. "You think I lied to you?"

"The thought did cross my mind." He hadn't followed her into the deeper shadows, so Harley grabbed his hoodie and yanked. He came, willingly enough, and stepped into the darkness with her. "You look suspicious as hell." Sexy as hell, too, but that wasn't the point.

"You're the one who just pulled me into the dark."

She ignored that true point and huffed on, "Skulking around in a hoodie and sticking to the shadows as you slink your way through the city."

"Slink?"

"Fine. Creep. You *crept* your way through the city like some kind of criminal intent on getting to his target." Only the target was the cemetery? "My, my, but you are certainly adopting more and more of your new persona, aren't you?" She leaned in closer. "But a big, bad crime boss doesn't do the dirty work himself. He doesn't creep out on the streets alone. He has people who take care of the nitty gritty work for him. Going out on your own? That just puts a big, old target on your back. I don't know what Fabian promised you..." *Because I didn't read the text. You didn't show it to me.* "But you need to get it through your head that you can't trust him."

"I don't trust him." He reached out. Caught her hood. Lifted it back up and carefully tucked her hair beneath it. "When it comes to trust, the one person in this city I do trust is you." He adjusted her hood a little more. "What I'm doing tonight is personal."

Harley knew a dismissal when she heard one. She also knew when to completely ignore him. "Then I guess we both have personal business." Her head turned as she looked at the waiting cemetery. "Hope you're good at scaling walls."

"This might not have been my final destination. I could be going somewhere else."

"You could be." She eyed the wall. What a pain in the ass this would be. "But I told you I had trouble sleeping, right? So instead of counting sheep to help me settle down, I took some time and did a little more research on you." Or specifically, on his mother. Because his mother's murder was a big motivating factor in Seth's life. "Imagine my surprise when I discovered that your mom is buried in this cemetery. Right here in New Orleans. The city you insisted we visit with barely any travel warning. And now, you're outside of this cemetery in the middle of the night. Not real hard to connect dots."

"She's not buried here."

Uh, according to her sleuthing, his mother very much *was.*

"They don't put people in the ground here because when it used to flood, the bodies would go drifting down the streets."

Something she already knew. "I should have been more careful with my wording. Your mother is *entombed* here." Because he was right. No bodies were in the ground in the St. Louis Cemetery. They were all locked in giant stone, above-ground vaults. A lot of tourists thought the place was just a historic site, somewhere you went to take cool and spooky photos, but it was actually still an active cemetery. Those who were well-connected in the Big Easy could have the cemetery become a final resting place. His mother had been one of those well-connected individuals.

"Your mother grew up in New Orleans." She should have done a deeper dive on his mom sooner, but she hadn't realized how significant his mother's long-ago death was to the actions that Seth was taking in the present. "When she died, her family wanted her final resting place to be here." The wind picked up, blowing against her. She doubted the wind was even slowing down the people on Bourbon Street. "If we're going in, let's go." Because the drizzle was picking up, too. The weather was going to switch from bad to worse soon. "Just keep your eyes open, got me? Everyone knows these places are dangerous as hell at night. You're likely to get us both stabbed if you're not careful."

"No one is getting stabbed tonight."

"Promises, promises."

A rough sigh burst from him. "I'm not ditching you, am I?"

She started across the street. "Nope."

He didn't give her any other arguments. And the man turned out to be very, very good at scaling walls. He even gave her a hand, not that she needed it, but she was hardly going to argue if he wanted to make the scaling process easier on her. The minute her feet hit down on the other side of the massive stone wall that surrounded the cemetery, a shiver skated down her spine.

"Harley?" Concern roughened his low voice.

"Oh, don't mind me. Just being mildly creeped out because we're in a haunted cemetery on what looks to be a stormy night."

His fingers took hers. "Surely you don't believe in ghosts."

"Why not? I believe in plenty of things I can't see."

Her answer seemed to catch him by surprise. He turned toward her. "Like what?"

"Like love." Okay, there were entirely too many places for bad guys to hide in that cemetery. Zero light in there, so she used her free hand to pull out her phone and shine it at the ground.

His hold tightened on her. "You're in love with someone?"

Clueless man. "Seth, Seth, *Seth*. If I were in love with someone, I wouldn't have kissed you at the hotel."

"You're working a cover." Gruff. "The kiss didn't mean anything."

"Okay, that's an asshat thing to say." She snatched her fingers from his. "Don't know what ladies you are used to, but when I kiss someone the way I kissed you, it means something. It might mean, *damn, this is some serious chemistry*. Or it might mean *what the hell am I getting myself into?* But I don't kiss someone as if I can't breathe without that person just for fun. I don't play that way." Actually, come to think of it... "I don't play at all. And no one was there but us, so the cover line is total bull. I kissed you because I wanted to do it." She took a few steps forward. The place was like a maze. "Tell me you know exactly where your mom is entombed."

"Tell me that you're not involved with anyone."

Harley whirled toward him. "You picked one hell of a place for this chat."

"I'm pretty sure *you* started it." His hood was up. The darkness concealing far too much of him. He looked big and dangerous. And...scary.

How could one not look scary in a cemetery after midnight?

She heard something scrape. Like…like an old chunk of stone being moved. The sound made her jump.

A soft laugh came from Seth. "You really are scared of ghosts."

Her light swept toward the faint sound she'd heard. "No, I'm afraid of the living jumping out at me and killing me because my crazy boss thinks cemetery strolls at night are super fun." Something whistled. Her shoulders stiffened.

"It's the wind blowing through the old tombs." He strode closer to her. "I haven't been here since I was seven years old, but I remember exactly how to get to her crypt. Some things stay with you."

"Great. Then lead the way. Let's pay our respects and then get the hell out of here. Though why you decided to come here now, as opposed to, oh, I don't know, daylight, is beyond me." *So tell me, Seth. Give me the real reason you're out here because I do not buy for a single second that you just had the overwhelming urge to pay a post-midnight visit to your mom's final resting place.*

He didn't lead the way. They were in a narrow pathway—if it even *was* a pathway—caged on both sides by high, imposing tombs. He hesitated and said, "Her murderer was never caught."

Those five, rough words had her heart twisting for him. Even though she'd already known this was true. "I'm sorry."

"Why? You didn't know her."

"You don't have to know someone to be sorry they're gone." He was standing there, all stiff and hard in the faint rain, and she gave into impulse and wrapped her arms around him.

"What in the hell are you doing, Harley?"

"Hugging you. And if you had to ask the question, then you are obviously not hugged enough." She squeezed him a little tighter. He made no move to hug her back. "She mattered to you. You loved her, and I'm sorry you lost her when you were so young. I know you must wish you'd gotten to spend more time with her. I certainly feel that way about my mom." Then, because she was hugging him but he was stiff as a board, she realized she'd overstepped enough. Harley pulled back.

Just as his hands lifted to hold her.

But she'd already retreated, and his arms brushed over her, a fleeting caress that had her catching her breath and staring up at the darkness of his face.

"Your mom?" Seth asked, voice careful.

She swallowed. "I'm sure you did background work on me. You know my mom died when I was a kid, too." Barely five years old. "This isn't the place to rehash my past, so how about we get moving, hmm?" Harley turned away. "You said you remember where she was? Impressive, considering this place is like a giant maze."

"I remember because of Marie Laveau's vault. I can still see the X's drawn onto it in my mind. X marks the spot. From there, we turn right. My mother isn't far."

"I know where Marie is." Or rather, her vault. Because there was a whole lot of dispute regarding whether or not Marie was actually inside it. Harley's pace picked up as she headed through the maze. Finally, she had some guidance in the dark. Even at night, she could find her way to the tomb reputed to belong to Marie. She'd visited the spot more than a few times when her brother Ford would come to town. Talk about someone obsessed with voodoo.

But as she bobbed and weaved for her destination, she heard more whistles of the wind. And...scurries? Like insects or small animals scampering away. *So should not be here at night.* They were almost at Marie's when a powerful bolt of lightning lit up the sky. It streaked left to right, illuminating everything, and because she was looking straight into the shadows of a crypt before her—

The sudden, glowing sight of a person standing there had her heart nearly flying right out of her chest. One minute, the figure was spotlighted by the streak of lightning. She had a fast impression of height, strength, power, and then the lightning vanished and darkness flooded back.

His footsteps thudded as he ran away. Automatically, Harley surged after him.

Seth caught her hand. "He's not after us."

He *could* have been, until the lightning had revealed him. He could have been hiding and waiting to attack, maybe not them specifically, but anyone dumb enough to be in the cemetery at night. Drunk college kids. Tourists who wandered over from Bourbon looking for a thrill. "We should *not* be here."

"That's Marie's tomb."

Thunder rumbled in the distance.

Her phone's light flew to the side. Illuminated the X's that had been written on the tomb. She sidled closer. Tall, with X marks scribbled on the surface. Her light slid over the X signs and dropped down to see the offerings. Okay, so they'd found Marie. Now they were supposed to go right. Her light angled to the right. "Tell me why we're here again," she groused at him.

He took the lead, sliding in front of her as they advanced. Every crypt they passed had her doing a doubletake. Was someone else hiding in the shadows? Where the hell had that man gone? He'd been wearing a thick poncho, one that had hung loosely on his body. She knew lots of ponchos like that one were given out by the people who worked the shelters in the area. The ponchos were pretty damn important for plenty of folks. Because what did you get a lot of in New Orleans? Besides the heat? Rain. Lots and lots of it.

"Answers," she heard Seth breathe from in front of her. "That's what I want and why I'm here."

Answers? In the middle of the night? She craned to see around him just as another bolt of lightning split the sky. This time, she saw the crypt. The family name of Trahan was boldly stamped at the top—his mother's maiden name, she knew that. But that wasn't all she saw.

Someone sprawled in front of the crypt.

The lightning faded.

Harley inched to the side of Seth so she could better see that figure. This person wasn't wearing a poncho or a slicker. In fact, that sure looked like a wet business suit to her. And that body was awful big.

And familiar?

Thunder rumbled. Her phone's light hit the person on the ground.

Seth advanced and reached out a hand to touch the figure. "Hey, buddy, you—"

She grabbed Seth's hand before he could make contact. "*Don't.*" Her phone shone onto the person, and she heard Seth's brutal curse fill the air as recognition hit for him.

Justin Florent. His eyes were closed. His body curled on the ground. His way, way too still body.

"Don't touch him," she ordered as she tried to take in the scene.

But, surprise, surprise, Seth was already reaching down. He grabbed Justin's shoulder and rolled him over. The man's body flopped, his right arm dropping low, and her light hit him in the chest.

Red. Red covered the white dress shirt that he wore.

"Fuck." From Seth.

Yes, indeed. Fuck.

A dead body—with what appeared to be a whole lot of stab wounds—had been left right in front of Seth's mother's crypt. Was this the gift that Fabian had promised him? Talk about a twisted-as-hell present. "Did you know?" she demanded.

"What?"

"What game are you playing?" Harley snapped. A dead body was at their feet. *Dead.* Her light slid to the left, and she could see that the small pools on the ground weren't from water...they were from blood.

"What the hell?" Seth breathed.

Footsteps rushed nearby. A fast, frantic pounding. Someone who'd been lurking in the dark. The killer? Or a witness?

"Who told you to come here tonight?" Harley demanded. "And don't you dare give me some BS about randomly wanting to pay respect to your mom's resting place!"

He turned to go after those fleeing footsteps just as she heard the wail of a siren pierce the night. A wail that sounded entirely too close. She looked back at the body. Then over at Seth as he darted around a crypt.

Trap. That was exactly what this nightmare was. She'd thought the cemetery was a big maze. They were the rats trapped in the maze.

They had to get the hell out of there. Harley bolted forward. She caught Seth's shadow bobbing and weaving through the dark, and she grabbed him, locking her arms around his waist. "*No.*"

"Harley, what the fuck? The killer is getting—"

Doors slammed. She could hear them on the other side of that big wall that enclosed the cemetery. The sirens were blaring, too, and when she looked to the left, she could see the flare of blue lights reflecting in the sky. The cops were already there.

Because someone had *told* them to be there. The same someone that had lured Seth to a murder scene? "Do *exactly* what I say."

"The killer—"

"You're missing the big picture. You're the killer." She let him go. "Follow me, *now*."

He'd frozen. So she grabbed his hand and yanked him into motion. The cops would go through the main, front gate. That gave her and Seth a little time, but not much. They needed to haul ass out of that cemetery and vanish before things went from bad to worse. And the worse that she feared? That would be Seth getting locked up on a murder charge.

They reached the wall. "Boost me up, now." That would be way faster.

He didn't question her again. He boosted. She hit the top of the wall, twisted her legs around, and dropped. A moment later, he landed on the ground beside her. The swirling lights from the cop cars were so much brighter out there. She caught voices drifting on the wind.

"Suspect is inside." From one cop. "Caller said they saw him near the Trahan crypt."

What a helpful prick of a caller...who had probably been the real killer. She checked to make sure there were no cops watching, then Harley ran across the street. Seth was with her. Every single moment. Actually, she had to double-time it to match his stride. As soon as they cleared the street and got to the safety of the sidewalk and the buildings that waited on the other side, they both ducked around the corner and immediately flattened into the shadows there. *Away* from any streetlights or gas lanterns.

"What is happening?" A rasp from Seth.

"Oh, the usual. You ignored my orders for the night and nearly got arrested for murder." Someone was coming down the street. A couple swaying a little too much and humming and not seeming to care that the drizzle had turned into harder rain and that lightning kept streaking across the sky.

Can't let that couple see our faces.

She whirled, brought Seth in front of her so his back was to the couple, and demanded, "Kiss me. Now. *Kiss me.*"

CHAPTER EIGHT

Step Eight: Protect the client at all costs. Do what you have to do, but remember, it's not personal. Repeat that line. It's not personal.

"Kiss you?" He'd heard wrong. They had a dead body. Cops swarming. There was no way that Harley had just asked him to—

Her hands grabbed his hoodie, fisted, and she yanked him forward just as he heard a woman's laughter behind him on the street.

His mouth crashed onto Harley's. *Not a real kiss. She's trying to hide us.* Okay, he got that, now. His mind was all over the freaking place because he didn't make a habit of finding dead bodies. Shit. He was trying to navigate in this insane new world, but finding a man covered in stab wounds—*at my mother's grave*—was not par for the course for him. Everything was spinning out of control. Nothing seemed real or solid.

Except her. His hands clamped around her hips, and his mouth opened on hers. His tongue thrust past her soft lips. The kiss was a ruse, so why did it feel so powerful? Why did he kiss her and his whole body immediately tightened and hardened with need? She twisted against him, pressing ever closer, and the lust burned hotter within him.

"Gone." Her mouth tore from his. "They're past us. Now we need to get the hell out of here. We are not going back via Bourbon. I'm not going to count on the lightning having scattered people. People don't scatter on that street, no matter what. So we're going an alternate route. We have to stick to the shadows and hope no one sees us. The last thing we want is to explain why you're near a murder site."

"I didn't kill him."

"I know you didn't. I was there with you, remember? But I'd still rather not have to deal with cops because your life is already complicated enough, so how about we just get moving? Sound like a great idea to you?"

"The killer is out here." He could have been in the cemetery with them. Could have? Hell, he *had* been. The body had still been warm.

"Yes. The killer is close. Another reason to move. We can't stay out in the open."

This shouldn't have happened. It hadn't been the plan. Only the plan was splintering apart, and he had no choice but to follow her through the city. The sky erupted after they'd gone about fifteen feet. No more light rain but a pounding fury of a storm as more lightning streaked overhead. Luckily for them, most of the buildings on that street had balconies, so they were sheltered from the worst of the storm. Harley moved quickly, nimbly, seeming to know exactly where she was going.

But then again, she'd gone to college at Tulane. One year, anyway, before she'd transferred to a school in Texas. That had been the story of Harley's life. Always moving. Never staying in one place too long. Yes, he'd researched her.

Because he'd needed to be sure he could trust her.

They were at the corner when another police cruiser blasted by. Harley immediately turned into his arms and pulled him toward her.

The kiss was quick. Should have meant *nothing*.

Only his body didn't respond that way. Whenever she touched him, whenever she kissed him, it seemed to mean everything.

Her mouth slid from his.

Thunder rumbled.

"You can let go now," she said.

He didn't want to let go.

"We're gonna zig and zag, and I know my route is going to take us twice as long to get back, but we need to go this way. Just—get ready to hide in the shadows whenever I say, okay?"

"We could have just talked to the cops."

Her breath rushed out. "That was an option, yes. But how about we save that until we make sure you're not going down for murder? Besides, if my instincts are right, they'll be coming for you soon enough."

Coming for him? "The Feds—"

"Let's get moving. The sooner we're back in our hotel room, the sooner we can figure out a plan."

Fine.

They rushed down the streets, hid in shadows, and stayed beneath the shelter of balconies as much as they could. Sometimes, they had to run in the open, and the rain felt brutal when it blasted down on them.

But soon he saw the lights from their hotel. The doorman wasn't outside, no big surprise considering the time and the thundering storm, so Seth yanked open the door for Harley. They left a trail of dripping water in their wake.

As they approached the lobby, the security guard looked up from his phone. His gaze swept over them.

"We weren't here." Harley slapped something down next to the guard. *Cash?* "We were in all night long, should anyone come asking."

The money vanished. "Course you were, Harley. Who would go out on a night like this?"

"Thanks, James."

She was on a first-name basis with the night guard? Since when?

"Security cameras might be a problem, though," James mused. "If anyone comes looking. Unless, of course, they went offline. Sometimes, those damn things do, especially in storms."

"If they could go down tonight, that would be greatly appreciated."

James sent her a little smile. "Pretty sure they already did. Wiring in this historic hotel is shit."

A quick nod from Harley, then she was dripping her way across the lobby, and Seth staggered in her wake. He'd touched the dead man. Felt for a pulse that wasn't there. And the image of all that blood...

The elevator doors opened. Shaking her head, Harley grabbed his hoodie and half dragged him inside. As soon as those doors shut, Harley glanced toward the left corner. She pulled her hood up, concealing her face even more from the small security camera perched up there.

His hood was already up. He'd made sure of it before coming into the hotel. Was the camera in the elevator still working? Or was it part of the system that had already gone offline? Why did it matter? "*I didn't kill him.*"

She huffed out a breath. Didn't speak. She did use her keycard to access their floor and to get the elevator moving.

Water dripped onto the floor. Drip. Drip. Her eyes were on him. His on her.

"I figured out a plan," she whispered. "Go with it, okay?"

Uh, what?

The elevator ride seemed to take freaking forever, but finally, finally, it stopped and dinged. He was already stepping forward even before the doors opened. No one else was out in the hallway. The corridor was dead silent as they made their way back to their room.

She unlocked the door. Rushed inside. "Give me your hoodie. Strip off all of your clothes, *now*."

What? This was her plan? "Uh, Harley, I think we should take a moment..."

She started stripping. Right in front of him. Her raincoat hit the floor first, revealing her holster. Harley ditched the holster and gun, shoving them into a nearby drawer. Then she grabbed the hem of her shirt and yanked it up, revealing a sexy black bra that cradled curving, absolutely gorgeous breasts.

She kicked off her shoes. No socks. Her hands went to the waistband of her jeans. "You aren't stripping."

Because he was having a majorly hard time following along. And because watching her undress had completely frozen him. "Are we...having sex right now?"

"We're saving your ass right now. Strip."

"We just found a body. We need to talk." He should stop staring at her breasts as they thrust against the silky cups of her bra. *Stop looking*. His gaze inched up. "Are you one of those people that gets turned on by dead bodies?"

"*What?*" She stared at him as if she questioned his sanity. Considering he didn't feel particularly sane in that instant, he hardly blamed her. "No, dammit." She surged forward and pushed up his hoodie. "I'm one of those people who recognizes a setup and is trying to cover your ass. You wanted protection? I'm giving it to you. Strip."

He helped her yank the wet hoodie over his head. It hit the floor and her hands slid down his chest. The touch of her fingers against his skin seemed to electrify him into action. He didn't exactly get how this was helping things, but a gorgeous woman was nearly naked in front of him and he was stripping with her.

His control was razor thin, and if Harley wanted him naked, he'd be naked.

"We need to hide the wet clothes." She scooped up the hoodie and her discarded raincoat. He kept stripping, and she snatched his jeans from him. "I'll hide these in our suitcase, and you get in the shower."

He still had trouble following along with her plan. Maybe if she explained more? "Uh, Harley—"

"I'll be joining you."

Harley in a shower with him. That image was strong enough to banish the sight of the dead man from his mind.

"I don't think we're gonna have a whole lot of time." Worry threaded in her voice. "Turn on the hot water and wait for me inside."

Sure. Fine. Right.

She rushed away, giving him a quick, unforgettable view of her pert ass covered in a scrap of black silk that matched her bra. For a moment, he just stood there, admiring that view. Then he turned and hurried into the bathroom. The shower was huge, fancy, with two shower heads that he had spraying hot water in moments. The water pelted down as he finished stripping, ditching his boxers and kicking them to the side. Harley was clearly setting some kind of stage, and mental note, when the woman went in with a plan, she went *all in*. Naked, he stepped into the shower and pulled the glass door shut behind him.

Immediately, the hot water slammed into him. It poured over his skin, chasing away the chill that had lingered on him ever since he'd entered that cemetery. Then, when he'd found the body...

Fuck. Yes, he knew a setup when he saw one. And the way those cops had swarmed...

If Harley hadn't been there, I'd be in custody right now. Except, he could have talked his way out of things, right? He hadn't needed to run unless…His head turned.

Harley stood on the other side of the glass door. As he stared at her, her breasts thrust forward as her hands rose behind her back and she unhooked her bra. She gave a little roll of her shoulders, and the bra fell to the floor.

His hands fisted. She had the most incredible breasts he'd ever seen. Round, high, with tight little nipples. He wanted to taste them.

Her hands went to her hips, and she shoved down her panties. Instantly, his gaze dropped. For a moment, he stopped breathing.

I want to taste her. Every single inch of her. And she was reaching for the shower door. Hauling it open and stepping inside with him. The water hit her from the shower head on the right, sliding over her body, sending beads dripping over her creamy skin. She turned her head, letting the stream soak her hair, and he could not move as he watched her.

"Put your hair under the water," Harley ordered.

He was pretty sure his hair was already wet. The hood hadn't protected him completely.

She stepped forward. Put her hands on him as if to push him beneath the spray.

His hands flew up and curled around her wrists. "This is a bad idea." Seth barely recognized his voice. More growl than anything else. Rough with too much savage desire.

"Probably." A nod from her. "But it's the only plan I have at the moment."

She was wet and warm and right there. "You're naked."

"Super astute of you to notice."

"Harley..."

She stepped closer. Her body rubbed against his. There was no way she missed the giant dick bobbing so eagerly toward her.

"I'm trying to save you right now." She licked her lower lip. "Do you trust me?"

"Yes." A hiss.

"Great. Then get your head under the water."

He wanted to get *in* her. Instead, he freed her wrists, backed up, and let the spray hit him. Maybe if the water had been ice cold, it would have helped him. But it wasn't cold. It was hot. She was hotter. His hand rose, and he shoved his fingers back through his hair. "Better?"

"No." She followed him. Her hands curled around his shoulders. "If I'm right, we're going to have company very soon."

The water kept pounding down.

"You were here all night." Her slick body edged ever closer. *So close.* "You never left my sight."

He didn't put his hands on her. He *needed* to keep his hands the fuck off her.

But all I want is to fuck her.

"Don't you think..." *Do not touch her. Keep your hands fisted at your sides. Act like you are not naked in the shower with the woman you want more than you have ever wanted anyone in your life.* "This is..." Dammit, talking was hard.

All he could manage were growls. *I want in her.* "This is...extreme?"

A shake of her head. "Better safe than sorry."

Uh, no. This was not safe. "There is nothing safe about what you are doing with me."

Her short nails sank into his shoulders. "I trust you."

Maybe she shouldn't. "I want to fuck you."

Her breath sucked in. "Did notice that."

"You're naked and your hands are on me. How the hell can you think this is *safe?*"

Steam drifted in the air around them. "I want you, too." A rushed confession from her.

That confession had him jerking.

"But I don't fuck for an audience."

What audience? It was just them. "No one is here. Just us." Her mouth was right there. His control—the control he valued so much—was shot to hell and back. Too much had happened that night. The attack at the mansion. The body in the cemetery. Running frantically through the city with Harley. And now...

Fuck it.

His mouth crashed onto hers. The water kept pounding, and he didn't care. He had Harley right in front of him. Harley with her sweet mouth and her wicked tongue, and he couldn't hold back. She moaned low in her throat, that sexy, husky sound just driving him over the edge even more.

She met him. No, challenged him. Kissed him back with a ferocity that had the blood practically boiling in his veins. Hotter, harder, that was what she made him. His hands grabbed her waist, and he lifted her up. Her legs wrapped around his hips, even as he turned slightly and pinned her against the wall of the shower. Over and over, he kissed her. Deep and hard, and with her legs up, with her hips arching toward him, the head of his cock lodged right at the entrance to her body. It would be so easy to thrust into her. To take what he wanted so badly...

Then he heard a crash. From somewhere beyond the bathroom. The sitting area? His mouth tore from hers, and his head whipped toward the threat.

"You never left," Harley whispered.

The bathroom door flew open.

CHAPTER NINE

Step Nine: Working around the clock with your client may require some...intimate moments. But you must still remain professional, no matter the situation.

Or at least pretend to be professional. This goes back to step one. Appearances are everything, remember? Especially when things get wild.

"Freeze!" A hard bellow that reached them even over the pounding streams that came from the double shower heads.

Seth's whole body stiffened. And, honestly, the man's body had been plenty stiff and hard already. Surely he'd heard her last whisper? He knew to play this scene like they'd been, ah, busy all night.

"Oh, jeez." Not a bellow any longer. More a startled realization and... "Uh, you can cover up."

She peeked around Seth's shoulder. His very broad shoulder. He still had her lifted against the wall, and from this elevated position, she could look over and see the little crowd of people who'd come barreling into their bathroom. First was the man with the gun. The tall and glaring guy in the rumpled and rain-soaked suit. A badge gleamed from his hip, and his intense, dark eyes glittered.

Had to be a detective with NOPD. Behind him stood a much shorter man with carefully styled, red hair. That fellow wore the hotel's spiffy uniform, the one that she'd seen several of the concierge members sporting, and, while he didn't flash a badge, he had a shining, gold name tag above his right breast pocket. *Cayden.*

A rain-splattered beat cop—female, with short, black hair—waited in the rear. Her expression was half horrified, half confused.

"There had better be one incredible explanation for this," Seth rumbled.

Oh, his voice was dark and deep and ever so delicious.

"Step away from the woman," the detective ordered.

"Uh, no." She smiled, like there was nothing at all embarrassing about this situation. "I'm naked. In case you are not getting an incredible view of his ass, Seth is naked, too. You're the ones who need to step away. As in, step away from our *private* bathroom. We'll put on our robes—"

"And then you'll tell us what the hell is happening," Seth snarled. Oh, yes, he'd moved from a rumble to a snarl. Nice. Great transition. The man's acting kept impressing her.

He also turned his head more so he could glare at the people gaping in the bathroom entranceway. "It had better be a good explanation, because otherwise, I'm suing you to hell and back."

The concierge guy swayed. "Told you this was a massive mistake." Cayden wiped his sweaty forehead. Sweaty from stress or from the thick steam in the room? Harley had no idea and didn't care. "We need to give them privacy, now," Cayden urged.

The detective didn't move. "Ma'am, does he have a weapon?"

He could not be serious.

"*Are you fucking kidding?*" Seth threw back. "I'm unarmed."

Well, technically, she didn't count that giant dick of his as being *unarmed*.

"I'm naked and fucking my girlfriend—*get the hell out,*" Seth ordered. "Out of my bathroom. Out of my hotel suite. When I'm dressed, *we will damn well talk.*"

The female cop and the concierge had already retreated.

The detective glared. "Ma'am? Are you safe?"

"Safe as can be," Harley assured him. "Thanks so much for asking."

His head jerked, and he spun around. "I will be waiting in the sitting area of your suite. We need to talk, Mr. Wellington."

Seth slowly lowered Harley until her feet touched the shower floor. He reached out and turned off the blasting water. "About what?"

"About the little matter of a murder." The detective stomped away, but he paused long enough to swing the door shut behind him.

Without the warm water pouring onto her, goose bumps rose onto Harley's arms. She shivered.

Seth's gaze locked on her. Then his head dipped down toward her. With his mouth at her ear, he rasped, "That guy got here damn fast."

She nodded.

"Too fast."

Again, she nodded.

"How'd you know he'd be showing up here?"

Because it had made sense. "Someone set you up for murder. If you weren't caught at the scene, then the next step would be to catch you off guard here." Her words were as low as his had been. "I knew a cop would be hauling ass to get here once they didn't find you at the cemetery."

"But there should have been nothing at that scene that tied to me." His breath slid over the shell of her ear. This time, her shiver wasn't from the cold.

"If the cops were told to bring *you* in—you specifically—it wouldn't matter." And that was her fear. "At the mansion, I was told by someone that Fabian controlled a whole lot of the cops in this city. I can't let them take you in." Because her fear was…

If they take you away from me, I might not see you again.

"No one is taking me anywhere." He pulled back. A muscle flexed along his jaw. "You don't fuck for an audience."

She shook her head. *No.*

"You knew they were coming. Everything you did from the minute we set foot in this suite was designed to throw them off."

No, not everything. In fact, *everything* had gone way past control for her. "I want you." There. Done. Said. Just so there would be no confusion. "My response to you wasn't and will never be faked."

His eyes widened.

"Just so we understand each other. Because, yes, I do give you huge props for your acting ability." The man was a born chameleon, something that probably should worry her more, but didn't. "You could totally have made a major career on the stage or screen. Talk about a waste."

"*Harley.*"

"But I do understand there are some things that can't be faked. I'm talking about my reaction and yours." She glanced down. *Wow.*

"There won't be an audience later," he pointed out.

Her gaze flew right back up.

Challenge blazed in his eyes.

So she...nodded.

Challenge accepted.

His whole face turned extra brutal and hard. "First, I'm dealing with the assholes waiting, then I'm dealing with *you.*" He backed away. Shoved open the glass door and yanked a towel down from the rack.

Her breath whispered out as she stood, naked and dripping, in the shower, and watched the powerful play of muscles as he dried himself off.

Promises, promises.

Seth discarded that towel, only to immediately grab another—and then he reached for her. He tugged her out of the shower and onto the plush rug. He looped the fresh towel around her body.

"What are you doing?" Harley tried to swat at his hands. "I'm more than capable of drying off—"

"Those bastards just saw you naked." His nostrils flared. He let her take the towel, but then he just grabbed an enormous, fluffy, white robe and draped it over her shoulders. His big hands went for the belt, and he tied it quickly around her waist. He stepped back, frowning. "Too sexy."

He was kidding.

"Put on clothes before you come out."

Bossy. He'd already swung around, and, seeing as how *he* was still naked, she figured it was wise to tell him, "You should do that, too."

Seth stilled, as if just realizing that he'd been striding out buck naked. His hands flew out to grab a towel, and he hooked it around his waist.

Harley decided to fill him in on a few other details. She was helpful like that. "Just so you know, your body was blocking mine. With the steam and your body in front of mine, I don't think anyone saw much of me. Not like anyone got a full frontal view of my glorious self. So you don't need to worry on that score."

He looked back at her. "I saw plenty."

But you're different. She swallowed. "I do think the female cop was admiring your ass. And perhaps Cayden was, too." How could she blame them? It was a great ass. Meant to be admired.

He growled, and the sound reminded Harley of the hungry rumbles that had come from him while they were in the shower. A scene that should have just been a cover, but had turned into so much more.

Oh, come on, woman. Like you didn't know it was gonna be more the minute you decided to strip with him.

And the way his eyes seemed to blaze as he stared at her right then... Her left hand rose to pull the edges of her gaping robe closed. "You don't have to say anything without a lawyer."

"I know."

Of course, he knew. He'd grown up with an army of lawyers. "We never left the suite. Remember that." Barely a breath of sound.

"There is no way I will ever forget anything that happened tonight." His gaze dipped down her body. "Some things are burned in my mind."

Like the dead man at the cemetery? But she didn't say that. She'd already said too much and didn't want to risk being overheard.

"Like the way you look and the way you feel when you're naked against me."

She cleared her throat. "They're waiting."

"We'll talk to them, then kick them the hell out. And there will be no audience. There will only be you and me." With that, he marched for the door and yanked it open.

As he left, the steam drifted out after him.

Her breath exhaled. *Promises, promises.*

***

"Why the hell did you break into my hotel suite?" He'd yanked on a t-shirt and sweats, and Seth figured the best defense was truly to go all out on a massive offense.

The three people in the sitting area of the suite whirled at his words, and Seth kept stalking forward like the extremely pissed and injured party that he was. *Just a few more minutes, and I would've had exactly what I wanted.*

Harley.

He stopped as that thought fully sank in.

Wait. Dammit. This wasn't about screwing Harley. His head shook. He felt drunk on her.

"I'm sorry, Mr. Wellington." The man in the hotel uniform took a few rushed steps forward, then paused. His hands twisted in front of him. "I-I only allowed it because the detective assured me it was an emergency. A life-or-death situation. I used my card to try and gain access, but the additional lock was secured, so the detective kicked open the door—"

Cayden. Seth read the name on the guy's tag. "There is no emergency. You were misled."

"I'm so sorry." Cayden's shoulders slumped. "Please, please don't sue the hotel. *Please.*"

"I make no promises." He wasn't going to sue the freaking hotel. His gaze swung to the watchful detective. "Emergency? What kind of emergency sent you rushing here?"

"A murder, like I said before."

"Before? You mean when you were in my *bathroom* while I was fucking my girlfriend?" That seemed like something he would say. Or rather, his character. Because he knew to keep playing the con.

Harley clearly didn't trust the cops. And that meant Seth didn't, either.

The detective straightened his shoulders. "I had reason to believe you might be in danger."

Seth narrowed his eyes. "What reason would that be?"

The detective opened his mouth to speak.

"What murder?" Harley's sharp voice came from behind Seth.

Be dressed. Be dressed. Be completely covered from head to toe so I don't lose my shit with another surge of jealousy. The jealousy wasn't faked. That smothering, body-churning spike of rage was all too real. He didn't want anyone else seeing Harley naked.

His head turned so he could eye her.

Thank Christ. Harley now wore jeans and some kind of flowing, silky, blue top. His breath expelled on a rush as he nodded toward her.

She came to his side. Pressed against him. "What murder?" she repeated.

The detective fired a quick glance at the female officer. "Why don't you escort Cayden back downstairs now that the situation is secure?"

"Sure thing." She motioned toward Cayden.

"I don't want to lose this job," Cayden said. "It is very important to me." His hands twisted some more. "I thought you were in danger."

"You're not losing your job," Harley assured him. "Relax. You were just trying to help."

Cayden's head bobbed. "Absolutely. Help. I was *concerned.*"

"We will need that door repaired immediately, though," Harley continued breezily. "Or, actually, we may be switching rooms. Because that repair probably won't happen tonight, will it?"

"I'll get you the best suite we have!" Cayden vowed.

Harley angled her head toward Seth. "Is this not the best one? Darling, I thought you told me that you'd always give me the best."

His back teeth clenched. "Get the new room ready," he bit out. "And I won't sue the hotel."

Cayden practically flew from the suite. The uniformed cop followed on his heels.

Then it was just the three of them. Seth, Harley, and the grim detective. There sure was a whole lot of suspicion in the detective's eyes.

"He still hasn't said who was murdered," Harley loud-whispered to Seth.

The detective's lips thinned. "A body was just discovered in the St. Louis Cemetery."

Harley strolled away from Seth's side and meandered toward the stocked bar. She reached inside and pulled out a miniature bottle of wine. "Aren't there a lot of bodies in that place? I mean, isn't that the point of it being a cemetery?"

The detective's hard eyes narrowed on her. "This one is fresh. As in, still warm to the touch and sporting a ton of stab wounds to the chest."

Her fingers trembled. The wine bottle fell from her fingers. "That's *horrible*."

"It sure as hell is," the detective agreed. "And it will be even more horrible if his killer isn't stopped."

"Terrible crime," Seth said because he figured he had to say something. And a brutal stabbing to the chest? Even if he hadn't liked the man, it still seemed one brutal way to go. "I certainly hope the perpetrator is caught." He headed for Harley. He picked up the wine bottle and put it on top of the little bar. "You okay, love?"

"No, I'm shaken. So scared. You're right. Murder is a terrible, terrible thing." Her long lashes swept down to conceal her eyes. "Terrifying and terrible."

"Um." From the detective. "Do either of you happen to know a Justin Florent?"

Harley rolled back her shoulders. "Was he the victim?"

Ah, nice job. She hadn't answered the detective and had just distracted him with her own question.

"He was." The detective thrust his hands into the pockets of his pants. "You didn't say if you knew him."

So maybe she hadn't distracted the cop.

"I'm really bad with names," Harley revealed. "I...I don't think I caught *your* name. Or did you tell us?"

Seth was absolutely sure that Harley knew the detective had not identified himself.

"I'm Detective Zion Raye." He pulled out his ID. Flashed it nice and fast. Made it vanish in a blink.

"Nice to meet you," Harley murmured.

"Detective Raye." Seth edged in front of her. "I'm sorry to hear about a murder tonight, but I fail to see why you raced here and kicked in my door. Why did you come to me at all?"

"You still haven't told me if you know Justin Florent."

Someone had bulldog tenacity. Seth could admire it. Choosing his words carefully, Seth replied, "I've never been introduced to the man." Totally true.

Had he held a gun on the man just hours before? Yes. No wonder Harley had been convinced he'd look guilty as hell. Several people at the party had peeked out and seen that little bit of drama play out. Would those people talk to the cops?

Maybe. That's why my answers have to be careful.

"Interesting." The detective advanced. "If you've never been introduced to him, want to tell me why I found *your* ID beneath his body? Your driver's license, covered in blood, was just discovered at my crime scene."

Shit.

"Want to explain that?" Zion pressed.

"You said the St. Louis Cemetery?" Harley's breathless voice filled the room. "Oh, Seth, we were there earlier today! When you went to show me your mother's resting place." Her hands fluttered in the air. "You must have lost your ID then."

"Your mother?" Zion prompted.

"Charlotte Wellington." He paused. "Charlotte Trahan Wellington."

The faint lines near Zion's mouth tightened. "We found our vic right in front of the Trahan crypt."

"How horrifying," Harley said. "Just horrifying. That poor man...I-I've heard there are a lot of crimes in those cemeteries. That they are so dangerous at night. Drug dealers, gang activity...you just never know what could happen there."

Zion didn't glance at her. He seemed too busy studying Seth. "You didn't realize you'd lost your ID?"

No. Not until you just told me. And he wondered how the hell his ID had gotten in the cemetery, beneath a dead man, when it should have been secured in his wallet.

"Did you lose your whole wallet?" Zion questioned. "Or just your license?"

His wallet was in the bedroom. He'd seen it when he changed. Harley had dumped his wet clothing somewhere, but she must have taken the time to put the wallet on the nightstand.

"Seth has his wallet. I-I saw it a moment ago." A long exhale from her. "This is my fault."

Now Zion's attention went completely to her. "A murder is your fault, miss? And I don't believe I caught *your* name."

"Harley." A quick smile that showcased her disarming dimple. "Because my father loves to ride them. Nothing like the open road." Her features sobered. "I wanted to leave an offering."

"Excuse me?" Zion took a step forward.

"For Marie Laveau. I didn't have coins on me, but Seth said he had a few shoved in his wallet. At the time, I thought it was lucky. I left them on Marie Laveau's grave and then we went to see his mother's resting place. He was putting his wallet back up, and that..." Her head turned toward Seth as she stared at him with wide eyes. Her breath shuddered out. "That must be when you lost your ID."

Wow. She'd certainly, ah, pulled that cover story out of her gorgeous ass quickly. Impressive.

"That is a possibility." Though another possibility also blasted through his head. One that he would be discussing only with Harley.

"An offering." Zion didn't seem convinced.

"You know people leave coins for Marie all the time." Harley's voice was rushed, nervous. "We did, too. I'm sure you saw a pile of coins there tonight. I couldn't help myself. I just—it seemed like it was okay. Please tell me that I'm not going to get arrested for leaving a few coins behind?"

"You're not getting arrested for anything." Seth rubbed her shoulder. *Neither one of us is getting arrested, thanks to your plan.* But back to the watchful detective. "You found my ID." He let his brows climb. "And you came here because you were worried I was...a victim?"

"Something like that." A grunt. "Glad to see you're unharmed." His gaze went to Seth's forearms.

He's looking to see if I have any injuries.

"I'm certainly glad, too. But I'm still confused. You have my ID, but how did you know I was staying at *this* hotel?"

Zion rubbed the bridge of his nose. "Recognized your name. Knew that if I wanted to look for you, I should start with the swankiest hotel in the city. Talked to Cayden and found you."

"Yes, you found me." He could clearly see the suspicion on Zion's face. "I'm alive and well. Thanks for the due diligence."

"Can we get his ID back?" Harley asked.

A negative shake of Zion's head. "That ID is now part of a murder investigation."

Fantastic.

"Where were you tonight, Mr. Wellington?" Zion questioned him.

Is this where you see if I had an alibi? "Well, I was here in my hotel, spending time with my lady."

"All night?"

Nope. "I've been civil. I've been more than accommodating, especially since you broke into my room without a warrant and interrupted me at a most inconvenient time." He held Zion's stare. "I haven't murdered anyone, I haven't been murdered, and I really think that's all there is to say about the matter. It's extremely late, and I'd like to get to bed."

Zion's stare flickered to Harley.

"He was with me," she said simply. "Barely let him out of my sight. And we were busy tonight, as I'm sure you saw."

A muscle jerked near the detective's jaw.

A sharp rap sounded at the door. Then Cayden poked his head inside. "The Governor's Suite is ready for you."

"We'd better get moving," Seth murmured.

Zion didn't move. "I have more questions."

"It's closing in on two a.m. Harley and I are getting into a *secure* room, you know, one with a door that is actually capable of still closing and locking, then we're going to bed. Any other questions can wait until a more rational time." He paused for just a moment. "I'll be sure to have my lawyer follow up with you during daylight hours."

"Lawyering up?" A tight, taunting smile. "Thought you didn't have anything to hide."

Seth smiled in return. Not taunting, yet with a whole lot of teeth. "I don't. But I also don't want the NOPD thinking they can burst in on me anytime without a warrant. That won't be happening again."

"Extenuating circumstances. I believed you were in danger."

And I believe I am, too. But Seth suspected he might be looking at one of the threats. "Do you happen to know a Fabian Butler?" Seth asked, deliberately throwing back the words Zion had used, only instead of the dead Justin, Seth asked about the man he suspected of setting up this new nightmare.

Zion's eyelids flickered. "I may have heard of him."

"Really? Only heard, huh?"

"Guy is mostly just rumors. Legend. Not like he's ever been collared. Plenty of folks aren't even sure he's real."

Oh, he was very real. They both knew it.

Zion tipped his head. "Good night, Mr. Wellington." He strode for the door and a gaping Cayden.

"Good night, Detective Raye," Harley's warm voice rolled out. "Good luck catching your killer."

At those words, Zion paused. "I don't need luck. I'll have the bastard in jail sooner than he thinks." He glanced back. Held Seth's gaze. "Count on it."

CHAPTER TEN

Step Ten: Remember that you are the one running the con. You don't get to become the victim. In other words, keep your enemies close, but never, ever let down your guard. You trust the wrong person, and the game is over.

The bellman and Cayden departed in a flurry of activity. The door to the Governor's Suite clicked shut, and Seth made sure to flip the top lock. "Not like this little lock gives us a whole lot more protection. Not when apparently one big kick from a detective can send the whole door flying inward."

Behind him, Harley remained silent. She'd been silent all during the room transfer. Silence from Harley worried him. He turned, put his back to the door, and locked his eyes on her.

There was a pensive, thoughtful expression on her face. He could practically hear the wheels spinning in her mind. Considering the way his brain was flying through possibilities and suspicions at about a hundred miles an hour, he completely understood.

Seth took his time walking toward her. Part of him wondered if she might retreat, but, no, this was Harley. She just straightened her shoulders, tipped back her head, and stared up at him with her amazing eyes. This time, as he stared at her eyes, the brown seemed more powerful than the gold. A troubled, worried gaze.

His hand rose and his knuckles slid down the silk of her cheek. "You lied to a cop for me."

"I don't remember lying. Not exactly."

No? "The coins?"

"I did put coins on Marie's tomb when we passed. You were just focused on other things, so you didn't notice." Quiet. "I do that every time I go to the St. Louis Cemetery. If Marie is gonna be granting favors, why not stack the odds my way?"

His brows shot up. "You believe in voodoo?"

"I believe you should be grateful that I put those coins there when I did." She swallowed. "If the cops should decide to collect the coins, they'll find my prints on some. Just remember what story I gave the detective. *I* took them from your wallet. I gave the wallet back to you at your mother's tomb. Your ID fell out then, *before* the murder occurred."

His hand dropped to his side. "You have things neatly worked out, don't you?"

"Hardly." A tight reply. "And we *did* go to the cemetery earlier today. We went there after midnight. That means it's today."

"You like to play word games with cops often?"

"No, I don't enjoy playing with cops at all. In fact, there is very little about this situation that I do enjoy." Her breath huffed out. "You get that one of the guards at Fabian's mansion must have lifted your wallet during your pat-down at the door?"

"I've realized that was an option, yes."

"It's more than an option." Her brows beetled at him. "It's a certainty, at least in my mind. One guard—the blond—distracted you by acting like he was going to do a hardcore frisk on me. Dammit, he distracted us *both* because I should have seen this coming." Her eyes squeezed shut. "I have to get on my game. This intense attraction I feel for you is messing with my head."

Intense attraction? Seth filed that info away for later. Harley's honesty could be quite the punch to the gut. "We're thinking the other guard lifted the wallet, took out my ID, then slipped the wallet back into my pocket. In order to do all of that," Seth mused as he tried not to focus on the intense attraction he felt for *her* and rather on the fact that he'd been set up for a murder, "the plan had to already be in place."

"The plan to frame you for murder?" Her eyes opened. "Yep, I'd say so. Though I do wonder if the victim changed. Not so sure that Justin was originally the one who was supposed to be found dead in front of your family crypt."

His body tightened. "Then who do you think the original victim was?"

Her lips pressed together.

"Harley? Don't stop now." She never stopped sharing her opinions. This was exceedingly un-Harley-like. And it worried him. "Who do you think the original victim was?"

"I think it might have been me."

His heart slammed into his chest. "What? Why the hell would you say that?" What could have been ice cold fear blasted through him.

"Because if I was a crime lord gunning to take down some competition, I'd do it in the most brutal way possible. I'd destroy something my enemy cared about." A roll of one shoulder, like this was a super casual conversation. No big deal. "There aren't many things you seem to care about in this world. I did my research on you, I know. Fabian would have researched you, too, and come up with the same results."

"What results?" No freaking way should Harley be a target.

"You don't date anyone exclusively. You have non-existent ties."

"I'm running an extremely high stakes undercover op! Not like there is room for ties." He couldn't afford any. His life was too dangerous. *All the more reason for me to keep my hands off her.* And, yet, what the hell did he keep doing?

Putting my hands right back on Harley.

"The person you're probably closest to in the world is Cooper Fairmont." Her tone was all unruffled. Calm as you please. "But now that world is buzzing with the news that your father killed his, well, I'm thinking your enemies might believe that the best friends have become best enemies."

He didn't change expression. Mostly because he was remembering the way Coop had looked when his buddy learned the truth. *My father did kill his.* His father had staged a car accident that sent both Cooper's father and a local prosecutor to their deaths. Then his father had swooped in and played the caring godfather to Coop and Coop's sister, Claudia.

His dad had been so good at playing roles.

I'm too much like him.

"Based on that recent turn of events, those gunning for you would think Cooper was out of the equation, and the only person who *seems* to matter? The only person close to you right now? That would be me. After all, you just flew me down to the Big Easy with you. We're sharing a suite together. We're going to shady meetings at night together. For all intents and purposes, I am the lover you're obsessed with. That's the cover we created, and it's one that is working extremely well. If someone wants to hurt you, if someone wants to send a message, then why not kill me and leave my broken body at your mother's crypt? Talk about an attack that hits you right in the heart."

Fucking fuck. "That shit is *not* going to happen." His hands closed around her shoulders.

"I could be wrong, of course. Totally off target with my suspicions. But I'm thinking any plans had to change after the big scene with Justin at Fabian's place. Add on the fact that you were promised a gift by Fabian, and then, bam, a dead man is left at your mother's tomb." Her breath expelled on a long rush. "If Fabian was behind the murder, I've got to say, the man delivers one heck of a gift."

"It wasn't a gift. It was a threat."

The brown—the darkness—seemed to deepen in her gaze. "Glad we're on the same page because that's exactly what I think, too."

His lips tightened.

"What did the second text message really say?"

He was the one to back up a step. The question had caught him by surprise. A deliberate tactic, he was sure. Harley could be ever so sly.

"You lied to me." She advanced. Her delicate jaw hardened. "I can't believe you did that crap. Seriously a jerk thing to do." Her hand rose. Her index finger jabbed into his chest. "After everything I've done to help you—you *lied* to me. That hurts, Seth."

It did? He'd never, ever intended to hurt her. "Harley—"

She jabbed him again. "You didn't just decide to go prancing to the cemetery in the middle of the night. You had a meeting scheduled. That second text from Fabian was about setting up the meeting in the cemetery, wasn't it?"

He realized she was furious. When Harley got mad, her eyes went very, very dark. "Uh, Harley…"

"*What did the second text say?*"

His own anger—normally so tightly contained—pushed to the surface. "I thought you trusted me."

"I just saved your ass from the cops. Without me, you would have been found over a dead body. They swarmed the cemetery—*while you were there*—because they got a tip. Someone killed that man and set you up. Someone who knew that you would be at that crypt tonight. The cops would have rushed inside, you would have been there with the body, and then you would have gotten tossed into a cell." Her delicate nostrils flared.

"Then you would have either faced an eventual murder trial or you never would have *made* it to a trial. Cops who are connected to Fabian would have delivered whatever punishment he wanted. *I saved your ass,*" she snapped again. Her voice had definitely frayed at the edges.

He tried to hold on to his own fraying control. "You think all cops are dirty?"

"What?" An immediate, negative shake of her head. "No. Absolutely not. My brother Steele is a cop, and he is as true blue as they come. Heck, for all I know, Detective Zion Raye is the best person on the force. Maybe he did rush over here because he was legitimately worried about your safety. Or maybe he came because he had orders to take you in, orders that did *not* come from the NOPD." She stood directly in front of Seth, her body almost brushing his. "There are good and bad people everywhere, and I generally make a habit of not trusting folks until I see what their true colors happen to be."

"What are my true colors?"

She blinked.

"What do you think I am, Harley? Good or bad?" She'd said before that she didn't know if he was a good man, pretending to be bad. Or a bad man, pretending to be good. *Sometimes, I don't know either.* "If you're so convinced I'm bad, then why lie for me?"

A growl of frustration—weirdly sexy—broke from her. "Would I still be working for you if I thought you were bad? What kind of question even is that?" Her brow scrunched. "Did you hit your head when we were scaling that wall?"

"What do you think I am?" Seth repeated doggedly because it mattered. In this twisted world, her response mattered one hell of a lot to him.

"I think you're an asshole," she responded, voice flat. "An asshole who is lying to the only person who is seriously, one hundred percent on his side. Your buddy Brent? The Feds working with him? They have their own agenda. If they had to risk your life in order to bring down the big fish they're after, they'd do it in a heartbeat. You're expendable to them, and expendable is the most dangerous thing to be."

"I know they're using me." *I think you're an asshole.* That hurt more than it should have. "I'm using them, so that's probably only fair."

No surprise flashed on her face. "Of course, you are. Trying to right all the wrongs left by your father. Ridiculous hero or martyr complex."

He did *not* have a martyr complex, and he was no one's hero. "You don't understand me."

"Oh, I think I do. You're just not understanding *me.* How about you try listening to me one more time? *You are not your father.* Whatever he did, it's not on you. You don't get to wash the blood away or balance the scales by putting yourself in danger or by locking up a ton of bad guys. No matter what you try, you can't undo what he did. His crimes will never go away." Now she did back up a step. "You still haven't told me what was on that second text." Determination hardened her gaze. "Let me see your phone."

"Harley..."

"You get that the authorities can subpoena your phone? They can read your messages? Heck, they can even do those crazy searches now where they find out which phones were near a crime to help pinpoint the perps. Something I will worry about *later*. Right now, I'll focus on us finding the real killer and clearing you before anything else can happen."

So they were hunting for a person who just brutally stabbed his enemy and left the body in a cemetery. "You didn't sign up for this."

"I signed up to be at your side. Now just tell me what the message said. What text had you running out on your own? Running to possible *death?* Because I'd already told you Fabian was gunning for you. You knew the risk, and you still went *anyway*." Her voice cracked. Fury. Pain?

He blinked. "Harley?"

"I can't keep you safe if you're lying to me."

Holy shit. Were those tears in her eyes? No, no, he was not the kind of man she should ever cry for. *I am not worth it.*

"This won't *work* if you lie to me, Seth. I'm trying to keep you alive. But you're running a second agenda. Or maybe even a third or fourth agenda. I can't decide! What do you expect me to do? Working blindly is an impossibility on this case. I told you that before." She spun away. Started marching toward the bedroom because, this time, there was only one bedroom. A pullout couch, too, sure, yes, and he'd planned to bunk down on it. The bellman had just left the luggage in the bedroom, and now Harley was striding in there.

He found himself following her. And when she went toward the luggage—

His heart seemed to stop. "Are you leaving me?"

With her back to him, she froze.

Maybe it would be for the best. It certainly *would* be for the best if someone was going to target her. Bringing Harley on as his bodyguard—sometimes, Seth thought it was the best decision he'd ever made. At other moments, he thought it was the fucking worst choice of his life.

Fabian knows she's tied to me. I took her into that mansion. Shoved her under his nose. Even if Harley left him now, would that stop a target from being put on her?

What the hell have I done?

"Is that what you think I'm doing?" Low. "Leaving you? Running because the going has gotten a little rough?"

"I think murder qualifies as more than a *little* rough." He grabbed the doorframe. Started to answer, then stopped. *I don't want her to leave me. She thinks I'm as bad as my father, and she wants to run.*

But I don't want her to leave.

He was so screwed up.

"Asshole." Harley spun toward him. Her blazing eyes fired daggers at him. "What is it about me that makes you think I'm the type to cut and run at the first sign of trouble? We have a contract." She stalked her way to him. "How many times do I have to remind you of that fact? And you..." Harley came to a dead stop right in front of him. "You have a death wish. Why else would you run out into the middle of the night? Why else would you agree to this horrible deal with the Feds? Why would you—"

"I was there."

"In the cemetery? Yes, I know. I was with you. Your alibi. Your ride or die. Your superheroine for the night and don't you forget—"

"When they killed my mother, I was there."

Her mouth hung open. Then she shook her head. "That...that wasn't in the reports I read about you."

No, that detail would have been omitted. "Because my father made sure it wasn't in any report. I was in the car with her. I was in the back seat. I saw the big, black SUV pull in front of us, blocking the road. I saw the van turn sideways behind us, so she couldn't reverse. So we were trapped."

"Seth." She reached out. Took his hand.

But he'd started this brutal walk down memory lane and couldn't stop. "A man got out of the SUV. I heard her say that he had a gun."

He's got a gun, Seth. Oh, God, he has a gun. She'd looked back at him. He'd never seen his mom so terrified. *Get on the floorboard, baby. Stay down. No matter what, stay down.*

"She got out of the car. Ran toward him. I was supposed to stay down, but I didn't. I looked up and when I saw her getting close to him, when I saw that he was lifting his gun to shoot her, I jumped out of the car. I screamed for her." The memories would never stop. "She looked back at me. There was so much fear on her face. That fear was the last emotion I saw from her. Because while she was looking back at me, he fired. He shot her three times that day." Seth could still hear the shots.

Boom.

His feet had flown over the pavement. "Mom!"

Boom.

Her body swayed. Her eyes were on him. So much fear. No, no, his mom shouldn't be afraid.

Boom.

The blood hit him because he was so close. Then she fell. Even as her hand reached out to him, she fell.

"She fell before I could catch her." But he'd still grabbed for her. Still screamed for his mother only to look up at the man who'd shot her, with rage pouring through his veins. "I looked up at her killer only to see that he had his gun pointed right at me."

Her hold tightened on him. "He was going to shoot you?"

His mother's blood had been pouring out on the pavement. "He stared at me and said, 'I didn't get paid to kill no kid.'" Words that had haunted him. Still did. A gruff, growling, southern accent. A man with too pale skin. Tats on his neck. A shaved head with just the faintest of red-brown buzz growing out. "Without another word, he turned and walked away. Left me there in the road, holding my mom, and screaming for help. Screaming that I would get him."

The bastard had laughed as he walked away. The van had screeched behind Seth as it reversed and peeled from the scene. The man who'd shot his mom had climbed into the passenger seat of the SUV. As the driver took him away... "He smiled and waved bye to me. I was holding my mom's body on that road, her blood all over my skin and clothes, and he *waved* to me."

She threw her body against his. Held him fiercely. "I am so sorry."

He wanted to wrap his arms around her. Never let go. But he had to finish this. *Because she thinks I'm evil, just like him.* Maybe he was. Hard to say for sure. He'd been sliding deeper and deeper into the dark so often lately. "I don't know how long I was on that road with her." Begging her to live. To come back. Making all the promises that a seven-year-old could make. Offering deals and prayers and in the end...

In the end, there had been only one promise that mattered. "I swore I'd find him."

Her head lifted. Her eyes seemed to swirl with tears. No, no, that couldn't happen. Her eyes shouldn't fill with tears. Once more, he had the thought...*I'm not worth them.* "Don't cry." Not tough Harley. She should never cry. Certainly not for someone like him.

"I'll cry if I want." She sniffed. A tear slid down her cheek. "This wasn't in *any* of the intel, and Wilde is normally very, very good at intel gathering. The best, in fact."

"My father was the one who eventually found us. I have no idea how long I was out there. But he came rushing to the scene, he grabbed me, pulled me away from her, and told me... 'You were never here.'"

You were never here.

"He told me I saw nothing. Told me that I was never there."

She flinched. "I practically told you the same stuff tonight. No wonder you were freezing me out."

"What?" His head shook. "No, I wasn't." Freezing was the wrong word. He'd been burning alive for her in that shower. Nothing had been able to cool him down. When it came to her, he suspected that nothing ever would. He'd want Harley with a burning intensity that consumed, until the very day he died.

She seemed about to argue, but stopped. Her arms still curled around him. He liked it when she touched him. *Like* actually didn't begin to cover things.

But Harley cleared her throat and slowly retreated. One step. Two. Her arms fell to her sides.

Come back to me.

Another delicate clearing of her throat. "The police report said your mother's attack was random. A carjacking gone wrong."

More lies. "There was nothing random about my mother's murder. She was targeted. Taken out. And my father told me to bury every memory and never talk about it. When I was a kid, he even told me..." Seth's hands fisted. To stop from touching her? Or because the past enraged him? Maybe both. "Told me that I had to stay quiet for my own protection. See, I wasn't supposed to be there that day. My mom had picked me up early from school. I-I don't remember why. Don't know what she told the people in the office. She was supposed to be alone that afternoon. But she wasn't."

"And the man hired to kill her hadn't been paid to kill you, too." So much sadness whispered in her words. "Oh, Seth."

He tensed. "I don't want pity from you."

"You think that's what I feel? Pity?"

"My dad told me to bury it. He grieved publicly, demanded all sorts of criminal justice reforms. What a slick sonofabitch he was." He choked down the fury that flared. Like he always choked down so many of his emotions. Acting wasn't a talent. It was a defense he'd had to learn. *Act like you don't care. Act like you don't feel. Then maybe things won't hurt so much.* "It was after my mom's murder that he started me on my 'training' each day. Said I wouldn't be weak again. That I had to learn to protect myself. Over and over again, I'd train. So many days. Brutal years." Bouts that had left him bloody and with broken bones. His father had never relented. Just kept up the regimen. "No matter how much it hurt, I kept going. Hell, part of me *liked* it." More than that. When he'd started taking down opponents, when he'd moved onto weapons in his teen years, when *he'd* started to be the one who left his opponent hurt on the ground... "I enjoyed it too much."

She just watched him with a mix of emotions swirling in her eyes.

"I wanted to learn as much as I could. I wanted it because..." But he stopped.

She didn't. "Because you planned to find the man who murdered your mother and make him pay."

Yes. But to be more specific, just so she would know exactly what kind of man Seth had become... "I planned to find him and kill him." Full disclosure? "I still do."

CHAPTER ELEVEN

Step Eleven: There should be a bit of truth in every lie. Makes it harder for people to know you're conning them that way.

What will the lie be tonight? Better question, what will the truth be?

"You're not a killer." She was adamant. And trying to deal with the barrage of devastating info he'd just dropped on her. *Mental note, when Seth keeps secrets, he keeps them helluva deep.*

"You don't know what I am." He turned away from her.

Just turned away. Like he was going to drop his little I-plan-to-kill bombshell and stroll off. "Nope. Not how this works." So she grabbed his arm.

His steely muscles tensed beneath her touch. "It's how I work."

"You don't get to casually confess a murder plan to me and walk away."

He looked down at her hand on his arm. Heat seemed to singe through her fingertips. She ignored the flare because that burning awareness tended to happen whenever she touched him. Such a bad sign.

Another bad sign? Seth planning to *kill.*

"There is nothing casual about my plan. It's something I've been working on my whole life." His jaw flexed. "Then my dad dropped *his* bombshells on me. The night of his murder, he told me—no, enough. Enough fucking soul baring for one night. I get that I have to rip myself open to keep you, but *enough*."

He had to rip himself open? "Who told you that?"

He pointed toward the luggage. "You were leaving."

"No, Mr. Jump To Conclusions, I wasn't. I was getting my gown." She put her hands on her hips. "So we're both on the same page, you thought confessing that you intended to *murder* someone was what would get me to stay if I did happen to be leaving you? Those were your magic words?"

His hand dropped. "You weren't leaving me?"

"You are planning to *kill* someone? You get that just dropping that in a conversation isn't normal, don't you?"

His eyes glittered. Tension and fury poured from him. "My mother didn't die right away. She had bullets in her back. One bullet had torn through her chest on its way out of her. My mom's blood was all over me, and she kept trying to speak, but she couldn't. She didn't *die* until those bastards had left us alone. She died with my hands on her and with me begging her not to leave me. There were no magic words that would keep her with me. There *are* no magic words in this world."

Oh, damn. Her chest ached. No, she ached. For him. Harley wished she could take away all of his pain.

"Stop it!" A sharp order from Seth. He surged toward her. His hand lifted, and, with a touch so tender it took her breath away, he wiped away the tears that she hadn't even felt sliding down her cheeks. "You're supposed to be tough."

"I am, asshole. Tough people cry, it's a thing."

"Sometimes, you say 'asshole' the way other people say 'sweetheart.'"

Only to him. Because her voice had softened. She'd softened when he touched her. Her hand rose and curled around his wrist, keeping his fingers against her skin. "I'm so sorry about your mother." She'd told him that before. The ache she felt for his loss hit extra hard because of what had happened to Harley's own mother.

"She didn't get justice. I'm gonna give it to her."

Her lower lip trembled. "That's why you're doing everything, isn't it? This whole deal with the Feds isn't just about you trying to right the wrongs your dad committed. This isn't about his sins."

"It's about my own sins. The ones I intend to commit. That shooter was a hired killer. I find him, I get him to talk, then I find his boss. *That's* the person who started everything." Each word seemed torn from him, as if he hadn't intended to tell her more. "I'll take them both out before I'm done."

"You want me to stop you." That was why he was telling her. Had to be. Did he even realize it?

Seth knew he was going over the edge, and he wanted her to help him before he went too far.

"Oh, baby." *Baby* breathed out as a caress. So gentle. Covered with emotion. His head lowered, and his lips feathered over hers. Such a tender kiss.

Her eyes fluttered closed. Her lips parted.

But his mouth lifted. "You are so dead wrong." He backed away. Stopped touching her completely.

A chill skated over her skin as her eyes opened. "What?"

"I didn't tell you so that you'd stop me. There is no stopping what's already in motion. I told you so that you wouldn't get in my way."

His words seemed to echo around her. Pierce through her. She shook her head. "No, no, you want me to stay with you." He'd just said that to her.

"Damn right, I do. But I don't want you in my way. If I have to leave on my own, you let me leave. If I hold back from you, you don't question me. If I—"

"Decide to kill a man, I just stand there and applaud?" Harley finished angrily. Not happening. "No. No, you have the wrong woman."

"What if it had been your mother?"

Oh, that had been a hit. A dirty, mean, direct hit.

"You weren't like me, were you? Harley Adaire, the youngest child of General Chason Adaire and his wife Megan. The beloved baby of the family who grew up with *five* older brothers always surrounding her with love and protection.

Your dad was a decorated war hero. Mine was the killer who lied to everyone he met, but he was the *only* family I had. You had a dream life. I had a nightmare. What if, though, Harley, what if it had been different? Would things be so black and white for you then?"

Her fingers wanted to tremble, so she balled her hands into fists. "If my world was black and white, do you think I would have lied to a cop tonight? And you might *think* you know my family because you read a file or two on me, but you don't. You know nothing about the sacrifices my family made. The risks they took. The blood my brothers and my father have shed. You know nothing about me."

"I know I want you more than I have ever wanted anyone else in this world."

He just kept throwing her off balance. Had to be a deliberate technique. She needed to stop underestimating him.

Except he wasn't done. "I know that I am wrong for you in so many ways. But I have wanted you from the first moment I saw you." His lips twisted. "Or, from the moment my body stopped shaking because you'd just pumped me full of electricity and I looked into your eyes and you told me that you bet I would never forget you. I knew you were telling the truth. There is no way in the world I could ever forget you."

Just as she knew she could never forget him.

"A woman like you doesn't wind up with a crime boss's son. A woman like you doesn't go off into the sunset with a man who has spent his whole life planning revenge and murder. I knew that going into this partnership with you."

"I just told you…" she began.

"Good night, Harley. You take the bed. I'll be on the couch. Tomorrow—hell, later today, when the sun is actually up—we'll figure out what we should do next." And once more, he swung away. "I'm sure our friendly federal agent will be at the door come dawn."

She watched him walk away. The dull drumming of her heart filled her ears with every step. He headed into the sitting area. Lowered onto the couch. Just sat there.

Her foot tapped against the floor.

He didn't look her way.

So she stalked after him. "You're adorable."

"The fuck I am." His head whipped toward her.

"Right. I was lying. See, I do that, too. What you actually are is aggravating to the extreme." She didn't cease her stalking until she was directly in front of him.

Seth's head angled so that he stared up at her.

"It's been a big night," she told him. "Had a crime party, a real-life game of Clue, a dead body in a cemetery. So big. Lots of stuff happening."

"All the more reason for you to go back in the bedroom. Shut the door. Lock it. And get in bed."

"Lock it?" One eyebrow lifted. Just one. It had always driven Ford crazy that she could do the one-brow lift and he couldn't. "If the door is locked, how will I protect my client?"

"Maybe you're the one who needs protection from your client."

"Oh, right. Because you're so big and bad."

"Bad for you." His hands rose. Curled around her hips.

That singeing awareness flew through her. "Do you feel it?" she asked, curious.

"Feel what?"

"The heat that surges when we touch. For me, it's like a wave that goes through my veins. It fills me until I could swear that every part of my body is completely tuned to you."

If possible, his jaw clenched even more. "Bedroom." A rough rumble.

"What's wrong with right here? Right now?"

His fingers pressed deeper into her hips. No pain. With him, there was never pain. "What are you saying?" he growled.

"You didn't answer my question. Hardly seems fair for me to answer yours when you just leave me hanging." She waited for his lashes to lift and for his eyes to find hers. The man had long, thick, dark lashes. They did nothing to soften the brutal intensity of his gaze as it fixed on her. "Do you feel it, too?"

"Yes." Another rumble. Even deeper and darker than before. So stupid sexy.

"I've never crossed the line with a client. Never even been tempted, and let me just tell you, according to every gossip site in the country, that rock star I protected was supposed to be helluva good in bed."

"Sonofabitch."

She rolled one shoulder. "He was actually a really nice guy, not a sonofabitch at all."

Seth growled. Again, those rumbles and growls were so hot. *No, you just think he's hot. That's the problem. You're not thinking clearly because you want him. He's not thinking clearly because he wants you.* So maybe they should both stop thinking.

Harley wet her lips. She'd started this little chat. She'd end it. "Considering my awesome rock star option, you would have thought that if I was going to cross any lines, it would have been with him."

"Don't want to hear about him."

"Because you're jealous."

His hazel eyes burned even more.

There was no need for jealousy. "I didn't want him. I want you. *You,* the man who is so intent on letting me know you're *not* nice."

"I'm not."

"You're doing this whole undercover, potentially suicidal mission, because you want justice for your mom. I don't think that's such a bad thing." She didn't think it was bad at all. Misguided? Yes. Dangerous? Helluva yes. But wanting justice for someone you loved? *That doesn't make you a monster.* "There's something you should know about me." Her hands rose to curl around his shoulders.

"Why are you letting me touch you?" The question seemed torn from him.

She lifted her right knee. Put it beside his thigh on the couch. Moved her left to a similar position on his opposite side. Straddling him put her in a much better position. His hands remained curled around her, but now she was much, much closer to his mouth. "The something you should know...is that I'm not one of those women who falls for the bad guy."

Then she leaned forward and kissed him.

Fire. Lust. Her whole body charged at the touch of her lips to his. Rational thought? She waved goodbye to that petty issue and just held tightly to him. She hadn't been able to think *rationally* since joining this partnership with him. Desire beat in the air between them when they were close. Need pulsed.

She'd tried ignoring their attraction.

A failed effort.

So why not give in? Maybe rational thought would come back...*after*. And maybe not. Screw it. She was taking what she wanted.

His mouth was open. So was hers. Their tongues met. Desire exploded. He yanked her hard against his hips, and there was no missing the powerful, thick length of his cock. Their clothes were in the way. A problem that would have to be rectified very, very soon, but for the moment, she rode his cock through their clothing as her hips rocked up and down against him. And she kept kissing him with a voracious hunger that had been building inside of her for too long.

His mouth wrenched from hers, only to press a fiery trail of kisses along the sensitive skin of her throat. "You don't want this." A rasp.

She tipped back her head to give him and his wicked mouth better access. "There is nothing I want...more than you." Total truth. This wasn't about forever. This wasn't about anything but need and passion. A passion she'd never felt before because never, ever had she been so reckless with anyone.

Oh, sure, on the outside, she might look all bold and devil-may-care, but when it came to her personal relationships...

"You don't go for the bad guy?" he gritted. She felt the score of his teeth against her skin.

Harley shuddered. The good kind of shudder.

"If you don't, then why are you almost fucking me right now?"

"Such a dirty mouth." Her nails pressed into his shoulders. "Because I know you're more. I can see through your mask."

His head lifted. Torment flashed on his face. "Harley..."

"How badly do you want me?"

"If the cops rushed in again, I wouldn't stop."

She smiled at him. "Good thing they won't be coming in. Told you before, I don't perform that way in front of an audience." There was no audience now. Just her. Just him. It took a little shimmying—especially since she didn't want to lose her perch on his lap, she was enjoying the ride too much—but Harley managed to lift her blouse over her head and toss it to the floor. "Unhook my bra for me?"

His gaze seemed to drink her in. His big hands left her hips. Slid up her back. She felt the faint calluses on his fingers and loved the slight roughness against her skin. No, what she loved was his touch. The way everything else had vanished except the desire between them.

Danger could wait. Death could wait. This was happening.

He unhooked her bra. Fumbled just a little, but she wouldn't hold that against him. His hands were freaking huge, and the bra clasp was tiny. She was probably lucky he hadn't torn the thing. The bra joined her blouse on the floor. Harley licked her lips. "Thanks, I—"

He spun her around. Put her beneath him on the couch. One of his powerful thighs braced between her legs. He had her pinned beneath him, and his mouth went right to one breast. When his lips closed over her nipple, heat surged to her core. Her hips jerked against his thigh, but it wasn't his thigh she wanted to be riding. "Seth!"

He kept licking and sucking. First one nipple, then the other. Her breath came faster and faster even as her hands snaked down his body. She shoved his t-shirt out of the way so she could touch his skin. Warm skin. Powerful muscles. Down, down, she went, and her fingers eased between their bodies as she reached the top of his sweatpants.

Those pants were not hiding his arousal. Not even close. "Ditch the clothing," she urged. "It's in the way." Her jeans. His sweats. They had to go. She wanted to be naked with him.

He rose up.

She drew in a deeper breath.

"I want to taste you."

Okay, yes, his voice was sexy. So deep. And his expression had gone way into the brutal-desire stage. So hard and fierce.

"*All* of you."

His hands went to the snap of her jeans. He yanked open that snap, hauled down the zipper, and tugged the jeans over her legs. The fabric was tight, though, and she had to twist a bit to help him. "See," her breathless voice, "if you'd let me change into a gown earlier, this would have been so much easier." Good thing she didn't have shoes on. She'd kicked them off shortly after getting in the new suite.

When he hauled down her jeans, he also caught her panties. But before yanking them off completely, he froze.

Nope. This was not the freezing time. Not when her heart pounded, her breath rushed out, and her whole body clamored for release. "Seth?" *Keep things moving.*

"You planned to fuck me then?" He tossed away her jeans and the pesky panties. "When you were going for the gown? I thought you were leaving me."

Back to that? And why did his words make a pang shoot through her heart? She was spread out, naked, on the couch. He still had on his sweats, and this wasn't the time for a heart-to-heart. But... "Told you, I'm not the kind who leaves." She licked her lips. "And I've wanted to make love with you for a long time. Tonight just tipped the scales."

"Why?" His hands weren't on her.

Why weren't his hands on her?

"*Why?*" Seth demanded again. "What changed?"

She'd kissed rational thought goodbye earlier. Why was he trying to make her explain *now?* "Don't you want me?" Harley knew that he did.

"More than anything."

"Then don't make me wait." Since he wasn't doing any touching, she did. Her hand reached out and she caressed his arousal through the soft fabric of his sweats. She could feel his power. She wanted him inside of her.

"Will you hate me after?" His hands fisted. "Am I going to be your mistake?"

"You get chatty during sex. Noted." Her fingers dipped beneath the waistband of his sweats. No underwear. She immediately touched his hot, eager cock. "I already know all your dark and dangerous parts. If I don't hate you now, how could I ever?"

His breath hissed out at her touch. Then he leaned over her.

She stroked him. Base to tip. Squeezed.

His mouth hovered over hers. "You don't know how dark I can get."

That sounded interesting. "Show me." She wanted to see that crazy control of his splinter.

And splinter, it did.

It started in his eyes. She saw the emotions swirl and burn. His face hardened more. Hunger—raw need—covered his expression. Then his hands were on her. Sliding between *her* legs just before his mouth crashed onto hers. Feverishly, possessively, he kissed her.

And touched her.

One finger slid into her.

Another. Two big, strong fingers flexing in her.

She still had his cock in her hands. Still was stroking him. And he was stroking her, and her hips arched and twisted and he—

Withdrew his fingers. Damn him. "Seth!"

He caught her wrists. Pulled her hands off his dick.

"Now that's just gonna make us both unhappy," she groused.

He pushed her hands up. Eased down her body. Parted her thighs more and put his mouth on her.

"Happy," she gasped in correction as his tongue pierced her, then withdrew to swirl against her clit. "Happy, very, very—*Seth.*"

He licked her with a ravenous desire. Over and over. Thrust his tongue into her. Strummed her clit with his fingers. His fingers and mouth both worked her sex as she thrashed beneath him on the couch. Her hands grabbed the cushions and fisted them. Emotions and a desperate need churned through her, and as the tension peaked, Harley knew she was about to come. "Seth! I want you *in* me!"

He didn't let up. If anything, he went harder on her. Tasted more. Took more. Sent her careening into an orgasm that blasted through every single cell in her body. She trembled. She quaked. She came against his mouth.

And as her breath shuddered out, as the eyes she'd closed slowly fluttered open, she looked down and saw him raise his head.

She expected some sort of lull. Some slight after-orgasm awkwardness. The man was still between her shaking thighs. Her core still quivered. And he—

Hungry.

That was the only way to describe his expression. A sort of almost feral, primitive sexual hunger.

Not awkward. Fierce.

He climbed off the couch, off her. Only to then lift her into his arms. Her own arm automatically looped behind his neck. The last time she had been carried had been...um, she didn't remember. He acted like her weight was nothing, though, and that was hot.

The fact that she still quivered for him—that was hot, too.

That he'd made her come so fast? *So super hot.*

He took her into the bedroom and lowered her onto the bed. "Don't. Move."

Where was she gonna go? Did she look like the kind of woman who ran when amazing orgasms were being handed out?

But she did lever up, with her elbows behind her, so she could enjoy the view. The man *still* had on his sweats. His feet were bare. No shoes. She had no idea when he'd ditched those. No shirt, too. He'd shoved that off a moment ago. Harley vaguely remembered pushing his shirt up so that she could touch his powerful chest—that had been when she'd gone wild on the couch. She was glad he'd tossed it aside now. As he bent over the luggage, Harley took a moment to admire the ripple of his abs. Lickable abs. She would definitely be licking them at the first opportunity.

He opened one of the pieces of their luggage. Pulled out a small, toiletry bag and palmed a foil packet.

"Prepared," she murmured. "Were you a Boy Scout?"

His head turned. His eyes locked on her.

All of the moisture seemed to dry from her mouth. No man had ever looked at her with so much absolute lust in his stare.

"No, far from it." He headed back to the bed. To her. He stopped at the edge and stared at her. She could feel that stare like a touch on her body. "You sure I'm not bad?"

"You're pretending to be."

"That's cute. The belief you have."

She didn't find anything *cute* about their current situation.

"Bad or not," Seth put the packet on the nearby nightstand, "I'm fucking you."

Oh, was that how he wanted to play things? She moved to her knees, turning her body to face him. Her hands slid to his shoulders. "Good guy or not, I'm fucking you." *But you are good. I can see it, even if you can't. Your dad just did one serious number on you.*

She kissed him. Light dips of her tongue into his mouth. Teasing. Taunting—

"*Harley.*" A warning.

She ignored his warning and kept right on teasing until he tumbled her back onto the bed. She would have laughed in delight, but his rougher, more consuming kiss stopped her. Instead of laughing, her hands flew greedily down his back. Such a strong, broad back. The suits he usually wore disguised the full power of his body. Her mouth jerked from his. "Those sweats need to go."

He pulled away. Stepped back. Stripped the sweats off.

Her tongue slid along her lower lip. It was probably unladylike to stare so hard at his dick. Sue her. She kept staring.

He reached for the little packet. Ripped it open and rolled on the condom. "You won't regret this later?"

Now her gaze did come to meet his. "I know what I'm doing."

"I won't let you go after this."

Maybe an alarm bell should have rung at those deep, possessive words. All she could hear, though, was the pounding of her eager heartbeat. "Good thing we have a contract."

Another thing that should have sounded an alarm. He was her client. He was—

He climbed onto the bed. Onto her.

Hers. Seth was *hers.* Her arms wrapped eagerly around him, and Harley hauled him close to her. Her legs parted, but he still pushed them open even more, lodging his hips between them. The head of his cock pressed against her, and she arched, taking him in. Just one inch. Then two, then...

He slammed all the way inside, and she was gone. Her legs wrapped around his hips, and she met him as they began a fast and frantic rhythm. No part of her wanted him to slow down. Every part of her wanted him to go faster. Harder. Harley wanted him to the point that nothing else existed.

She'd known passion before. Sure, she was selective with her lovers, but she'd still had some great times in the past.

This wasn't just *great*. This was like being swept away by a hurricane. Getting completely lost in the storm. Passion overwhelmed her. Need took over. Primitive instinct dominated. His hand moved between their bodies, stroked her already way too sensitive clit, and she went off like a rocket. The orgasm twisted and churned and had her crying out his name.

His hips pistoned against her. Harder. Faster. And she stared into his eyes when he came. Passion shone so brightly in his stare. Lust. Pleasure.

So much pleasure that she knew it was going to consume them both...

And it did.

I might have just made a major tactical mistake.

***

"It doesn't mean anything."

His rough, grating, and *wrong* words had her cracking open an eye. After that body-shaking orgasm, she *might* have drifted off to sleep. Technically, Harley had a vague memory of Seth getting out of the bed and ditching his condom. Maybe she even recalled him being all sweet and thoughtful as he tenderly put a warm cloth between her legs.

Then she'd drifted to sleep because it was who-knew-what o'clock and her satiated body had been ready for dream time.

But those unfortunate words pierced the veil of sleep. They also pissed her off. "Excuse me?" Her voice emerged a little sleep husky, but there wasn't much she could do about that situation.

"You don't have to tell me. I already know."

"Know what?" One breast was peeking out. She knew because he was staring at that peeking breast. A very intent stare. She yanked up the sheet, the better to help him focus. "Yo, eyes on mine."

His eyes immediately met her stare. *Lust*. Still burning brightly. Good. But he swallowed and with that killer jaw of his clenching, he told her, "The sex didn't mean anything."

"Is that a question or a statement?" She settled more comfortably against the soft mattress.

He stood beside the bed and glowered. "It's what you are supposed to tell me. I'm just..." He waved his hand toward her. "Saving you the effort. I get that it didn't matter to you."

Her brow wrinkled. "I have not gotten enough sleep for this conversation."

Seth turned away and headed for the open door. "Get your sleep." Rough. "We'll talk later."

"Or now. Seeing as how you woke me up." And made her angry. "Did it not matter to you?"

Seth stilled. "Fucking you was the best thing that has happened to me in...years."

Those words had her sitting up and hauling the sheet with her. "If that's the case, then why are you walking away?"

He spun. "Because I am not good for you! Because I'm your mistake, and *you don't fuck clients*, remember?"

"You gonna fire me?"

Seth bounded toward her, then caught himself. "What?"

"You probably should. It would make things a whole lot less complicated." A determined nod. "Fire me. Then you can't say I'm having sex with you as part of the job."

His head shook. "Harley..."

"You often say my name like that. Like you're confused. It's cute." She huffed out a breath. "Fine. You don't want to fire me because you're worried it will hurt my feelings or something."

"I...am?"

A determined nod. "Yes. Because you care about me. I'm pretty sure that scares the shit out of you."

He took a step back. "You—no."

"Liar, liar." Obviously, action needed to be taken. She climbed from the bed and wrapped the sheet around her body. "I'm wearing this sheet for you, by the way, because if you see my full naked body again, speech will become impossible for you and we'll wind up rolling in the bed again."

His brows climbed.

When she was right in front of him, her shoulders fell. "My brother says that I get extra flippant when things matter to me. It's some sort of protective instinct I have or something. Wade's got a PhD in psychology, and he thinks he knows everything about what makes people tick. To tell you the truth, he can be pretty annoying."

Seth shook his head. "I don't know what's happening right now."

After grabbing her courage, Harley blew out a long breath. "I don't get brutally honest with a lot of people." She could count those people on one hand. Correction. Two hands. Her five brothers. Her dad. Now, Seth. "I care about you."

His head shook again.

"And that scares the shit out of *me* because I don't care about people easily. I don't let my emotions lead me. I don't get involved against my better judgment. And as I've told you before, I don't sleep with clients."

"We didn't sleep."

She had, for a very brief period. But she knew what he meant. "We made love." Deliberately, she called it love, not fucking. Would he notice that important detail? Another long exhale. "I'm really sorry about this..."

"Harley?"

Staring straight at him, she delivered the news, "I quit."

CHAPTER TWELVE

Step Twelve: Keep the enemy guessing. You keep them off-balance and they will never see the attack coming until it's too late. Magicians use the art of misdirection. You can, too. Get someone to look one way, while all the action is occurring somewhere else completely. Boom.

Bet you didn't see that coming. God, I love magic tricks.

"I quit."

Seth staggered a little because the world must have just tilted hard. Wobbled. Or maybe there'd been an earthquake. Granted, he'd never heard of a quake hitting New Orleans, but stranger things had happened. Could have been a tremor. A sonic boom? *Something* had just happened because his normally perfect balance had been completely thrown off.

She can't quit.

"That eliminates one problem." Wrapped in a white sheet, with her dark hair tumbling over her shoulders and her eyes more gold than brown, Harley gave a determined nod of her head.

"I'm...a problem?" Why the hell was he just standing there and growling out words? *She just quit.*

"In so many ways." Her sheet dipped. She straightened it with a casual flick of her graceful hand. "Me quitting gets rid of the absolute weirdness that would come from you *paying* me while we're sleeping together. You weren't firing me—sweet, really—so I had to take the initiative and get things done."

He blinked. "You're not leaving me?"

"You are obsessed with that point." Her mouth tightened. "I thought you trusted me."

He did.

"Want me to say all the words? Fine. I have zero intent of leaving you. I have one hundred percent intent of having sex with you again. Since you are not paying me for sex, and I don't want anyone to so much as ever suggest that was the case—I'd have to kick someone's ass—"

"I'd do it for you," Seth heard himself say.

She sent him a delighted grin. Her dimple winked.

He rubbed his hand over his chest.

"Since I'm no longer working for you and any professional conflicts won't be an issue, I am now back to my wonderful streak of not sleeping with clients. Win."

Maybe it was because he'd just had an orgasm so intense that it had obliterated some of his brain cells, but Seth had trouble following along. "You're not my bodyguard any longer?"

Her dimple vanished. "I am absolutely still your bodyguard. I am in this with you for the long run. You think I'm letting you face Fabian on your own? Letting you face potential murder charges without me at your side?"

"No?"

"*No.* I am still your bodyguard. You're just not paying me for the service." With that, she whirled around and headed for the bed. "We both know this bed is big enough for two. Pretty sure we just proved that fact, so there is no sense in you bunking on the couch."

His feet felt rooted to the floor.

Without looking back, she added, "You do know you're completely naked, yes?"

Seth glanced down. *Fuck it.* "Why?"

"Why are you naked? You'd have to tell me. Though I suspect it's because once wasn't enough, you're now going to be physically obsessed with me, and you are planning to pounce on my nimble body again." She slid into the bed. Fluffed the covers. Then sighed and let her shoulders sag. "I'm doing it again. Being flippant to protect myself. I'm the one who is probably physically obsessed. Not you. Was that some projection thing I was doing?"

"You're making my head spin." His feet had unfrozen, and he shuffled toward her.

Harley's fingers fiddled with the covers. "I'm sorry. I think I have that effect on people."

Sweetheart, you have all kinds of effects on me. "When I asked why..." Seth stopped and cleared his throat because the sight of Harley all tousled and sexy in that bed made his whole body flood with arousal. Who was he kidding? He'd been aroused during her whole confusing talk. "I asked why because I wanted to know *why* you are staying with me. If I'm not paying you, then why would you still want to help me?"

Her hand reached out and curled around his. "You have value beyond your money. You get that, don't you?"

"Sure." He looked at their hands. Hers was so much smaller and more delicate than his own. "I have value to the Feds because of who my father was. I've got connections that have let them close half a dozen cases so far, and now we're going after even bigger threats."

Her hold tightened on him. "I'm talking about *you*. I care about you, Seth."

Why? No, he wasn't saying that again.

"You've been through hell. You've lived a life that I think must have been torture, but you still have good shining in you."

Automatically, his head shook in denial.

"Let me believe what I want."

Even if she was wrong? Or did she need to believe that in order to justify sleeping with him? And a deep, dark part of him—because he had so many dark parts—thought...*Let her believe any lie, if it means I get to keep her*.

With that thought, a jolting realization hit.

Oh, fuck. Fuck. I intended this all along. Seth stared into her eyes and understood that he was truly far worse off than he'd believed. He'd brought an innocent woman into hell...*and I think I did it because I wanted her so badly*.

He'd wanted her ever since he'd heard her taunting line...

Betting you'll never forget me, huh?

No, no, Seth would never be able to forget her. Would she ever be able to forgive him? "I'm sorry."

"Sorry for what? Keeping me up? Giving me an awesome orgasm? Be super specific, then get in bed. At this rate, Brent will be at the door before we get any beauty sleep."

He didn't get in the bed. "I wanted you."

"I hope you still do." She winked. "Do me a favor and turn off the bedside lamp before you hop into bed with me?"

"I will *always* want you."

"That's better." She let go of him and slid back down against the mattress.

"I shouldn't have ever brought you onto this case."

He expected anger. Harley just yawned. "Why not?"

"Because...I think I did it just because I wanted you."

No change of expression.

"I wanted you so much, and I know you're a good bodyguard—"

"I'm better than good."

"But I think I let my personal...attraction to you overrule my thinking. I should have stayed away, and now I've got you in this mess with me. My danger is reaching out to wrap around you."

Another yawn. "I'm pretty used to danger." The lamp light spilled onto the bed. Onto her. "Doesn't faze me that much. But you're telling me you've had this super, overwhelming personal attraction for me ever since our electric first meeting?"

"*Yes.*"

"And you let that attraction consume your common sense and you hired me when there are a ton of other bodyguards out there—granted, not as good as I am, but still, plenty out there—yet you hired me because you just couldn't stay away?"

"*Yes.*" He wanted in that bed with her.

Her dimple winked again. "Stop being sweet. You'll make me want to jump you again, and I am *trying* to get to sleep. Got to be semi-rested and refreshed for tomorrow so that I can be ready if the bad guys attack."

Seth shook his head.

"Okay. Let me tell you what happened from my perspective. Right now, you're in your own head and missing what is right in front of you."

She was in front of him. She was everything he wanted. *I wanted you so much that I pulled you into my hell.* Because he was a selfish bastard.

"Let me recap. Fast." An exhale from Harley. "You say you brought me on because you wanted me so badly, but *I* was the one to make the big move tonight. I went after you. I seduced you on that couch. I was the one to change things between us. All me. And I have *no* regrets."

"*Why?*"

Another yawn. Her voice began to slur as she said, "Probably because I've been falling in love with you."

No. He had not heard correctly. No way. Impossible. There was nothing about him she could love. His life was a lie. *He* was a lie. A monster. The son of a killer. A man who'd told her that *he* planned to hunt down his mother's murderer and issue some bloody justice of his own.

She could not love him.

"Why else would I have broken my sacred rule and slept with a client?" Definitely slurred, and her thick eyelashes fell as her eyes closed.

"But I'm not your client any longer. You just quit." *So...you could be my lover?*

She didn't speak. Her chest rose and fell, and Seth realized Harley had slipped away from him. He could leave. Go back to the couch. Give her some space.

But she *had* told him the bed was big enough for two, and, brutal honesty, there was no other place that he wanted to be. So Seth turned out the bedside lamp and slid into the bed with her. He pulled her against him. Inhaled her scent. Savored her softness.

And closed his own eyes.

He was such a bastard. Straight to his core. She didn't get that truth, but he'd tried to tell her. Now it was too late. Whatever it took, whatever he had to do...he was keeping her.

Before he'd taken her body, he'd tried to warn her.

I won't let you go after this.

His hold tightened, and he fell asleep with her in his arms.

***

"Someone is at the door," Harley muttered. The banging penetrated the rather amazing dream she'd just been having. A dream about her and Seth. Her, Seth, and sex. Her eyes reluctantly opened as she kissed the dream goodbye.

She found Seth's face just inches from her own.

His eyes opened. Confusion showed first. Then a flash of surprise.

Yep, it's me. I'm in bed with you. No dream.

And then…satisfaction. He even started to smile as he stared at her.

The banging came again.

His smile slipped.

Alas, Harley knew the moment was lost. So she rolled over, slid from the bed, and strode naked toward the luggage. "Figure our guest could be Brent, our favorite federal agent. It could also be Zion, our new detective friend. Or it could be Fabian, our current lead suspect and enemy." She tugged on fresh panties. "My money is on Brent."

Seth jumped from the bed. He grabbed his sweats, hauled them on, and darted from the room.

"Good morning to you, too!" Harley called after him. "Don't open the door without looking first!" Jeez. Now she had to haul ass, too. She yanked on her jeans and a new shirt. No time for the bra. She'd add that later. *After* a shower. Harley hustled after him just in time to see the suite's door swing open. Brent stood in the hallway. "I win," she muttered.

A muscle ticked along Brent's jaw.

Uh, oh.

Seth sighed and waved the agent in.

Brent stomped across the threshold and kicked the door shut behind himself. "What the *hell?*" His voice came out as a low, angry snarl. "Why are you in a new room, Seth? And why am I hearing buzz that a detective from NOPD was questioning you?"

"Because the Feds get good intel?" Harley asked. "That certainly would explain the buzz. By the way, how's that clearance going for me?"

He glared at her. Then...looked at the open bedroom doorway that was behind her. His stare flew around the suite, assessing things and reaching a fast conclusion. His eyes widened. "Does this suite only have one bedroom?"

"Um. No one can ever say you're not observant. It does. Just one. But there's a pullout couch, too." She pointed to the couch.

He studied the couch. "It looks unused. Not pulled out."

"I fixed it already." Seth rolled back his shoulders. "We're in a new suite because of that NOPD questioning you just mentioned."

Brent's gaze was still on the couch.

Harley sighed because she could almost hear the wheels turning in his head. "Bigger fish, man. Bigger. Focus on the NOPD visit."

His stare jumped to her.

But it was Seth who helpfully finished the update by saying, "We had to switch rooms after the detective—"

"Detective Zion Raye," Harley supplied helpfully.

Seth nodded. "After he kicked in the front door of our previous suite. The place wasn't secure so the hotel let us switch. And we wound up here."

"*Why* did he break in the door?" Brent wanted to know.

Harley tugged down the hem of her shirt. "You didn't hear that bit of buzz? I would have thought that you had. A dead body was found. Remember that charming gentleman who chased us out of the mansion last night? He was murdered."

"Sonofabitch." Brent squeezed his eyes shut.

"Indeed, he was. But he's also a murder victim," Harley pointed out. "And he was stabbed quite a number of times."

His eyes flew open. "How do you know that?"

Because I saw the body.

"Because the detective was here," Seth rumbled. "The body was discovered in front of my mother's crypt at the St. Louis Cemetery."

"You are shitting me." Brent began to pace.

"Wish I was." Seth lowered onto the couch. "I'm not. And, in addition to being dumped right in front of my mom's final resting place, my ID was found beneath the body."

Brent whirled toward him. "Your ID? How?"

Harley strolled over to perch next to Seth. Her stomach rumbled, reminding her that she had not eaten in a very, very long time. "We think it was lifted during the pat-down last night. I'm sure you recall the lovely experience Seth and I had before we were allowed into the mansion. And if that's actually when the ID was taken..."

Horror flashed on Brent's face. "Then Seth's cover is blown. Fabian is trying to frame him for murder, and we are all fucked."

Harley turned to glance at Seth. "He summed that up nice and fast, don't you think?"

Seth's lips curled down.

"We'll have to get you out of town." Brent went back to pacing. "You won't be safe here. The Feds already stepped in once when you were suspected of murder. We can't step in again."

"You did that in North Carolina." Seth's voice held no emotion. "And that was when I was *mistakenly* being accused of killing my own father."

"Doesn't matter. We barely kept our involvement quiet there. Hell, Francesca had to take a back seat on the investigation because she was photographed by the media. We didn't want her getting tied to you, and that's why I'm the agent running interference between you and the Bureau now. I kept myself out of the press. But if you are miraculously saved from *two* murder investigations, we might as well consider our undercover op dead and buried."

Better the op than Seth.

"That's it. I've got to report this to my boss. Not like he was a fan of the original plan anyway." Brent yanked out his phone. "He is going to lose his shit."

Sounded like his mysterious boss needed to settle down, but, before Harley could voice that opinion, another knock sounded at the door. A knock this time, not impatient banging. Harley's brows climbed. "We expecting another early morning guest?"

"No." Seth was already on his feet. He went straight to the door and put his eye to the peephole. "What in the hell?"

Harley automatically tensed.

He swung the door open. She jumped to her feet in case he needed her, but she just saw—a very, very large gift basket. One that was being precariously carried by Cayden.

"Good morning," he called. He flashed a nervous, weak smile. "I, um, have a delivery for you. May I come inside?"

Seth waved him in. "By all means."

Cayden came inside, struggling a bit with the basket, so Seth took it from him. Harley hurried forward, truly curious. She couldn't help it. She'd always had a weakness for really good gift baskets. Through the plastic wrap, she could see wine bottles, fine chocolates, a bottle of whiskey, beignet mix, and—

Seth put the basket on the small dining table. A card was tied to the ribbon at the top of the basket, and he pulled it free. "When did the basket arrive?"

"Just a few moments ago." Cayden's curious gaze darted to a watchful Brent. "Ah...good morning?"

"He's our driver," Harley explained, voice breezy. She wanted to see the card. "We'll be going out soon so Seth asked him to come up."

"Right. Yes. I, um..." Cayden's stare darted toward the bedroom, then back to Harley. His red hair looked particularly disheveled, and shadows lined his eyes. "Did you enjoy a good night's sleep?"

"*After* the detective broke my door, you mean?" Seth shoved the card into his pocket. "Great. The stuff dreams are made of." He strode into the bedroom.

Cayden jerked on his collar.

"He means that," Harley reassured the man. "He's not just being sarcastic." Okay, he had been. "His dreams were fabulous. We got plenty of rest." It was only a little after six a.m. so "plenty" was definitely a stretch. "Cayden, just how long is your shift?"

"Going home now." He straightened. "Just wanted to bring that gift box up personally to Mr. Wellington and see if there is *anything* at all I could do to make up for the inconvenience you both suffered last night."

Seth strolled out of the bedroom and headed straight for Cayden.

"I, um," Cayden tugged on his collar again. "I believe there might have been a mention of *not* suing last night? Are we still in that frame of mind?"

"I'm not suing," Seth said, voice rough. "I'm tipping you. Thanks for the delivery." He held out the cash.

Relief flashed on Cayden's face even as he made the money vanish. "Thank you. And I certainly hope you have a wonderful day in the Big Easy. If there is anything I can do to assist you during your stay, do not hesitate to reach out to me." He turned for the door.

"Did you see the person who made the delivery?" Seth asked.

"Ah, yes." Cayden looked back over his shoulder. "I took the basket personally at the concierge desk."

"Did you get a name?" Seth pushed.

"No, but, he was a nicely dressed gentleman. Big. Blond hair. Very, ahem, well built. Not the typical delivery personnel we see. He was actually rather...intimidating. Had a very, very penetrating stare."

To Harley, that description sounded a lot like the blond goon who'd been doing the searches at Fabian's place. Of course, she was sure there were plenty of big, blond men running around New Orleans so it *could* have been someone else.

Cayden hurried out, and she started unwrapping the basket. Those chocolates would be perfect for breakfast.

"I wouldn't eat those," Seth advised her. "The basket *is* from Fabian, and seeing as how he might want us both dead..."

She needed to stay away from the expensive chocolates. Her shoulders sagged. "I worried about that as soon as Cayden mentioned the blond delivery guy. For the record, anyone who would poison chocolates that expensive and tasty is an absolute dick."

Brent sidled closer. "Fabian Butler just sent you a freaking *gift* basket? What in the hell?"

Sadly, Harley turned away from the basket and its offerings. "The man has to cover his ass. Fabian told Seth he'd be getting a gift. Sure, we might all be thinking he meant the gift of his goon's *dead body* in that cemetery, but thanks to this big basket, the man has proof that a gift was, indeed, delivered." *And now Fabian gets to act like he didn't leave a dead body for Seth to find. He can play innocent and say his message was misinterpreted.* Clearly, not the man's first ball game.

"The basket is nothing but a cover. He wants to meet," Seth said. "And he's giving me thirty minutes to show up."

Seth's words had both Brent and Harley whipping their heads toward him. "Where?" Harley asked. *Please be in a very public location. Please be…*

"Café du Monde." A roll of one shoulder.

"I thought *you* were going to pick the next meeting location." Brent sounded worried.

Good. He should be worried. Harley was worried, too.

"Guess the *buzz* about the murder reached Fabian, too. And he's calling for the meeting ASAP. The note said we meet in thirty minutes or we don't meet at all." His gaze flickered over Harley. "You still in, *bodyguard?*"

Hell, yes, I am. Even without a contract, I will protect him. Just as she knew—with certainty—that Seth would protect her. "Try to keep me out."

Because that just wouldn't happen.

An early morning meeting with the bad guy who *might* have left a dead body for them last night? No way would she miss that date.

But first, she had to take one super fast shower.

CHAPTER THIRTEEN

Step Thirteen: Personal involvement is dangerous. When emotions get involved, you stop thinking straight.

But who are we kidding? My emotions have been involved from the very beginning.

The million-dollar question: Have his?

"I don't remember saying to bring your bodyguard along."

Seth didn't tense at those words from Fabian. He'd headed to the far outside seating area at their meeting location and not been even mildly surprised to see that Fabian's goons—uh, guards—had managed to clear the space out. Sure, it was still early enough that a whole lot of people weren't out and about, but the guards—including the blond from last night—were making sure that no one else joined this little private party on the small terrace.

"Did you expect me to miss beignets?" Harley asked. "Don't be crazy. Who in their right mind would miss them?"

Seth noticed she hadn't said a word about being called a bodyguard. He walked past the goons and when the blond looked a little too intently at Harley, Seth stilled. "Even *think* of frisking her, and I'll break your fingers."

The blond stiffened.

"It's hard to be a pickpocket with broken fingers," Harley murmured. "That will suck for you."

The blond's face reddened.

Hit. So the bastard *had* lifted Seth's ID? His flushing response sure was suspicious. The lead in Seth's gut settled even heavier. He knew that Brent had eyes and ears on this little meeting, but things could still go sideways in an instant.

"We're meeting for breakfast. No need for anyone to be searched. I mean..." Soft laughter from Fabian. "It's not like one of us is working undercover and wearing a wire or anything, am I right?"

Fucking hell.

Seth turned his head to stare at Fabian. The other man had on sunglasses that shielded his gaze, but a mocking smile curved Fabian's lips.

"Isn't that what you accused me of doing last night?" Fabian carefully continued. "Wearing a wire? But I can assure you, I am not." A delicate pause. "Can you say the same?"

He knows. They were screwed. And Seth figured aborting the operation was long past being a possibility.

"I suppose Seth could strip right here and right now," Harley murmured. "But other than giving a few tourists a delicious eyeful, there would be no shocking discovery made. He's not a Fed."

Fabian's head turned toward her. "But *you* are a bodyguard."

Seth pulled out a chair at the table for Harley. As she settled in, he considered and discarded explanations to offer Fabian. But then he realized...

Truth was easier than fiction in this case. "Sounds like a statement, not a question." He took the chair next to her, the one that put him closer to Fabian. "Been digging into my life, have you?"

Fabian's lips curled a little more. "I like to investigate people that I might potentially engage in business enterprises with. It's always important to understand a potential business partner's strengths and weaknesses."

He couldn't be sure because of the sunglasses Fabian wore, but Seth had a sinking feeling the guy had just looked Harley's way when he said *weaknesses*. Taking his time, Seth pulled out his own sunglasses and perched them on his nose. "What a coincidence," Seth returned. "I like to look for those very same things."

Fabian laughed. "Shall we cut through the bullshit?"

"I do hate bullshit," Seth allowed.

"You could be wired right now."

Do not tense.

"Tech these days is so small that even if you stripped, it could still be hidden on you."

"Or on you," Seth fired back.

"Feds can certainly have their uses, but I don't wear wires for them."

"I am starving," Harley confessed and flashed her disarming smile. The dimple was in full effect.

"What are the odds that one of your guards—hello, gentlemen—would go and snag us some beignets?"

"Already ordered." A shake of Fabian's head. "I mean, really, why come here if you're not going to eat? I picked this place because I do enjoy starting a day with a beignet."

And do you enjoy ending your nights with a bit of blood and murder? Not that he could ask that question...yet. "Got to tell you..." Seth settled more comfortably into the chair. Considering it appeared to be an ancient, wrought iron chair, there wasn't exactly much comfort to be found. "You are not what I expected. When I was told that if I visited New Orleans, I'd have the chance to meet a...like-minded professional, I didn't expect a guy who sent gift baskets and ate beignets as the sun rose."

"I hate living up to expectations," Fabian demurred. "Makes life boring. And I can't help but note, I didn't hear a thank you for the gift."

Seth's fingers curled around the arms of his chair. "Quite unexpected, I assure you."

Fabian leaned forward. "Was it? And here I thought it would be exactly what you wanted."

"Ahem." Harley delicately cleared her throat.

Both men looked her way.

"Are we talking about gift baskets?" Harley asked sweetly. "Or the dead body in the cemetery? You know, the one that you and blondie over there tried to stage so Seth would get tossed in a New Orleans jail cell?"

Leave it to Harley to cut through the BS and ask the million-dollar question.

Fabian's chin lifted. "I was notified of the tragic news." A bite entered his voice. "I had nothing to do with that attack, and, I can assure the person who *is* guilty that those actions were quite unnecessary." His jaw clenched as his head angled toward Seth. "I was going to handle the situation on my own, and I certainly don't take kindly to someone else stepping in. You're new to this town. You sure as fuck don't own it yet, so stop acting like you do."

Whoa. Seth held up a hand. "You think *I* did it?"

"You certainly announced your arrival very publicly, didn't you? So much for maintaining a low profile. First you get your bodyguard to neutralize one of my best...employees in *my* home. Then you created a spectacle in front of my assembled guests last night by holding a gun on that same employee, obviously trying to show that you aren't afraid to break all of my rules."

This conversation was *not* going as planned.

Fabian's quiet fury hardened his voice as he continued, "Then *you* dumped his body in front of your family's crypt. A sure sign that you wanted everyone to know that when you fucked with Seth Trahan Wellington, you would get sent to the grave." He whipped off his glasses to reveal his furious, narrowed eyes. "Did I cover everything? Or did I leave some shit out?" He grabbed the edge of the table with his left hand and loomed toward Seth even more. "Because let me be clear, new *friend,* I will not be intimidated in my own town. I will not have you coming here and making me into some joke. I don't care who the hell you think you—"

"Beignets walking," the blond guard announced.

"Fuck, thanks, Andre." Fabian heaved out a breath even as he slapped the sunglasses back over his eyes.

Seth glanced to the side, and sure enough, a waitress was bringing a tray filled with two giant plates of beignets their way. She set them down quickly, her fingers trembling with nerves, and some of the powdered sugar spilled onto the table—and onto Fabian.

"OhmyGod." The waitress shuddered. "I am *so* sorry."

"Think nothing of it. If you're going to have beignets, you have to pay the price." He sent her a charming smile.

Mental note, the guy is even more of a chameleon than I am.

"Bring some coffee, would you?" Fabian murmured.

Head bobbing, she practically ran away.

Fabian exhaled slowly. His rage seemed to have vanished. "Nothing is free in this world. Every action has consequences." Fabian made no move to take a beignet. "We all have to pay, in one way or another."

Harley helped herself to a beignet. A little cloud of white powder dusted the air around her mouth as she let out a moan that could only be termed sensual. *Fuck.*

Then she devoured her beignet.

Seth didn't move. The atmosphere was far too charged, and he had no idea what stunt Fabian might pull next.

Fabian's head swung between him and Harley. Seth, sitting tense and at attention. Harley, relaxed, seemingly having no care in the world, in beignet heaven.

"Worked up quite an appetite last night," Harley confessed with a breezy shrug. "Needed to eat."

"That will happen," Fabian pounced, "when you spend the night running through the city."

The sonofabitch was watching us.

"Oh." Harley blinked, eyes wide and innocent. "I meant when I was fucking Seth like crazy. Didn't your detective friend tell you about that?"

Seth *almost* choked.

Delicately, Harley patted her powder-covered fingers on a napkin. "He interrupted us at an unfortunate moment, but we managed to get things going again, no worries."

Once more, Fabian's head swung between Seth and Harley. Then his attention lingered on Harley. "You're his bodyguard. One of the waitresses recognized you at my place. At first, she was saying that you were the ex-girlfriend of some rock star, but when I did a little more work, I realized you'd been photographed with quite a few powerful men."

"I have a type." Blissfully unconcerned, that was Harley.

"Of course, you do. Your type is men with money who want a beautiful and deadly bodyguard at their sides. A woman who can blend perfectly at social functions and still allow them to be protected at all times. You sign a contract, you take a job, and you develop no personal connection to your employer whatsoever." He seemed to tick off his version of the facts in rapid succession. "Sure, you play a good game. You look perfect in public, but the appearance ends when the door closes." He smirked. "You're not personally involved with Seth Wellington. In fact, I suspect you probably don't even like the man. From all I've gathered, both he and his father are extremely unlikeable individuals."

"Sitting right the fuck here," Seth growled.

"Coffee," Andre announced.

Seth, Harley, and Fabian took a breath and stopped talking while the waitress poured everyone coffee. If possible, her fingers shook even more now, and Seth thought it was a miracle they didn't all end up burned.

As soon as she hurried off...

"I can offer you fifty grand to walk away right now, Harley. I'm sure protecting someone so connected to the criminal underworld isn't what you'd prefer to do, but since Seth claims to be an honest businessman, I'm thinking Wilde—that *is* your employer, yes?—I'm thinking Wilde couldn't deny him when he came looking to hire you."

Harley didn't reach for her coffee. "Wilde can take or ignore any case. We're fun like that."

Fabian stirred his coffee. "Fifty grand. It will be in your bank account by the time you get back to your hotel. Walk away right now."

Her head tilted. The sunlight hit her hair, pulling out the red highlights hidden in the darkness. "You want me to split town. Interesting. Does that have anything to do with me being Seth's alibi for last night?"

"He wasn't fucking you."

"I've got an unforgettable orgasm that says he was."

Andre started coughing.

"I think your guard is sick." She did her *tsk, tsk* sound that Seth now found oddly adorable. "Better watch it, you'd hate for him to bring you down."

"*You're* Seth's bodyguard, not—"

"I'm not his bodyguard." Her words rang with sincerity. "Not in any official capacity. Hook me up to a lie detector, and I will pass with flying colors."

Because she'd quit already. Had she done that deliberately? Knowing Fabian would discover the truth? Interesting question, one that Seth would consider later. For now... "You know, it's weird. You seem to be looking at the world in a very black and white manner." A shake of his head. "Harley assures me that we shouldn't do that. But here you are, Fabian, saying that she has to be my bodyguard. That she can't be my lover. I don't get it. Why can't she be both?"

Fabian lifted the steaming mug of coffee to his lips.

"We're all more than one thing," Seth continued easily. "Why, just take a look at yourself. You're an entrepreneur and a murderer. Two things. Not either-or."

"A murderer?" Fabian repeated carefully. "Just who are you accusing me of killing?"

"Oddly enough, the same man *you* just accused me of killing. Your employee, Justin Florent. When I look at you, I see a guy who got pissed and took out his own man last night." He sent a grimace toward Andre. "Be careful. You might not have as much job security as you think, even if you did pull off a solid for your boss and lift my ID."

"*Enough.*" Fabian slammed down his mug. Hot coffee immediately flew out and landed on his fingers. Hissing out a breath, he grabbed a napkin.

"Be careful. It's easy to get burned." Seth stared straight at his enemy.

The moments ticked by in thick silence. On the river, a steamboat slowly chugged past, and a long, blasting horn sent birds flying overhead.

"I didn't kill Justin." Fabian tossed down the napkin.

"Neither did I."

"He was found at *your* mother's crypt. Found with your ID—"

"That *your* man took from me." Now they were finally getting somewhere. "Why? What was the point of that little maneuver? Except, of course, to set me up for a crime." *Only Harley thinks he initially planned a different victim.* "That setup didn't go so well, did it?"

"I have no idea what you're talking about."

Seth rose, and the chair legs grated over the stone flooring. "We're done here." He extended his hand toward Harley.

Graceful as a ballerina, she rose and slid her hand into his.

"*Wait!*" A fast order from Fabian. "I'm not lying to you. I didn't kill Justin."

"Neither did I." A pause. "So if we're both innocent, then who drove a knife into your guy over and over again?"

"I don't know." Fabian made a shooing motion toward Andre and the other guard. Immediately, they both rose and left the terrace. "I didn't order Andre to take your ID. I have no freaking clue how it got to the cemetery. Maybe you should realize that I'm not the only enemy you have in this town."

"Give me a name."

"Harley fucking Adaire."

Seth leapt at the SOB.

Harley grabbed his arm. "*Seth*. He's trying to provoke you."

"Then consider me provoked." To the extreme.

Fabian jumped to his feet. "You're a stranger in a strange town. What I'm trying to do is to be your friend. You see, I think we could have a good friendship. We could turn the world upside down." A faint exhale. "But not if you're being manipulated. That's what's happening, see. You're being tricked. Because you fucked her, but really, I think she fucked you."

Seth's head turned toward Harley. "Let go." Because he was about to rip Fabian's annoying head right from his shoulders.

"*Think* about it," Fabian snapped as he edged away from the table. "Who had access to your ID? She did. She's touching you right now. She could lift your ID in a second, and you wouldn't know.

She also is the one who got into a fight with Justin. The person who, according to him, nearly killed him last night when he was just chatting with his girlfriend."

"Chatting?" Harley repeated. "Try choking! Because that's what he was doing. Then he tripped over his own feet and fell. Granted, he had a little help falling, but it's still his fault."

Seth moved to stand toe-to-toe with Fabian. "Does this usually work?" True curiosity filled him. "Are the people in your world such dumbasses that they let you play your divide and conquer games so that you can make them vulnerable and easier to take out?"

Fabian's sunglasses just threw Seth's reflection back at him. "Maybe I'm honestly trying to help you. Your *bodyguard* had the opportunity to snag your ID. She'd already been in one fight with Justin, and maybe...maybe when she misinterpreted some rough foreplay as an attack on Mae, she decided to take justice into her own hands." His lips pressed together. "Do *you* know where Harley was all night? Can you alibi her every second?"

He'd found Harley right across the street from the cemetery.

But that's because she was following me. Not because she got there first.

Right?

"Be careful who you trust," Fabian warned him. "Maybe, deep down—or hell, not so deep—Harley thinks you and your old man are bastards who deserve to rot. Her brothers throw terrorists in jail. You really think she's down for guarding *your* back? Hell, no. She hates you. She hates me. If she had the chance, I fully believe she'd set you up so that you could spend the rest of your life in prison."

Silence. No, there was the faintest hint of jazz music drifting on the wind. Very, very faint.

"Seth?"

He turned his head to look at Harley.

"We should go." Her voice was soft, careful.

Harley was not a soft and careful woman. Alarm bells rang. And he moved close to her.

"I get that you don't know who to trust," Fabian muttered. "But maybe don't just go all in with a woman simply because you like the way she fucks."

Yeah, like he was just gonna take *that*. Not him, and sure as shit not the persona he was supposed to be projecting. Without any hesitation, he whirled back around and drove his fist straight into Fabian's jaw. Fabian staggered to the side, hit the edge of the table, and sent white powder flying.

Footsteps pounded toward them. The guards, rushing to the rescue. But before Seth could spin toward the new threat, Harley was already in action. She pulled a small gun from her handbag and aimed it at the approaching men.

"Andre, I believe it was? Freeze," Harley instructed politely. "Your friend needs to freeze, too."

Both men froze.

Seth took a step to the side so he could view both those two jerks and Fabian. Fabian rubbed his jaw and glared.

"Be very, very careful what you say about Harley," Seth grimly advised him. "When it comes to her, I can be quite uncivilized."

Fabian's jaw slid to the left. The right. "Noted."

"I trust her completely, so play your games somewhere else. Harley didn't kill Justin. I didn't, either."

"Neither the hell did I!" Fabian snarled.

The man actually seemed serious. And that led to a very big problem. *Who else could be setting me up?* A question that had to be solved, fast.

But first, he needed to get Harley out of there. "I'll assume we aren't doing business, Fabian." Brent would be pissed. Seth hadn't gotten anything he could actually use in this little chat. "If I see you again, I'll just take your presence as a threat."

"That a promise?" Fabian rumbled. "Am I supposed to be scared?"

"Yes."

Fabian's stare turned contemplative. "You really didn't kill him?"

"Again, you make me think you're wired. And if that's the case, then let me just speak nice and loud...*I had nothing to do with Justin's death.*" Disgusted, he turned away and grabbed Harley's free hand. The hand that wasn't gripping a gun. "Why the hell would I want to murder him? Harley had already handled the bastard. I had no reason to want his ass dead."

"Of course, you did."

Seth kept walking, pulling Harley with him. He was so done with Fabian's games—

"You wanted him dead because Justin's dad was the hitman who killed your mother."

Seth's heart thundered in his ears. No, he had not just heard those words.

Fabian's soft laughter trailed after him. "I happen to think that might be one hell of a reason. Justin's dear old dad got taken out in a drive-by about five years ago. Since you couldn't unleash your vengeance on him, why not turn to the son?"

Justin's dad was the hitman who killed your mother.

Seth looked back at Fabian. There was no missing the rage on the other man's face.

"If you don't have the father to punish," Fabian added, voice silky, "then why not just take your rage out on the son?"

CHAPTER FOURTEEN

Step Fourteen: When you trust the wrong person, immediately take steps to correct the situation. In other words, get that traitor out of your life, STAT. As my father would say, do let the door hit him in the ass.

"Drive," Harley breathed to Brent as she dove into the limo and hauled Seth inside with her. He'd pretty much turned to stone with Fabian's reveal, and she'd needed to drag the man to safety.

He'd wanted to stay. Wanted to play more of Fabian's game and demand answers.

Nope. They needed to get the hell away.

Brent slammed the door and flew around the front of the vehicle. She peered through the window on the side to make sure that two hulking goons weren't coming for them. Luckily, all she saw was a few early morning tourists.

And not Andre with a big gun.

Her own gun was back in her bag. For a moment there, things had certainly gotten dicey. "Was the punch to the face necessary?"

"One hundred percent." He yanked off his sunglasses and tossed them onto the seat. His eyes blazed. "Didn't like the way he was talking about you."

She winced. "You know he was taunting you? Deliberately trying to push you past your control?"

"I was in perfect control." His hands flattened on his thighs. "If I hadn't been, he would be dead right now."

Okay. That was a pretty chilling statement. What chilled her even more? She thought he was serious.

The limo pulled away from the curb and eased forward. Harley tried to figure out where the hell she should start. Or, actually, she knew. Inching forward, she checked to make sure the privacy screen was in place. It was, or at least, it appeared to be. Her head turned as her gaze flew around the interior of the limo. "You want to take that wire off?"

Because he'd been wired for the whole exchange with Fabian. Unfortunately, Fabian hadn't exactly said anything they could use against him.

But Brent and his Fed buddies had been able to hear everything that went down. If things had gone to hell—which they almost had—the Feds *should* have come to the rescue. Only Harley now had some doubts about that situation.

Seth shoved his hand onto the front button of his shirt. He grabbed hard and yanked the whole button from his shirt. Not that the button itself was the listening device. No, the listening device was a tiny, black object that had been hidden *on* the black button. It had blended perfectly.

The days of actually wearing a wire were long gone. Tech had gotten far too advanced for anyone to actually need a giant listening device that would be taped to a chest, like you used to see in the old TV shows. Now listening devices could be practically microscopic. You could have a full body search and still miss them, Fabian had been right on that score.

She swiped the button—and the listening device from Seth—and dropped the items onto the limo's floorboard. Then she used her high heel to stab the device and obliterate it.

"Uh, Harley?"

"We have a problem." Once more, her gaze darted around the limo. There could be other devices back there. In fact, odds were high that the Feds had hidden them. *In the limo. Maybe even in our original hotel room.* Hell. She should have been more suspicious sooner. This was on her.

She leapt across the vehicle and curled her hands around Seth's shoulders.

"What are you doing?"

Her mouth went to his ear. Making her voice as soft as possible, she whispered, "We have an issue." A big one. "Someone in the government is feeding Fabian intel."

Beneath her hands, she felt his body turn to stone. "How?" Barely a breath from him.

But she knew what he meant. *How do you know? How did you figure that out?*

She swallowed. Brought her mouth even closer to his ear. She hoped that any listening device that might have been installed in the rear of the limo wouldn't be able to pick up this soft exchange, but she couldn't be sure. Again, tech had gotten damn advanced. "*No one should know what my brothers are doing.*" That information had been classified. Classified at the highest of need-to-know levels.

The twins, Ryder and Rafe, had been working classified ops ever since their SEAL days. No one outside of the highest echelons of the US government should have known about the cases they'd just completed—cases that had involved deep undercover work as they ferreted out domestic terrorists. Only someone with the highest government clearance should have been able to get even a hint of their dangerous activities.

But a New Orleans crime boss knew what they'd been doing. And that meant...

He's in bed with someone in a high position of power.

Seth's hands rose and curled around her waist.

Harley kept her lips at his ear. "*He's working with someone in the government.*" Had to be. And if that was the case... "*He may have known all along that you were trying to bust him.*"

Seth's hold tightened.

The limo pulled to a stop. She looked out the window. They'd been twisting and turning through the streets, and she wasn't exactly sure where they'd wound up. They definitely weren't back at their hotel. Her head craned.

She caught sight of an infamous bar. A bar that was, of course, closed at this time of the day. From the outside, the place looked like an old house, its gray walls fading to reveal red bricks that were pushing out for freedom. The shutters were closed tightly at the last bar on Bourbon Street, Lafitte's. The whole street would be quiet and empty at this time.

This is my brother Ford's favorite bar. But no one came to the bar in the morning hours. You would only go inside there now...

If you're looking for an empty place where no witnesses can spot you.

Her gaze flew toward the front of the limo just as the privacy screen rolled down. Her body tensed for action, but it was too late.

Sighing, Brent aimed his gun right at her and Seth. "I'm really sorry about this," he said. The man actually sounded as if he meant those words. "But orders are orders."

Her little bag was on the other side of the limo, still in the seat she'd occupied moments before. And even if she could leap over and snag it, what was she going to do? Haul out her gun and shoot an FBI agent?

Seth lifted her up before she could figure out a plan, and then the crazy man tucked her *behind* him as he faced the threat.

Obviously, he still had a big problem with the whole understanding of what a bodyguard was supposed to do.

"Why are you pointing a gun at us, Brent?" Seth asked, his voice surprisingly cool and calm, given the situation.

"Because I have to take you in, Seth, and in light of the conversation I just heard between you and Fabian, I suspected that you wouldn't come without a fight."

She peeked over Seth's shoulder and saw that the gun hadn't wavered. Right then, it was pointed straight at Seth's chest. A situation that would not do. At all. "Exactly where will you be taking him?"

"Into the bar, of course. So, do me a favor, when the door opens, don't fight. Just step out and let's handle this situation with a minimum of fuss." His lips tightened. "There is no need for anyone to get hurt."

"So says the man with the gun," Harley retorted. "How about you just put it down and we talk like the *friends* we are?"

"But we're not friends," Brent said, expression firming. "I'm doing a job, even if that job happens to suck."

Great. *Jerk.* He was—

The limo's right rear door opened. A man in a beige suit peered inside and motioned with his gun. "Get out."

"There are an awful lot of people suddenly pointing guns at us," she muttered. "I hate that first thing in the morning." She leaned across the vehicle, as if she was preparing to exit, and her hand casually extended toward the bag she'd left behind. *Almost got it. Almost...*

"No, Harley. You pull your gun, and I might have to hurt you." Now Brent's voice was *definitely* regretful, but determined.

"*You fucking hurt her, and I might have to kill you.*" From Seth. Only he did not seem regretful at all. Just coldly furious *and* determined.

Her breath shuddered out as she lifted her hands. "We all need to take a moment to calm down." She sent her dimpled smile to Brent. "I wasn't reaching for a gun. Why would I do that when I am a law-abiding citizen who intends to cooperate with the two FBI agents who are with her?" The guy in the beige suit? He screamed FBI with his short, no-nonsense haircut and slightly dour expression.

Brent's jaw hardened. "Out of the car. Now."

She climbed out of the car. And, unfortunately, she had to leave her bag behind. No worries. Well, some worries. But as she'd once told Seth, she was always armed. She just had to wait for the right moment to attack.

Seth followed her out instantly, as if he didn't want her getting out of his sight, and as they rounded the limo and went toward what *should* have been an empty bar, the door swung inward.

A woman bustled out, wearing jeans and a baseball cap over her head. She passed Brent—because he'd slipped out of the limo, too—and he handed off the keys to her. "Make sure the car isn't seen," Brent ordered.

The ball cap dipped in a nod.

Brent glanced around, probably trying to make sure no one was watching from anywhere nearby.

A witness or two would have been wonderful, but that wasn't happening. He'd picked a good spot. The area was dead empty at this time of the day. *Dead* being the keyword.

Harley's gaze darted to the open door of the bar. Inside, the area appeared cavernous and dark. When they walked in, they could be heading straight into an execution. Sure felt that way.

Seth's arm curled around her shoulders.

Maybe she should make some dramatic, last-minute confession to him. Tell him how she'd felt more alive with him than she ever had before. How the case had always been personal, that she'd only agreed to the crazy charade because she'd wanted to help protect him.

That she'd meant what she told him during their explosive night.

She *was* falling for the guy.

She could tell him all of that. Get it off her chest before the end came.

Harley spun in his arms. Stared up at him.

"Get inside," Brent snapped. "For the love of God, why can't you follow simple orders?"

Harley stared into Seth's eyes. Saw the emotions swirling back at her. The barely contained rage. And she decided...

Nah. No last-minute confessions from her. She yanked him toward her and kissed him with every bit of passion she had.

His arms locked around her. His hands slid straight to her back. The back of the sexy red dress she'd selected...a dress to go with her black heels and black bag. *A dress that lets me be armed and ready.*

And she was thrilled his fingers were stroking her back. Thrilled because—*aw, he remembered.* Seth knew exactly where she liked to hide her weapons. And as he kissed her so passionately, she knew he was sliding a small knife from the back of her dress. That sweet little hidden spot.

"Stop it!" Brent blasted. "You've got a gun on you—stop kissing! Jeez, just get in the bar!"

When they didn't stop, Brent grabbed Harley and pulled her away from Seth. Brent shoved Harley forward. The other agent—the one in the bad, beige suit—lingered nearby, but he looked uncertain. Good. People who were uncertain were often slow to act.

The female in the ballcap had already ducked inside the limo.

Harley climbed up the two stone steps that led to the bar's main door. She let her heel catch on a step, and she cried out as her body twisted a little. Bending, she grabbed the heel, as if the shoe had broken, and she brought up one of her favorite weapons even as she whirled and drove the spiky heel right toward Brent's chest.

And as she launched her attack, she saw Seth lunge forward with the knife he'd taken from her. They moved in sync and—

"*Dammit, Harley!*" Hard arms grabbed her from behind, stopping her before she could do some serious damage to Brent the Betrayer. *He threatened to hurt me.* Those arms hauled her inside the bar, pulling her into the cavernous darkness even as Seth roared her name.

"*Stand down!*" A furious order from her captor, then his voice blasted to her, "*Tell your bastard of a boyfriend to stand down, too!*"

That voice was familiar. So familiar that the shock had her dropping the high heel that Harley had intended to use as a weapon.

The voice was familiar. The *blasting* of it was familiar...because the man holding her so tightly had yelled at her plenty of times over the years. Just as she'd yelled back at him.

How could she not? Ford was the brother who often drove her the craziest. And he was definitely driving her beyond mad right then. Because he shouldn't have been there. He should have still been working his case in Colorado. He shouldn't be in a little bar on the edge of Bourbon Street and he shouldn't be trapping her in his massive, too tight hold. She opened her mouth to rip him a new one—

"*Harley!*" Seth leapt into the bar, the knife gripped in his hand.

"Stand the fuck down, boyfriend," Ford thundered. "My sister is not in any danger, but you threaten one of my agents again, and I will have you thrown in the deepest, darkest cage I can find."

Seth took a step forward, heading deeper into the darkness of the bar. Someone needed to turn on some freaking lights. "Seth, drop the knife," she urged him. "We're safe."

Her brother brought his mouth close to her ear. "The hell you are, Harley. The hell you are."

CHAPTER FIFTEEN

*Step Fifteen: When you have something to lose,
your enemies can use your weakness against
you. The weapon of choice for most? Family.*

*Ah, family...Can't live with them. Can't let
anyone else even so much as think about
hurting them, either. Not. Ever.*

Brent and the Fed in the beige suit closed and bolted the bar's front doors. He glared at Seth as he took the knife from him. "Really?" Brent snapped. "After all we've been through? You were gonna slash me? And where the hell did you even grab the knife from? Freaking magic trick. One minute, your hands are empty, and the next, you're coming at me!"

"The knife belongs to my sister."

Sister.

That word again. The giant bastard with his arms around Harley dropped the word like the bomb that it was. Seth couldn't see much about the guy. After being in the bright, morning sunlight, coming in the shadowed, shuttered bar was like stepping into a tomb.

Then lights flashed on overhead. A series of hanging bulbs that had been strung up along the ceiling illuminated the scene.

Seth finally got a good look at the man holding Harley. *Her brother?* He was trying to process that situation—

Just as Harley drove back her elbow and plowed it into the guy's stomach with brutal force.

"You asshole!" Harley snarled.

The man's grip loosened on her, and she spun around.

Harley drew back her fist. "You've been pulling strings on this op? *You?* You were supposed to be in Colorado!" Her fist flew.

The big guy with her—he easily outweighed Harley by at least one hundred pounds—caught her fist and his fingers curled around hers.

Harley didn't even take a breath before she blasted at him, "And if you were in charge, I should have had instant clearance! This is such BS!" Harley jerked her hand free of his grip. She staggered away from him, glaring her fury. "Do you get that I thought Seth and I were being led into this place so we could be shot in the back of the head? Do you understand that?" She snatched up a fallen high heel and jerked it onto her little foot.

Her *brother's* hands went to his hips. "If I wanted you dead, don't you think I would have killed you a thousand times over by now? Growing up with you was the opposite of easy." He inhaled. "Brent, Jamal, go outside and make sure no one breaches the perimeter. If you see any sign that you were followed, I want an immediate alert."

Brent and Jamal hurried to obey. Huh. Well, Seth figured that meant Harley's mysterious brother had a whole lot of power.

The door slammed shut behind the two Feds after they exited. Seth rolled back his shoulders. Harley was currently standing mid-way between him and her brother. The silence in the bar stretched a little too long. Finally, Seth decided to get the ball rolling even as rage twisted inside of him. "Which brother are you?" Harley had five. All older.

"Ford." A growl.

His eyes narrowed. "When I did my search on Harley, you were listed as being a college professor."

"Yeah, that's called a cover." Ford's gaze assessed him even as a faint, mocking smile curled the other man's lips. A slash appeared in his cheek. Not a dimple, just a hard, taunting line. "I'm sure you can understand what that means. You know, considering the high crime life you've recently been living."

"Don't be a dick, Ford." Harley strode toward the bar's long, gleaming counter. "How long have you been involved in this operation?"

"Since Special Agent Francesca Garcia had to take a back seat. That would have been on your previous Wilde case, Harley. When the fact that Seth's dad was involved in the criminal underworld up to his eyeballs—when that little trivia tidbit became public knowledge. People in power at the Bureau worried that Francesca had been spotted too publicly with him. She needed to be reassigned, fast, so I took lead. But, before I could have a nice meet and greet with my new undercover operative and introduce myself properly, who else should enter the picture in bold life? My baby sister." Disgust. "Seriously, what the hell? Since when are you supposed to be protecting bad guys?"

"He's not bad." An instant denial from her. "And Seth shouldn't even be an undercover operative. The Feds are using him. *You* are using him." Her hand slammed down on the counter. "And you've also been using me. Because you kept hiding when you realized I was his bodyguard. You stayed out of sight instead of telling me the truth."

Seth's gaze shifted between Harley and... "Ford." The oldest brother. Former marine turned college professor. *Bullshit.* Former marine turned Fed. "What in the hell is going on? Why did you have Brent pull the gun on us and force us into this place?"

"The gun was Brent's idea." Something that seemed to piss off Ford. "No way would I tell the man to pull a gun on my sis. Rest assured, Brent and I will be having a talk about that crap." He stalked over to a nearby table, pulled out a chair, and flipped it around. After straddling the chair and sitting down, his hands rose to curl around the chair's back as he studied Seth. "I can tell you why you're currently in this bar with me, though."

"We're here because you love this place and you visit it every time you're in New Orleans." Harley hopped onto a bar stool and glared. "When I first looked out and realized where we'd stopped,

I thought of you. Then low and behold, you were lurking inside."

"I was *waiting* inside, not lurking." A sniff as he corrected her. "I can't be seen. Being seen would put me at risk. There are only a very few people in this world who know about the work I'm doing with the Feds. I don't exactly want all the bad guys in town getting wind of my business."

When he said *bad guys,* his stare lingered on Seth.

"I wouldn't count on a whole lot of secrecy if I were you," Harley retorted with a snort. "During our little chat with Fabian Butler today, the man let drop that he knew the twins had just worked to get those terrorists arrested. Someone in the government is feeding him information."

"I know." A sad shake of Ford's head. "I was listening to every word, and as soon as I picked up that detail, I knew we had no choice but to end this case. And *that* is why we are all having this lovely chat in my favorite bar right now."

Seth took a surging step forward. "End it? You're stopping the operation?"

A nod from Ford. "As of this moment, consider your debt paid to the Bureau."

"He didn't owe a freaking debt!" From Harley. "He's not responsible for what his dad did. Seth is different. He was *helping* you. If anything, the Feds owe him a debt. Get that stuff straight in your mind."

Ford's head swung toward her. "Got to say, I'm concerned about the way you're defending him. I understand that you had the cover of being his girlfriend, but there's no one here to see your masquerade any longer. You can drop it." His fingers tapped against the wood of the chair. "Unless I'm missing something?"

"You're missing a whole lot." She jumped from her bar stool and stalked toward her brother. "Someone is trying to set Seth up for *murder*."

"Know about that part, actually." Ford tugged on his collar. "Cayden reports to me. The concierge guy? Man chats up a storm." He grimaced and looked over at Seth. "Oh, what? Who do you think taught Harley the trick about making sure she has an *'in'* at a hotel when she's working with clients? She's paying off the night guard and I'm paying off the concierge manager. It's a family thing."

"*Ford*." Harley had almost closed in on him.

He held up his hand. "I am not the enemy here! Seth being set up is all the more reason why this operation is over. The man's cover is clearly blown to hell and back. Fabian Butler knows exactly who *you* are, Harley, and I'm not going to have you in any additional danger." He rose. "The operation is over. That's final."

"You're ending the operation because of me? That's your real reason?" Her heels tapped on the floor. "You can't do that! You can't pull the protective big brother BS and end a federal investigation."

"I can do anything I want. The operation is over, but *not* just because I'm your brother. It's over because Fabian Butler knows we're running a con, because our lead operative's cover is blown, and because..." His face hardened as he pointed at

Seth. "We can't trust him, and if we can't trust him, we can't use him."

Seth nodded. He tugged on the left sleeve of his shirt, straightened his shoulders, and then strolled toward Ford Adaire. He smiled at the man. "I think I like your sister a whole lot better than I like you."

"Is that because you're fucking her?" Ford inquired mildly.

"*Ford!*" Harley choked.

"I heard that part in the chat with Fabian, too," Ford added. "Really, Harley, you know better. You know—"

"I know that I trust Seth." And just like that, her hand was reaching for Seth's. Curling with his. "In this moment, I trust him more than I trust *you*. At least Seth hasn't been hiding in the shadows this whole time. You were watching me, listening to me, and you had no problem with that? I am your sister—"

"That's right. *My* sister. I'm your big brother. That means I protect you. Always. You come first for me." His voice roughened even more. "I'm putting you before a giant investigation, the biggest of my career, because you matter more to me than anything else."

Harley's fierce expression softened. "Ford..."

His expression reflected his determination. "I'm getting you away from here before you can wind up stabbed fifteen times and dumped in a cemetery. We picked up chatter, Harley. Justin Florent was in the family business. A hit man just like his father. The night he was found murdered,

Justin had just taken on a new job. *You* were the job."

Seth's hold on Harley's hand tightened. *No, fucking no.*

But Ford grimly continued, "While you were having your meeting with Fabian this morning, Detective Zion Raye retrieved texts from Justin's phone confirming that Justin had agreed to the hit. He was going to kill *you.* Justin's MO? He liked to get up close and personal with his targets. Loved to plunge his blades straight into them. *You* were supposed to die in that cemetery. You, not him." His breath shuddered out. "My sister isn't dying in some damn New Orleans cemetery. You're getting on a plane. You're going home. This case is over."

Seth shook his head. *You were the job.* He couldn't get the words out of his head.

Not Harley. God, no. But...hadn't he feared that very thing? Hadn't she even suspected it might be the case, too?

You were supposed to die in that cemetery. You, not him. Ford seemed so certain. Because he was. Because the Fed had evidence to back up his claims. Harley had been meant to die.

She gave a little gasp, and Seth realized—fuck, he'd squeezed her fingers too tightly. Immediately, he released her. Stepped back.

You were supposed to die in that cemetery. His chest burned. Every single breath burned.

"How did you get that info from the police detective?" Harley asked her brother.

"The NOPD is cooperating with the Feds." An easy reply from Ford. "Detective Raye is a good guy. He does some solid police work, and he understood the value in turning over the evidence he'd acquired right away." A pause. "He also told me about last night. Don't think he freaking didn't. I heard all about the shower scene."

"Ford, I'm a big girl. I'll fuck who I want, and the man I want? It's Seth. Deal with it."

Even though Seth had just put distance between them, she eliminated that space. She came right back to his side. Again.

She kept doing that. Showing where her loyalty rested. Her brother was on one side...*but she keeps choosing me.* Her brother, the war hero, the...*Federal agent in charge?* The man was telling her that Seth was bad, that she was in danger being near him...but Harley wasn't listening.

Because...

Her sweet, sweet words rang in his head...

I've been falling in love with you.

"No." Seth shook his head.

Harley's head immediately swung toward Seth. "Excuse me?"

He swallowed. "The case is over." *Say it. Get those words out now because if you have to look into her eyes for even a second longer...*His stare flew away from her. "That means our, ah, charade is over. We're done."

Silence.

He could feel Harley's gaze on him.

Ford cleared his throat, and then his hands came together in a single, awkward clap. "Well, good. Looks like we're on the same page. Harley, you'll fly home. Seth, I would seriously get out of town at the first opportunity and—"

"No." He wasn't leaving. "My job isn't finished."

Scratching his chin, Ford ambled closer. "Uh, it is. I just told you the case is over. Over as in...you will no longer have backup from federal agents. You will not have our protection."

"Didn't see a whole lot of that to begin with," Harley muttered.

Ford's eyes narrowed. Seth was staring—fine, glaring—at the man, and he finally realized that Ford's eyes were a similar shade to Harley's. Just more brown. The gold wasn't as strong in his gaze. They had the same dark, thick hair, but Ford's features were one hell of a lot rougher than Harley's.

"The case is over. The federal agents will be reassigned." Ford spoke grimly. "Of course, you can have an escort to get you out of the city. Originally, you were offered a new identity when the investigation concluded, but you refused—"

"And I still do. I don't need a new name and a new town. I'll stick with being Seth Wellington, asshole son of a criminal, but thanks for the offer."

A jerky nod from Ford. "Then we'll get you out of New Orleans—"

Seth cut him off by saying, "Not leaving, but again, thanks for the offer."

Harley's hand grabbed Seth's arm. "What are you doing?"

Finishing what I started. "I'll send a payment via Wilde."

"The hell you will. I already quit, and we both know it. You aren't paying me a dime." Her golden stare darkened as the brown took over. *Her eyes get darker when she's angry.* One of the many things he'd learned about her.

She was so beautiful to him. He could stare into her eyes forever, even when they were shooting dark daggers at him. "Go home, Harley, like your brother said. Next time, be a lot more choosy when it comes to the clients you take."

"You're pissing me off, Seth."

He knew that he was. It was deliberate. He had to get her to leave him and not look back. Because he knew Harley, dammit. She would stick by him. The Feds would leave town. Danger would come closing in, and Harley would face it with him.

You were supposed to die in that cemetery. Her brother's words would haunt Seth forever.

Harley had gotten a hit put on her because she'd been with him. Because others knew that she mattered. And she did. Mattered so much. Fabian had known. He'd pushed Seth so that he would react on the terrace and take that swing. His enemies *knew.*

His weakness? Harley Adaire. If something happened to her...

How do you protect your bodyguard?

You get her to turn away. To go far, far away from you. "It was fun. The memories will last a lifetime, I'm sure."

"Stop being a dick. I'm not like the others. I can see right through you when you're playing the bad guy."

"I'm not playing." Each word he said to her raked over his skin, hurt *him*. Because he didn't want to hurt her, not ever. But it was better for Harley to be hurt and hating him, than cold and dead in a New Orleans cemetery.

"You care about me," she told him, lifting her chin.

Yes, he did. That was why she needed to get away from him as far and fast as she could. "Goodbye, Harley." He stepped to the side, pulling away from her hold. She watched him with a little furrow between her delicate brows. Seth took a breath. *Stop looking at Harley*. His gaze shifted to her brother. "I don't need an escort from the Feds. I don't need a secure flight out of town. I'm not planning on leaving."

"Bad mistake," Ford warned him. "Your cover is blown. Fabian knows that you were looking to bring him down. You will be a dead man walking."

Funny. He'd felt like a dead man walking for a very long time. Until Harley. "Do you know who killed Justin Florent?"

"We think it was probably one of Fabian's enemies. The players in the area know that Justin was Fabian's executioner, so we figure someone looking to take over Fabian's territory got to Justin." Ford crossed his arms over his chest. "You know, I am curious about why you went to the cemetery that night."

"He *didn't*—" Harley began hotly.

Seth's jaw clenched. *She's still protecting me. I'm being a freaking dick to her, and she's got my back*. There was no way on earth he deserved her. Ever.

But he would damn well lie—or die—if it meant protecting her. *Maybe I'll kill instead of die. That option is one hell of a lot better for me.*

"He *did* go," Ford snapped. "I was watching. *You* were involved in this case, you think I was gonna leave your safety to chance? I had eyes on him. On you. I know he went to the cemetery and that you followed him. What I don't know is *why* he went there. Wanna share with the group, Seth? *Why* did you go to the cemetery at that specific time? Who were you meeting?"

Seth didn't speak.

"Do you know, Harley?" Ford asked, voice softer. "Did your new best friend confide that info to you?"

"Screw off, Ford," she told her brother with a jerk of her chin.

"I'll take that as a no." Ford exhaled. "And that leads me to my second suspicion. Actually, it's something that has worried the Feds for quite a while. It's the reason I know we can't trust the guy for even a second longer. You're working your own agenda, aren't you, Seth?"

Yes, he was.

"You brought down some players, even got us some tips on the big guns, but you were also working something private all along, weren't you? You were using the Feds."

Silence.

"And I'll take that as a yes," Ford concluded. "You wanted to find your mother's killer. Justin Florent's dad was the man who took her out. Only he was killed a few years ago, just like Fabian told you. So what's the next best thing to killing the dad? Pretty sure your buddy Fabian told you that part, too—"

"Why the hell does everyone keep focusing on the sins of the father being visited on the son?" Harley demanded. "Enough already. Seth was with me. He didn't kill Justin!"

"Maybe your best friend Seth hired someone to kill him." An immediate response from Ford. "Maybe he arranged the hit. Kind of a dark justice in that, don't you think? A hit man getting taken out by a hit. Maybe Seth scheduled the hit to take place at that time of night, in that specific location, and Seth showed up because he wanted to see for himself that the job had been carried out."

Seth stiffened. He more than got the feeling that Ford wanted to slap a pair of cuffs on him right then and there—*and shove my ass into the nearest cell.*

"There were a whole lot of players at Fabian Butler's house." Ford's voice turned musing. "Tell me, Harley, were you with Seth for the entire time that he was there? Or did you separate? Did he, say, have time to meet his contact—his *hired killer*—and give the order that Justin Florent was to be taken out that night? Because Seth wasn't wearing *any* listening device that night. Even though we have tech so tiny that no one would ever be able to discover it."

"It was my first meeting with Fabian," Seth pushed out through clenched teeth. "I was trying not to give the guy a reason for immediately putting a bullet in my brain. Not going in attached to a listening device that might have been picked up by some bit of tech *he* had seemed like the best idea. Your FBI agent Brent Marchello agreed with me." Not like Seth had gone rogue on the case. He'd played things by the book.

Mostly.

Ford's gaze hardened as it remained on Harley. "You didn't answer my question, sis. Were you ever separated from him?"

"Yes, *bro*, I was. Briefly."

"Your choice or his?"

She threw her hands into the air. "Fabian's choice. We could either play ball or look suspicious as hell! It's the same reason that Seth didn't go in with a weapon. *Because of Fabian.* His call. Not Seth's."

Ford gave a satisfied nod. As if some dark suspicion had been confirmed.

Harley, you didn't mention to me that your brother was a dick. Seth forced his jaw to unclench. "I didn't know that Justin Florent was connected to my mother's death. Not until Fabian told me this morning. I would've had no reason to put a hit on him, seeing as I didn't know." Something that was making the rage boil inside of him, though... "*You're* the one who had that intel. And I'm really, really curious about just how long the Feds have known who murdered my mom...and why you kept that intel from me." Curious and pissed. "Because I asked on day one—*day freaking one*—when I came to the Feds and offered to work with your agents. I asked if the Feds knew anything about her murder. I was told it was unsolved. I was told that you had no leads. I was told—"

"I wasn't the one telling you," Ford snapped. "So don't accuse me of lying to you. I wasn't lead on the case when you first came in." Ford backed up a step. "You were misled, but not by me. All right?"

"*What do you know about her murder?*" Because Seth was done being in the dark. He'd lived in the dark since he was seven years old, and he wanted out.

Ford's nostrils flared. "A review of case files revealed that your mother's death fit a particular hitman's MO."

"Justin Florent's dad," Harley said.

A jerky nod from Ford. "The Feds had long suspected him of being a hired gun, but suspecting the man and having evidence to convict him are two different things. Then, when Miles Florent was shot outside of his home in New Orleans about five years ago, the investigation on him ended. You can't punish a dead man." A shrug. "So the Feds moved on."

They had this intel the whole time I was working with them. "Moved on and *lied* to me."

"Your father fucking knew," Ford snarled. "So don't act like the Feds are the only ones keeping secrets."

Seth stiffened.

"Oh, what? Come on." A disgusted shake of Ford's head. "Put the pieces together, Seth. Your father was one of the most feared criminals out there. You really think he looked at your mom's murder and didn't tag the MO as belonging to Florent?"

"What was his MO?" Seth needed to know everything. *Can't stand being in the dark. Hate it here.*

"The kills that we suspect were his...Florent set them all up the same way. His targets would be pinned in on the road. His vehicle in front and another blocking any retreat. Seemed like he loved to trap them and take them out with three shots. Always three. That was like his freaking lucky number or some shit."

Three booms. He'd heard three that terrible day.

"His son grew up playing with knives and loving to get freakishly close to his kills. Both twisted bastards, and no one is going to be grieving for either of them. They're dead and gone, and there is *nothing* else for you in this city. Your mother's killer is gone."

Not so simple. "Who hired Miles Florent?"

Ford's hand sawed over his jaw. Once. Twice. "Is that what has you staying? You're trying to find the man who got Florent to pull the trigger on your mom?"

"If it was your mother, wouldn't you want to know?"

Ford's gaze swept to Harley. She gave the smallest of nods, and his attention shifted back to Seth. "Our mother died when Harley was five years old. One minute, she was there with us, loving us all with everything that she had, and then in the next, she was just gone. I understand grief, believe me, I do, but you can't let it consume you. You can't let it destroy you."

This bastard was comparing their lives? Oh, hell, no. "My mother was murdered, right in front of me, she was—"

"*What the fuck do you think happened to our mom? She was gunned down in a bank, right in front of Harley. Holding Harley's hand when it happened.*" Ford rushed to his sister, threw his arm around her shoulders, and hauled her to his side. "It took a fucking year for Harley to talk after that. But, Jesus, once she started talking, she didn't stop." He looked down at Harley, and there was absolute love in his eyes. On his face. "Got a mouth on her, I swear, it can drive you crazy. But that is a thousand times better than a year of silence from her. A year where my baby sister looked broken."

Shock rolled through Seth, and he found himself staggering forward, moving toward Harley. She hadn't told him. When he'd looked into her past...that *hadn't* been there. The information about her mother's death, it had... "The report I got said she had a heart attack."

Ford jerked Harley in for a hug.

"Great. Look what you did." Harley glared at Seth as she strained against her brother's hold. "You made him emotional. Do you know how annoying and suffocating Ford gets when he's emotional?"

He didn't know a damn thing about Ford. And he was starting to think he didn't know much about Harley, either.

"You are squeezing me to death." She shoved against her brother. "Not like you're in the middle of a big FBI reveal or anything. *Let go, jerk.*"

Grudgingly, Ford let go. "I love you." Said so easily and honestly as he looked at Harley.

Seth realized that he couldn't hate the Fed. Not even if the guy had been keeping secrets about the man who'd murdered Seth's mother. *I can't hate anyone who loves Harley so totally.*

Ford rolled back his shoulders. "In case you didn't realize it," he angled his head toward Seth, "our family is in the business of secrets. The people who shot my mother? They got away. Took my father five years to hunt them down, but he eventually did." His jaw flexed. "Like I told you, I understand the need for vengeance. But in your case, there is nothing else that can be done. You want the man who set things in motion? The person who hired out your mom's murder?" His lips thinned. "The other agents originally working her case knew, or at least, they suspected, and my own recent digging confirmed the details. But no one wanted to tell you because they were afraid you'd stop cooperating. You were pulling in intel that was too useful to give up. If you let rage take over, you weren't going to be any good to us."

"Why the hell would I stop cooperating?" He'd been all in. Working his own agenda, true, but, dammit, he *had* wanted to try and make up for the sins his father had committed—

No.

Seth shook his head.

But the truth was right there. And he wondered how the fuck he could have missed it all this time.

"I'm very sorry, Seth," Ford told him, and he seemed to mean those words. "But all the evidence I've uncovered points to the fact that your father was the one to put out the hit on your mother all those years ago. She was going to leave him, and he had no intention of letting her just walk away."

CHAPTER SIXTEEN

Step Sixteen: When things look the worst, that's when you dig in. You don't give up. You just fight harder. Another lesson from my dad...AKA The General.

"You weren't supposed to be with your mother that day." Ford's deep voice kept rolling on, but Harley didn't look at her brother. She was too busy hating the sudden pain that filled Seth's eyes. "But she took you out of school. Your father didn't know that she was planning to run away with you. He thought *she* was just leaving. Only your mom wanted you to escape with her. She'd found out what your father really was, and she wanted to start a new life far away from him."

"How do you know this?" Seth asked.

"Remember how the Feds offered you that nice, new identity somewhere far, far away?" A shrug from Ford. "I found some old files indicating your mom had a new identity waiting, too. Except she never got to use the one she'd had created for herself. Or the one made for you."

When Seth sucked in a shuddering, pain-filled breath, Harley jerked toward him. She could *feel* the hurt he was enduring, and it hurt her, too. "I'm so sorry."

His head whipped toward her. His mouth opened, then closed.

Of course, Ford kept talking. Harley wasn't the only chatty one in her family. In an emotionless voice, Ford revealed, "Your mother was supposed to turn over info she had in exchange for a new life, but she never had the chance to finish her deal. I don't know if someone on the federal side sold her out to your father or if he just had men watching her every move and they figured out what was happening...but somehow, he made the discovery, and then your mother was dead."

"He said..." Seth's hands clenched and released. Clenched and released. "The sonofabitch *told* me right after her murder that he was going to make sure I wouldn't be weak like she was. Then he started all the damn training. I thought he meant he wanted me to be able to fight in case someone came after me...but he didn't. He wanted me *to be like him.*" Horror burned in his eyes, replacing the pain. "And I am. I-I was going to kill the man who set it all up. No hesitation. *I am just like him.*"

She shook her head. "You aren't, Seth. You're nothing like him. I've told you that before. You were trying to get justice for your mother." Harley reached for him.

"You shouldn't touch me, Harley."

Her hand froze. "Why not?" He'd better not play that asshole routine again. She'd known exactly what he was doing moments before. Trying to drive her away so he could face danger on his own. No way. She could see right through his deception. Her hand pressed to his chest. Over his heart.

He looked down at her hand. "Because I am not good enough for you. I never will be."

"That's bullshit. You're plenty good."

A shake of his head. "My father killed her?" A question, rough. Lost. Then... *"My father killed her."*

"That's what I believe," Ford said, not pulling any punches. "I don't have a smoking gun. There were no transfers of cash I could trace back to your dad. Nothing that would conclusively tie him to the hit. If there had been, he would have been arrested long ago."

Seth kept staring down at Harley's hand. She could feel his heart racing beneath her touch.

"There isn't anything for you in New Orleans," Ford added. "Nothing but death. Fabian is after you. Your cover is blown. Be smart, Seth. Get on a plane and disappear."

He swallowed.

"Seth?" Harley said his name softly.

He kept looking down at her hand. "He didn't shoot me because he hadn't been paid to do it. A hitman not wanting to work for free is the only reason I'm still standing."

She didn't like the hollowness of his voice.

He swallowed once more. His head finally lifted. His gaze met hers. "Someone put a hit on you because I hired you to be my bodyguard."

"The hitman is dead." Didn't that mean the hit was dead, too? Canceled?

"I'm going to make sure there are no other hits. Go home, Harley."

"You come, too." She felt Ford's stare on her and didn't care.

Seth shook his head. "There isn't a place for me in your life."

"There is a place for you wherever I am. *Don't do this.*" She knew exactly what this game was. "I am so not in the mood for the martyr bullshit. Didn't I tell you that already? You don't get to leave me because you think it's safer. Don't you dare."

His hand rose and curled under her chin. "You have the most beautiful eyes."

Don't you dare do this to us. "I can handle danger. I'm not worried about it."

He smiled at her. "Have I ever told you that I think you're the most gorgeous woman I've ever met?"

Damn him. A lump rose in her throat. "You could have said that sooner, not at the moment when I think you're about to break my heart."

He licked his lips. "If I could've had a life with anyone, I would have wanted it to be you."

Fear blasted through her. "What the hell does that even mean? You have a life. Let the past go. *Move on.*" *Move on with me.*

"Someone put a hit on you, Harley. Do you think I'm just going to let *that* go? Walk away when someone wanted you to die?"

No, she didn't think he would. But she wished he'd run with her. "Seth...the Feds will figure things out. You don't have to—"

"I never told you why I was in the cemetery that night."

Her lower lip wanted to tremble, so she pressed her lips together. "I remember asking quite a bit about that very thing."

"It wasn't to pay respect to my mother's resting place."

It was her turn to give him a sad smile. "Not exactly a shocking reveal. Going after midnight to pay your respects when you could have done it during the day like a normal person? That would make sense. Your story didn't."

"I went there to give her justice."

She made sure her expression didn't alter.

"But someone beat me to the punch. I was told my mother's killer would be there that night. Sent a message on one of those damn apps where it disappears right after you read it. Someone knew why I was really in New Orleans. Someone knew I wanted her murder solved, and that person lured me to the cemetery."

"And I followed you. Gave you no choice but to have me tag along if you actually wanted to go inside."

"I intended to kill him."

"No, you didn't."

"*Stop thinking I'm better than I am.*"

She dropped her hand but just moved her whole body closer as they stood toe-to-toe. "Stop thinking you're worse than you are! If you had really planned to go through with the murder, you wouldn't have gone in the cemetery *with* me. You damn well knew I wasn't going to stand there while you committed cold-blooded murder."

"You wouldn't have been able to stop me." Grim. Certain. His hand fell away from her.

A shiver slid over her skin.

"I didn't tell you why I was there because I didn't want anyone to ever think you'd been an accessory."

You were protecting me, Seth? Didn't he even see what that meant?

And he did. She saw the truth in his gaze as he told her, "Turns out, I have this thing about protecting my bodyguard."

"Seth..."

"Someone beat me to the kill. I was furious. Then I find out that Justin had been hired to kill *you*." Rage seethed. Twisted his face. "I want to murder the bastard all over again."

"Ahem." From Ford. "Perhaps we should take a breath..."

"Fuck off, Ford," Seth said, never looking away from Harley. "You're about to get what you want. Me, far away from your sister."

She shook her head.

"It's not over for me," Seth told her. "You have a target on you. I'll get it eliminated." Another sad twist of his lips. "See, there I go again. Protecting my bodyguard."

"I don't need protecting."

"You do when you're with me. I thought I could keep you. I wanted you, all for me. I thought you could be *mine*."

Ford surged forward. "I do *not* like the way you're talking to my sister—"

"Fuck off, Ford," Harley said, never glancing his way.

"I've lied to you, Harley," Seth told her. "I've lied to the Feds. I've lied to *everyone*."

"Uh, you lied to Feds?" Ford asked. "What lies, specifically?"

"*Fuck off, Ford.*" An order that came in unison from Seth and Harley.

Seth tilted his head to the side as he watched her. "You asked me once if I was a good man pretending to be bad..."

She wet her lips. "Or a bad man pretending to be good?" But she knew the answer. She'd known even as she said those words.

He leaned closer. His mouth went to her right ear. His lips feathered over the shell of her ear as he told her, "I'm *good* at pretending, but I was never, ever a *good* man."

No. No. He was *lying*. Right now. She knew the truth.

"My father's son is a killer. You will be protected." Seth stepped back. "Goodbye."

This wasn't happening.

But he turned away from her and walked toward the bar's closed front doors.

"Seth?" Harley felt rooted to the spot. She stepped forward, only to have her path blocked by Ford. He'd whipped around her. When she tried to push past him, he shook his head and caught her arm.

Seth didn't stop.

Desperate, scared, hurting, her gaze flew to Ford. She knew he would see the plea in her eyes.

"Dammit," he growled. Her brother huffed out a breath and turned to look after Seth. Raising his voice, he said, "The offer of a new identity still stands. You can have a new life."

"Don't want it."

"You have a *target* on your back," Ford seethed. "Do you get that?"

"That's kinda the whole point." Seth's hand lifted and pushed against the wood of the door.

Ford let her go and took a hard lunge after Seth. "You won't have FBI protection when you leave. You will be on your own."

"I know." Seth glanced back. His eyes went to Harley. "But she won't be, right? Harley won't ever be on her own. You'll get her home and keep her safe. Because she's family."

"*Yes.*"

"Seth..." Harley shook her head. "I thought you said you weren't going to let me go." Did he think she'd forgotten those passion-filled words? He'd better not claim that had been some heat-of-the-moment BS. *You meant those words. Just like I meant it when I said I was falling for you.*

His mouth tightened. Then, "Turns out there is one person in this world who doesn't make me want to always be a selfish bastard. That person is you. Have a good life, Harley Adaire."

Then he walked out of the bar. Oh, the hell, no.

He walked out.

The door didn't slam behind him. Nothing so dramatic. It just closed ever so softly.

Ford turned toward her, grimacing. "I'm—"

"No." She stopped him before he could even speak. She didn't want an apology for him keeping her in the dark about his involvement on the case. She wanted help. Help that the special agent in charge could give her. "Get a man to follow him."

"Harley, I *just* told the guy that he'd be on his own. When I learned that Fabian Butler had inside information, the case was over. *Inside information.* You get how dangerous that is, right? The bastard has *information on you and our family.*"

"If you're not going to get someone to follow Seth, then get out of my way." Because she'd follow him herself.

But Ford didn't move to the side. If anything, he tensed and locked down his body. "Not happening. You're going home. You will be safe."

A bitter laugh slipped from her. "If I wanted safety, I would never have joined Wilde. Now either get out of my way, or I will be moving you out of the way."

"Harley, he is not good for you."

She lifted her chin and moved ever closer to her brother. "In all my life, have you ever known me to fall for the bad guy?"

"Harley..."

"I love him."

His eyes squeezed shut. "Don't. Do not say that stuff to me."

"Seth believes that he is like his father. And he's going down a very dark path." *If I don't stop him, Seth might just wind up becoming far too much like the monster who raised him.* Because once you started down that path, how did you stop?

"Yeah, he's going down a dark path. That means he's *bad*. Didn't you hear Seth when he said he'd lied to the Feds? To you? He's going off on his own. Let the man dig his own grave if that's what he wants."

She sucked in a sharp breath.

His eyes flew open. "Bad choice of words. What I meant was—"

"You think I don't know what you're doing?" And it was annoying to the extreme.

His head tilted a little. Kind of like an animal that had just sensed an attack coming.

"Right before Seth left, you said there was a target on him. That was the giveaway." She'd read between the lines.

"I don't know what you mean."

Her index finger stabbed into his chest. "You want to take down Fabian Butler."

"He's a criminal. Unfortunately, the man is also pretty much just a shadow. Nothing sticks. Witnesses vanish. Just like with Edward Wellington. You can't get cold, hard evidence to use against him."

"You can if you catch him committing a crime, right? Catch him in the act? And isn't that what this is *really* all about?" Rage almost choked her. "You pulled Seth into this bar right after his meeting with Fabian. We both know there were probably eyes following the limo all the way here. We didn't drive long enough to ditch anyone. And you put two agents outside who could easily be spotted. Sure, Brent was supposed to be our driver, but Jamal screamed Fed in that beige suit of his, and you could see his holster from miles away. *Too obvious.* A major mistake. Unless you wanted him to be obvious."

The lines near Ford's mouth deepened. "I brought you here because you had to be taken off this case. A plane ride is waiting for you."

"Let it wait." She had no intention of flying away. "You're using the man I love as bait, aren't you? Maybe that's what you were doing the entire time." Only she'd just seen the truth. "This wasn't about him being the crime boss who could get close to others in New Orleans. This was about your main target—Fabian Butler—coming after Seth. You just sent Seth out on his own, so he would look unprotected, like the Feds had abandoned him. Now you think a shark—Fabian—is gonna swim in your chummed-up waters and attack."

Ford didn't speak.

Fear made her voice turn hoarse. "What happens when he attacks? Will the Feds rush in, just in time, finally having their cold, hard evidence? Or will you be *too late?* Will Seth be on his own and easy prey?"

"He's not easy prey."

That was the terrible confirmation she'd dreaded. "Get out of my way."

"He's *gone* by now, Harley."

A minor problem. "Then I guess I'd better get busy hunting him, huh? Good thing I excel at that type of work, thanks to you and Dad."

Those faint lines deepened even more near his mouth and eyes. "Don't make me arrest you for interfering in a federal investigation."

Harley laughed. "I'd really like to see you try."

He reached into his suit coat and pulled out a pair of gleaming handcuffs.

CHAPTER SEVENTEEN

*Step Seventeen: Just remember to run the con
and don't let the con run you. What does that
mean? Hell if I know. But doesn't it sound good?*

Seth stood on the sagging front porch of a
sprawling home on the edge of a Louisiana
swamp. Night had fallen, and a thousand insects
seemed to be chirping around him. Every now and
then, he'd hear a distant rumble, kind of like the
faint roar of a motorcycle engine.

Once upon a time, he was sure the home had
been gorgeous. The bones of that beauty were still
there in the massive pillars along the porch and in
the sweeping staircase that waited just beyond the
foyer. Dozens of windows lined the front of the
house. A few months ago, most of those windows
had been boarded up because the glass had been
broken.

But then he'd had the repair work started.
New glass. New frames.

New hope.

He heard another rumble in the night, but
this one was sharper than the sounds before.
Sharper and coming closer. Seth glanced down at
the screen of his phone. Tapped a few times and
narrowed his eyes. Then he shoved the phone into
his pocket. He tensed as he waited, and soon he

saw headlights appear on the old drive that led to the house. His hand automatically went to the gun hidden under his coat. The shoulder holster was a light weight that he'd barely felt. Until now.

The car drew closer. A small sedan.

It stopped in front of the steps near the porch. The headlights died away as the motor shut off. The door swung open.

He started to raise the gun.

"Hiding out in a swamp, huh?" Harley's voice rang out, strong and slightly annoyed. "Great. You *know* how I feel about gators, and yet, here you are. I drove past an actual *swamp* on the way here. And you do see all of that green, slimy water behind the house, right? *More swamp.* We both know what lives in swamps. Gators."

He shoved the gun back into the holster and bounded from the porch. "You're not supposed to be here." He rushed around the car, and his hands flew out to curve around her upper arms. "You're—"

"Supposed to be where? On a plane, heading far away from you? Just what kind of bodyguard would I be if I left when you needed me?"

Seth shook his head. "Baby..." He'd walked away. Tried to act like his heart wasn't being ripped out of his chest. He'd gone away alone because he knew what had to be done.

And yet she was here.

"Don't act surprised and don't waste your breath telling me to leave. It took me damn long enough to track you. Then inspiration struck and I realized this whole thing was about your mother...so why not just go back to her?" Harley's head turned as she took in the house. "Your mother grew up here, didn't she? And you bought the place six months ago. That's how I found you, by the way. Got some friends from Wilde to dig into your financials." A delicate pause. "You realize, of course, that if I found you that way, others will know all about this place, too?"

"You shouldn't be here." He wanted to yank her close. To kiss her like crazy. To tell her that it had killed him to walk away from her at that bar.

"If you'd chatted with Ford longer, you would have learned that my whole life is a story of me rarely doing what I *should*." Her hand rose and patted his cheek. "And instead, I prefer to do whatever I *want*."

He tensed at the soft pat, knowing she'd done it deliberately. "Didn't I warn you about that?"

"Didn't I warn you about breaking my heart?"

In that instant, his own heart broke. *I am so sorry, sweetheart.*

"No?" Harley gave a faint *hmmm*. "Because if I didn't, I should have. *Don't* break my heart. Don't pull some ridiculous martyr scene. We both know what's happening here."

His head shook.

"My brother is using you as bait. You're the man with a big, bold target on his back." She studied him beneath the glow of the heavy moon. "I don't see any fake shock emanating from you. That's because *you* are using your fool self as bait, too."

"It's not safe for you here."

"Then you'd better go hide my car so no one knows I'm here." Her hand shoved into her pocket, then she dangled keys toward him. "Because I'm not leaving. You aren't facing a killer on your own. Someone happens to care whether you live or you die, and that someone is me. Maybe you don't love me. I get it. I'm a lot, even on my good days. I'm demanding, I'm grumpy, and I say whatever random thought comes into my mind. You haven't known me for that long, and the first few weeks of our acquaintance were certainly rough, but I thought you knew I would go to the mat for you. I would lie to protect you. I would risk any—"

He couldn't hold back. His mouth crashed onto hers. Furiously. Desperately. Hungrily. He'd thought for sure she'd been long gone after that scene at the bar. That her brother would have gotten her on the plane and that Harley would fly out of his life. "You're not a lot. You're fucking perfect." He kissed her again. "*Perfect.*"

"Oh." She pulled back a little. Studied him. "You're drunk. I see. That explains a few things from earlier today."

"*Harley.*" He was dead sober and dead certain. "I walked away once. How the hell am I supposed to do it again?"

"Simple." Her lips tilted up. "You're not. Now go hide the car and let's come up with a plan so that we can both stay alive. Sound good to you?"

A low, long rumble filled the night.

Harley tensed. "Company, already? I was certain I wasn't followed. I took lots of precautions, but—"

"I'm pretty sure that's the gators."

She tensed. "The gators. Right." An exhale. "You get that I must really, truly love you if I followed you out here?"

He wanted to lift her into his arms and run inside with her. "And you get that I must really, truly love you because walking away from you in that bar, leaving you behind, ripped out my freaking heart?"

Her lips parted. She didn't speak. His always-chatting Harley *didn't* speak.

"I love you," he told her again. "You're not a lot. I'll punch any bastard in the face who says that you are. You're mine. All I want is you but, baby, I have danger all around me."

Her arms looped around his neck. "It's a good thing I like danger."

"No, *no*. You have a hit on you because of me. I have to make you safe. I have to end this mess." It wasn't about justice for his mother. His mother couldn't know pain any longer. But Harley? Harley could be hurt. Everything he was doing—and, yes, he damn well knew there was a target on his back—it was to protect *Harley*. He had to send a message that no one could ever think of hurting her. You didn't hurt his Harley and get to walk away.

"You mean *we* have to end it." She rose onto her toes and kissed him once more. "Hide the car. Get in the house. And fuck me before the bad guys come in with guns blazing."

Wait. She had not just—*had* she just said—

She let go of him. Shoved the keys into his hand, and, whistling, she headed up the front porch steps.

The gators rumbled in the distance.

Fuck me before the bad guys come in with guns blazing.

Yes, yes, she had just said those words...

***

She'd bluffed that scene fairly well. Maybe Seth hadn't noticed the nerves that were practically shaking her apart. For hours, she'd been frantic as she hunted for him. Ford had given her zero help, the dick. Even when she'd texted him, asking ever-so-nicely. Only there had been no response.

So what if she'd locked his own handcuffs on his wrists and left him in the bar after a brief and dirty-fighting—on her part—skirmish? He *still* could have thrown her a bone at *some* point during the day.

Instead, the Feds had been radio silent on her. She'd turned to Detective Zion Raye, thinking he might have a lead. Nope. Zilch. The guy had only been able to tell her that a female caller had been the one to notify nine-one-one about the *fresh* body in the St. Louis Cemetery. The call had been traced to an old landline phone at a bar on Bourbon. Only no one there remembered a woman using the phone in the back office to make the call.

Luckily, her Wilde team had come through when they found the real estate purchase that linked back to Seth. But like she'd told him, if she'd found the house, others would, too.

I should have thought of his mother sooner. The place was his mom's. Of course, he'd come here.

She was just grateful that she'd arrived at the scene before anyone else had.

Harley glanced up. An old chandelier hung above her, big and massive. She stood in the middle of the foyer and a few feet away, a spiral staircase led up to the second level. The staircase's banister gleamed, looking absolutely brand new.

Probably because it was. Seth had been busy since he'd bought the place.

The front door squeaked behind her, and Harley whirled.

Seth stared back at her. Big, shadowy, with stubble on his jaw and fire burning in his eyes...Seth stepped over the threshold. He shut the door behind him. Reached back and threw the lock.

All of the moisture seemed to dry from her mouth. That last line she'd given about them fucking? It had just been to get the man moving. He'd moved.

Very, very swiftly.

Now he was closing in on her, and there was no missing the primal intent in his gaze.

Lust.

Harley sucked in a breath and started doing what she absolutely did best—talking. "I don't think I was followed. I kept a really close watch. I'm not saying I was perfect, but I certainly tried my gold-star best. Took lots of unnecessary side trips, probably looked like a lost tourist as I weaved my way out here." *Here*. The swamp. The gator-infested swamp.

He kept closing in.

He said he loved me moments before. Seth loves me. So why was she suddenly so nervous? He'd admitted the truth. She should be feeling great. Well, granted, bad guys were after them, so...*not great*. But she'd gotten Seth's confession, and some of her nerves should have eased. They hadn't.

So she kept talking. "It will be possible for others to find the location, though. They just have to get some people who are great at ferreting out financials, and it will only be a matter of time before this home is discovered." It could have *already* been discovered by his enemies. Wasn't that what terrified her? That the bad guys could close in at any moment? "No way you're gonna be hiding here long without getting unwelcome visitors." Hmmm. Speaking of... "Really hope I don't fall into the unwelcome category." Again, he *had* said he loved her. But that confession had come after she tracked him down. Why was her voice trembling? *Maybe it's just incredibly hard to feel welcome when the man you love ditched you in a bar*. Her chin lifted.

Seth was right in front of her. His hand rose, curling over her jaw, and his head bent toward her.

Harley's heart slammed hard into her chest.

He kissed her.

Her lips parted for him, and Seth's tongue thrust inside. The kiss was careful, tender. Oddly sweet. There hadn't been a whole lot of *sweet* kisses between them. Mostly because when they touched, fire ignited and she tended to want to rip his clothes off.

And fire was igniting within her right then. The desire stirred in her veins. It pumped through her, surging out until the heat seemed to rise from her skin. Her hand reached up and clutched at his forearm as she jerked back a bit. "Are you..." She licked her lips and tasted him. "Are you glad I'm here?"

His head shook. *No.*

Her heart sank as she let go of him. "No, please, don't try to spare my feelings. But you know, maybe also don't kiss me if you—"

He kissed her again. Not so sweet. Not tender. More consuming and hungry, and she wondered if the fire had gotten to him. Because there was so much desire in that kiss. A fierce, consuming desperation.

But desire hadn't been an issue for them. It was the emotional stuff that had been the problem. Her eyes had squeezed closed, and as she kissed him, Harley could swear she felt the pinpricks of tears behind her eyelids.

His mouth pulled from hers. "I'm not glad." A growl. "You walked straight into danger. You put yourself at risk for me. *For me.* I left so you'd be safe. You have to be safe. You should not be here with me. You should—"

Her eyes opened. Damn if a little tear didn't slide down her cheek.

His eyes widened in horror. "No." His right hand flew up, and he brushed the tear away. "Do not cry for me, Harley."

"Stop being bossy." She blinked several times. "I'm crying for me, asshole."

His face softened. "There you go again, saying the word like it's some kind of endearment..."

"I'm crying because you said you loved me, but now you're saying you're not glad I'm here. You're the king of mixed messages, Seth." A shuddering breath. "You didn't throw your arms around me when I arrived. You didn't hold me tight and tell me I'm the best thing that ever happened to you and that you are so, so happy that I *chose* you." Why was she doing this? Why did she put herself out there so much with him when she didn't with others? "I get you want me. I want you, too." Their attraction was one of those crazy, once-in-a-lifetime, off-the-charts deals. The sex was phenomenal. But...for her, their relationship was about more than just the phenomenal sex. *I want more.*

But maybe he didn't have more to give her.

She sucked in a breath. Maybe...maybe he hadn't been putting on a show for Ford. She'd been so confident that Seth was trying to protect her. That he'd been doing the whole self-sacrificing bit because...because he cared.

He said he loved me. He has to care. What was up with these doubts? She was never, ever like this.

"Stop." Seth's low voice. "Whatever is rolling through your head and making you go silent...you're wrong."

She'd been staring at his neck. Her eyes lifted.

"I think I have the steps down now," he murmured. "Forgive me for getting it wrong the first time. I was just fucking stunned because I didn't expect to see you. I thought you would have realized that I was trouble you didn't want."

She shook her head.

"I thought your brother would get you someplace safe."

Hard to do when she'd left him handcuffed. But she *had* stopped to tell Brent that his boss needed some assistance inside the bar. Jamal hadn't been outside when she left, but Brent had lingered near the door. She'd jerked her thumb over her shoulder and very straight-forwardly told Brent that Ford could use a hand...and maybe a key.

"I thought..." Seth continued gruffly, "that the best thing in my life was gone, and that I'd never get to see you again."

Hold up. Had he just called her the best thing?

Seth gazed into her eyes. "But even though the thought of never seeing you again ripped me apart, I was still certain you were safe so the pain was worth it. I knew that you'd get to be happy somewhere else. And that was enough for me. Knowing that you were going to be okay, that you had a chance to live a long, happy life—even if that life took you to some other bastard out there in the future—*it was enough for me.*"

Didn't sound like enough.

"You're still quiet. So un-Harley like." He sucked in a breath. Both of his hands were at his sides again. "I think I have it, now. May I try again?"

She managed to nod.

He threw his arms around her. Yanked her tightly against him. Held her as if he'd never, ever let go. "You are the best thing that has ever happened to me," he breathed. "I am so fucking, deliriously happy that you chose me." If possible, he squeezed her even tighter.

Breathing got a wee bit tricky.

He eased up, but only so he could look down at her. "I wish that you had waited to choose me until I had eliminated every threat to you, but you're here, baby, and I just don't have the strength to let you go again."

"I wouldn't go." She made her own choices. "We're partners, remember? I have your back. You have mine." She licked her lips. "You don't face danger alone, and neither do I. But we need to come up with a plan..." Because the danger *would* be coming. "A plan that doesn't involve us being sitting ducks far away from civilization."

He smiled at her. "I love you."

"You..." Her own smile flashed in return. "You do." She could *see* the love in his eyes and on his face.

His gaze went to her cheek. "That dimple. It gets me every time." Then he was kissing her again.

And she was kissing him back. Happiness seemed to explode inside of her. The kiss wasn't just about desire. A desperate lust. It was about love and hope. And...

She'd fought for him.

He'd sacrificed for her.

He left me to protect me. Such a dick move that he had better not repeat because there would be no more martyr days for either of them. They were a team. Together, they could face anything. Fight anyone.

And live happily ever after? Who knew? She'd never been the fairytale type. Not like her dad and brothers had ever spent a whole lot of time talking about those stories with her. They'd much preferred making up tales about blood and battles.

But a happy ending sure sounded appealing.

Provided we survive what's coming. And they had to survive. She wanted a shot with him.

He scooped her into his arms. Surprised laughter spilled from her as she pulled her mouth from his. "Seth?"

"Got to take you somewhere safe."

Then they should probably leave the house and get out of Louisiana. Except he wasn't taking her *out* of the house. He was carrying her up the stairs. "Do *not* drop me." She clutched him tighter.

"Never."

She stared at his profile. Such a hard, determined profile, and she knew he wouldn't drop her. He wasn't going to let her down, not ever again, and she wasn't going to let him down. She would have kissed him passionately and desperately right then, but Harley didn't exactly want to send them both hurtling down the stairs in a tangle of limbs, so she held onto her control.

Then they were at the landing. He turned to the right. Carried her to the third door. Opened it and stepped inside with her still in his arms.

And he took her right into security central. A line of monitors filled one wall. Two computers were at a desk next to another wall. There was a bed inside, yes, a big one, covered with a dark comforter, but this room was clearly more about intel gathering than anything else.

Seth slowly lowered Harley to her feet before he headed to one of the computers. He tapped a few buttons on the keyboard.

And all of those many, many monitors on the wall flashed to life.

"I didn't just have a team doing repair work on the house," he revealed.

Harley crept closer to the monitors. Surveillance images filled the screens. Images that stretched all the way out to the main road that had to be at least three miles away. Images from the twisting driveway she'd taken once she turned off that road.

Images of Seth's house from every angle. Images of the swamp behind the house. The little dock that waited to the side, sloping toward the swamp.

"No one is going to catch me by surprise. The place is wired to send an alarm anytime someone breaches the exterior perimeter." He tapped the screen that showed the road *three miles away*. "I saw your sedan coming. I have things set up so I can get a security feed and alerts on my phone."

She looked at all of those screens. Her head slowly turned toward him. "All along, you planned to use yourself as bait."

"All along, I knew I needed a backup plan in case things went to shit," he corrected wryly. "My father had too many enemies. I have them, too. I wanted a safe place to land." A shrug of one shoulder. "My mother's home seemed like a good idea. So I just took the precaution of making it as secure as I could. I figured if my enemies were coming, at least they wouldn't catch me by surprise."

He'd caught *her* by surprise. "I'm impressed."

"The house is wired inside, too." A long exhale. He went to the second computer. Did more tapping. And then she saw other images appear on some of those monitors. The foyer she'd just been inside. What looked like a kitchen. A library...

"Not this room," he added gruffly. "No one can see what happens in here."

Excellent to know. She scanned those monitors again. No sign of any unwanted guests.

She kicked off her shoes.

"Harley?"

She unhooked her ankle holster. Carefully put her gun near one of the computers. Then she put a hidden knife she'd had beside it. Quickly, efficiently, she stripped off all of her clothes.

"Harley..."

She smiled at him, working the dimple he'd referenced before. "Why are you acting surprised? Told you outside what I wanted to do. Now, seeing as how you have this fabulous security system in place that will let us know when our enemies are closing in, I think we have some time..." Who knew how long, though? "Perhaps you want to speed things along for me?"

He yanked off his suit coat, revealing his shoulder holster, but she'd already noticed the bulk of it earlier.

He's ready to fight. She swallowed. *He has plenty of security, but he's still thinking he'll have to shoot, maybe have to kill, before this is over.*

But didn't she think the same thing?

Seth removed the holster and his gun. He hauled off his shirt, sending buttons flying. So much for that refined look he'd had moments ago. He kicked his shoes away. His hands went to his belt—

"I can help with that," Harley offered. She wasn't the type to just stand there when someone needed assistance. Nope, not her. She dropped to her knees before him.

"Harley..."

She unhooked his belt. Unbuttoned his pants. She could see the thick length of his erection pushing toward her, so she used care when she lowered his zipper. Not like she wanted to hurt his money maker. Not when she had plans for it—for him.

No underwear. Good. That made things easier. Her fingers curled around the base of his dick, and she leaned forward. Her lips parted as she took in the head of his cock. Her cheeks hollowed. Her tongue swirled over him, and then she pulled him in deeper. She took more of him in her mouth.

His hands locked over her shoulders. *"I can't last."*

She sucked harder.

He shuddered. "Baby..."

And then she was in his arms again. He'd lifted her up and was carrying her toward the bed.

"I was having fun," she protested.

"So the hell was I...*but you're coming first.*"

Oh, had he been that close? Good to know. As far as her coming first...well, if he insisted...

Seth dropped her onto the bed, only to immediately follow her down on the bedding. She parted her legs, expecting him to get into position and take them both to oblivion. Not like they had a lot of time for foreplay. Hell, she had no idea how much time they did have before their world turned into a nightmare. She just knew that she needed this—needed him—with a stunning intensity that shook her to her very marrow. Seth was hers.

She was his.

Whatever was coming, whatever threat, she needed to have him once more. Once.

Like once more will ever be enough. I want a million more times with him, and that will just be the start.

But he didn't position his cock at the entrance to her body. Didn't thrust into her and send them both flying toward release. Instead, carefully, with a tender touch, his fingers slid between her legs.

"Seth?"

He put his mouth on her core. Not devouring and taking. And she'd been in a devouring mood. But he tasted her with light licks of his tongue. Delicate kisses. As if...

More worshipping than taking. That was what it felt like. So tender and good. As if she was something priceless to him.

So very precious.

Once more, she felt tears prick at her eyes. "Seth?"

His tongue slid over her clit. Still soft and careful. Over and over. Taking care of her.

And her orgasm rolled through her on a sudden wave that stole her breath. She couldn't even cry out his name because the pleasure took her. Her body arched and her hands grabbed for his shoulders. The pleasure churned and swirled, and it was so, *so* good, but she wanted him to feel the release with her.

"I love you."

Her eyes had closed, but now they flew open at his confession.

He stared at her and said again, "I love you."

She smiled at him. "Then come fuck me like you mean it."

Only...he just had. He'd fucked her with his mouth like she was the most precious thing in the world to him.

He pulled away from her. Took a packet from the small nightstand. She saw the tremble in his fingers as he rolled on the condom.

He is holding onto his control. Doing everything he can to be so careful with me.

Careful or rough, controlled or wild, she loved him every way. So Harley grabbed his hand and tugged him onto the bed. They rolled together, and she crawled on top of him. Harley straddled Seth, her knees pushing into the mattress on either side of his body. One of her hands flattened on his chest. Her other reached for his dick, positioning him, and then her hips surged down.

Already so slick and eager, she took him completely inside. He growled. She moaned. And then she let go of control. *Both* of her hands pushed against his chest so she could lift herself up and down easier. So she could move faster. Harder. Over and over again.

His fingers rose to tease her nipples. To pluck and stroke, and her head tipped back as need torpedoed through her. The first orgasm had been a gentle storm. The one building now?

Hurricane level.

Faster and faster, she rode him. His eyes stayed on hers, and she couldn't look away from him. One of his hands snaked down. Went to where their bodies collided.

She lifted up.

His fingers stroked her clit.

She sank down. Her body tightened.

Up.

He stroked her clit. Fast. Hard.

She came. Harley gave a choked scream as the orgasm detonated through her. Her body twisted and heaved.

Seth shot upward—still *in* her—and tumbled her back onto the mattress. She was coming and quaking as he lifted her legs over his shoulders and plowed into her. Faster. Deeper. Every thrust just made the orgasm still spinning through her feel *stronger and harder.*

Then he came. Erupted. Pleasure swept over his face even as his fingers bit into her hips.

"Fucking fantastic," he rasped.

Yes, the sex was.

He was.

They *were*.

And no one, *no one,* was going to take him from her.

She'd have him a million times and not be done. Never, ever would she be done with him. "I love you." Harley meant those whispered words with every fiber of her being.

Now, to handle the bad guys...

Please, please, let us live through this night.

Because it would really, deeply suck if she'd finally found the man of her dreams, only to lose him now.

CHAPTER EIGHTEEN

*Step Eighteen: When you have something worth
keeping, you fight for it.*

I can fight dirty really, really well.

Want to see?

"The Feds are watching," Harley said.

Seth remained seated on the edge of the bed, watching *her* as she dressed. It was an absolute shame—a sin—to cover up a body as gorgeous as hers. But since he didn't exactly want anyone else to have the same view he enjoyed...

Clothing is necessary.

She'd already put her ankle holster—and her deceptively small gun—back in place. Her black pants were back on, her flats, her black bra. As he stared at her, she tugged her blouse back on, too.

Also black.

He knew she'd chosen the outfit deliberately, so she'd be able to hide in the dark, if necessary.

He'd already dressed, too, and his shoulder holster—with weapon in place—was a weight that already seemed far too familiar to him.

"Seth?" Harley pushed back a thick lock of her hair that had tumbled forward. "You get that my brother sent you out—with a target on your back—

because he wanted to catch Fabian Butler in the act of trying to kill you?"

He nodded. "I get that." He would have been a fool not to see that one coming. "Good thing I have this place wired so well, huh? I'll have the full scene in living color for the Feds. They can run wild with the footage."

Her eyes narrowed as she edged closer to the bed. "Is that what you're planning? To get a confession and not to commit murder? Because I thought you were the one hellbent on the eye-for-an-eye justice method."

He had been. In fact, he still very much wanted to *destroy* Fabian. "If he put the hit on you, there is nothing more I want than for him to be in the ground." Wasn't that why he had a gun strapped to him? Why other weapons were strategically hidden around the house? If he had to kill, he would. But... "I don't want you to ever think I'm a monster." The way Harley looked at him? What she saw when she glanced into his eyes?

It mattered.

If he could be better, if he could be more...for her, he would be.

Her hand rose. She didn't fucking pat his cheek. She stroked his jaw. "You're trying to *catch* a killer for me? That is the sweetest thing anyone has ever done." She leaned forward and pressed a kiss to his lips.

He would hardly call it sweet.

Harley straightened, staring at him with the gold bright in her eyes. Looking at him like he was some kind of freaking hero.

It matters what she sees when she sees me. "Can't make any promises," Seth heard himself mutter. "Things could go off the rails. The Feds could wait a little too long to rush to the scene...or maybe they don't come at all. Maybe they decide me being dead is the evidence they need to use. A murder conviction could be the end goal for their case on Fabian." Only seeing as how Seth didn't plan to die... "I will defend myself. I will defend you." But he wasn't going to kill in cold blood.

That had been his father's way.

As Harley had told him and as he now believed...*I am not my father.*

"I will defend you, too. Always." Her head cocked. "But I still think we need to make sure our backup is close and *good*. I have a team from Wilde coming down—I made the request for additional agents after I got the address for this place, so it will take some time for them to get here. Holden promised me he would come in with guns blazing, as fast as he could."

Holden Blackwell. Her ex-partner. She'd been working with him when Seth first met her. "My father wrecked Holden's life. I can't imagine he wants to help me."

"Holden doesn't blame you. He's a good man. He will have your back. He'll have mine." Her hands went to her hips. "Another good man? My brother sure was singing the praises of Detective Zion Raye. Ford doesn't usually praise anyone, so I knew that meant he wanted me to trust the cop. I went to Zion earlier. He told me that a woman made the nine-one-one call that had the cops swarming at the cemetery."

A woman?

"I also wanted to get more info about the hit on me. Call me crazy, but I like to know as much as possible about attempts on my life."

He rose from the bed. "What did you learn?"

"The cops haven't traced the texts Justin received yet. They *weren't* sent from the phone Fabian had at his house—the one I'd tracked down before when I found you in the billiard room."

He fought a smile. "Pool room."

"I know, just wanted you to say it." An exhale. "The texts could be from a burner phone. Or they could be from one of the many numbers that Fabian probably has. Zion is working to discover more." She searched Seth's gaze. "I think we should call him and let Zion know where we are. I get that the Feds probably have a lock on your phone so they traced you here and the agents are out there, waiting, in the dark. Waiting behind your three-mile radius of protection. But I feel like it would be smart to have the detective on hand, too. He's not the enemy."

No, Seth didn't think he was. "Remember when I got that second text from Fabian? The one you thought I lied to you about?"

She nodded.

"I didn't lie. I read it exactly as it was. Figured the Feds would pull my texts—what would have been the point in lying?" Just to be discovered later? *No point.* "And the message I got on my app? The one that vanished? I told you the truth about it, too. I've tried really, really fucking hard to only lie a little to you."

"And what were those little lies?"

He swallowed. "At the bar, when I said the charade was over. That we were done. That whole scene—that was my lie."

"You count that as a *little* lie?"

He counted it as the hardest lie he'd ever told in his life. "I don't want to be done with you. I want to get out of this nightmare, and I want to have more—with you."

She reached out and squeezed his hand. "I want that, too."

Fuck, yes. *Yes.*

"So how about we get our backup, and we make sure that we survive everything that's coming?" She let him go. Moved toward the computer table. She'd put her phone there when she'd been stripping before, but hell if he could recall that moment. "I'll call Zion—"

Seth's phone rang.

"Oh, that can't be good," she whispered.

No, it couldn't be. Late night calls were never good. "Think Fabian is ready for another meeting? This time, I definitely get to pick the place." He pulled out his phone from his pocket, aware that Harley was firing out a quick text on her own device. Seth didn't recognize the number on his screen. How very shocking. *Not.* His finger swiped over the screen, and he turned on the speaker option so Harley could hear the conversation. "Who the hell is this?"

"It's pretty much the only friend you have," Brent Marchello snapped back. "And you should be exceedingly grateful to hear from me."

When he looked up, Seth saw surprise flash across Harley's face.

"Gonna lose my job for this," Brent added, "but I can't let you sit out there in that crumbling mausoleum of a house and die by yourself."

He knows where I am, but doesn't realize Harley is here. Brent thinks I'm alone.

"Fabian is on his way to you. For some reason, word is spreading through some informants that he is handling you personally."

Great. Because I'm so special.

"I'm not going to follow Ford's orders," Brent told him, voice thickening. "I'm not gonna just wait. I'm coming in. So turn off whatever fucking security you have so that the whole countryside isn't aware I'm arriving at your place. And, yeah, I know you were installing a security system out there. I've been driving your ass around forever. I heard most of your phone conversations. *Turn it off.* I'm coming in, and I'd prefer for things not to be blaring because I don't have much of a lead time on Fabian. Once I'm inside with you—and you have real freaking backup in the form of a trained agent—we'll get things operational again."

"You're coming in on your own? Where's Ford?" Seth asked. "If he's somewhere out watching the perimeter..."

"*He isn't.* That's what I'm trying to tell you! Ford has completely abandoned you. Guess he doesn't like that you fucked his sister. He's letting Fabian have free reign."

Harley shook her head.

"Ford left you to die, man, and I can't have that shit on my conscience. *I am coming to help you.* I just hope we both don't wind up getting a swift trip to hell." A ragged exhale. *"I'm the one about to turn on your drive.* Do not come at me with guns blazing, got it? I'm on your side." Brent hung up.

Seth rushed toward the computers. There was an alarm, yes, but the damn thing wasn't going to start blaring powerfully in the night like some kind of siren.

"My brother wouldn't do this." Harley's soft voice.

Seth typed in a few fast commands. He waited, tilting his head to the side and staring at the screen that would show him arrivals three miles out...

He saw the black SUV approaching. Saw it turn onto the path. *Brent.*

"My brother wouldn't leave you to die alone. I-I was sure he'd sent Jamal to follow you. When I left the bar and Jamal wasn't in sight, I figured Ford had already given him orders to tail you. Ford *wouldn't* leave you to die alone."

"Is this the same brother that kept his involvement in the operation secret from you?" Seth asked her.

She sucked in a breath. "He won't kill you for fucking me. I mean, he might want to. All of my brothers might because that's who they are—but he *wouldn't.* I'm telling you, this isn't Ford."

He looked back at her.

She had her phone to her ear. "I'm calling him," she said. "He's been dodging me ever since I left him handcuffed at that bar."

"What?"

"I get that he's pissed at me, but I have to talk to him—Ford?" Her voice kicked up in excitement, then, "*Dammit, voicemail.* Listen, stop jerking me around, Ford. I need to talk to you. Something is wrong. I don't—*I need my brother.* I need you now. Call me. Immediately." She hung up and hurried closer to the monitors. "You couldn't tell that I was the one driving the sedan. Was that because my windows were tinted?"

He didn't speak.

She cut him a glance. "You were going for your gun when I arrived. If you'd known it was me, you would never have reached for a weapon."

She had a point. "You cuffed your brother?"

"He was trying to stop me from coming after you. Nothing was going to stop me." Her focus whipped back toward the screens. "The SUV's windows are tinted dark, too. I can't see Brent's face."

"Maybe that's why he called. Maybe the call was less about potential alarms blaring and more about making sure I didn't shoot first and ask questions later."

"Maybe..." Her lips pressed together. "*I trust Ford. He knows I love you. He wouldn't do this to the man I love.*"

"Harley..."

"We can't know that Brent is alone in that vehicle. He could have someone else in there. Someone else could be driving or someone could be in the back seat." Her hand curled around his wrist, and her nails dug into him. "Someone was giving Fabian Butler information on my family.

Classified intel. I thought the person had to be placed very, very high up in the government, but maybe that agent just worked closely with my brother. Maybe Brent overhead conversations that Ford had—the same way he was listening in on your conversations."

Ice seemed to spread through his veins. "You're saying Brent is the enemy?"

"I'm saying..." She bit her lip. "I'm saying he doesn't know I'm here. I'm saying I will stay hidden because *I* am your backup. Your bodyguard. Your ride or die heroine, remember?"

He remembered that she was his freaking life.

"I stay hidden," Harley continued. "If anything goes south, I will come out with guns blazing. *Do not* lower your guard. You might think Brent is your friend..."

Alarms were softly beeping in the room. Beeping from the computers. From Seth's phone. Warning him that the perimeter had been breached.

He turned off the beeps. Made sure to silence his phone. *At the bar, Brent told me that he wasn't my friend.*

"You might think he is," she said once more, "but Brent could be your worst enemy."

***

Seth had a rifle hidden under the bed. When he showed her that sweet baby, with its wonderful night vision scope, she had to kiss him. Hell, yes, she knew how to work a rifle. Her father would have been embarrassed if she hadn't been a super shot by the time she was thirteen. Since Seth was supposed to walk out alone, she would be protecting his ass from upstairs. She found her perfect vantage point at the window, she got her weapon ready, and she stared through the scope as the black SUV slowly pulled to a stop in front of the old house.

Her heart raced in her chest, but her fingers were steady and relaxed around the weapon. Her brother Rafe was the best one at using a rifle. He could have been one hell of a sniper. But...

Other plans. Other dreams.

One day soon, Seth would get to meet all of her brothers. She hoped that meeting would go smoother than his first encounter with Ford had gone.

The SUV's door opened. The driver's door. Brent climbed out. He lifted his hands immediately, indicating he wasn't holding a weapon. Seth walked down the porch steps and headed toward him.

Her breath eased out, but she kept her eye to that scope.

***

"I've got a weapon holstered," Brent called, "but clearly there is nothing in my hands." He walked around the vehicle. The light from the moon fell onto him as he flashed a smile at Seth. "I don't hear alarms blaring."

Seth didn't smile back. "I think you overestimate my security system."

"Probably right." Brent edged closer to him. Still smiling. "I mostly just wanted to make sure you didn't shoot at the first sign of someone on your property. You're kinda unpredictable, you know?"

"No, I don't know." His own voice was casual. Brent stood directly in front of Seth. The back windows of the SUV were so damn dark.

Too dark.

Had he just seen a shadow move? Yes, yes, he fucking had...as if someone was *rising up* from the back seat.

Seth grabbed for his weapon.

"Do you want her brother to die?" Brent asked him.

Seth hauled out his gun and aimed it right at Brent.

Brent simply rolled his shoulders. "Her precious Ford is in the back seat right now, and Fabian Butler has a gun to his head. If you pull that trigger on me, Ford will be dead two seconds later. You think that will be easy for Harley to accept? Or do you think when the news hits her, she will break apart?"

"You're lying," Seth gritted out.

"Let's find out..." Brent turned away. Marched to the back passenger door.

Fuck, fuck, fuck.

He swung it open. The interior light didn't flash on.

It hadn't turned on when he climbed out of the vehicle, either. Bastard turned the lights off deliberately. So I couldn't see anything inside.

A low groan came from the back seat. And then...

Ford Adaire climbed gingerly from the vehicle. His hands were cuffed behind his back, and he limped as he moved away from the SUV. As he stepped into the moonlight, Seth saw blood pouring down the side of Ford's face.

But Ford wasn't the only one who climbed from that SUV. Fabian eased out, too, and he had his gun pressed to the back of Ford's head.

"Should I shoot him right here and now?" Fabian mused. "Or shall we take our business inside?"

***

"No," Harley whispered, but mentally, she was screaming...*No, no, no!* Because that was her brother. That was her overprotective, often annoying, always domineering, always *loving—damn him*—Ford. Ford with his hands cuffed behind his back.

With blood on his face.

Limping toward Seth.

I did this. She'd been the one to cuff Ford. He hadn't used his full strength in the fight against her at the bar. Growing up, no matter how many times she'd told him not to hold back with her, he always had. *And he'd held back in that bar.*

She'd left him cuffed. She'd sent Brent into the bar when she rushed out.

And Brent found him handcuffed and waiting.

Now Fabian had a gun at the back of her brother's head. As she watched, Brent pulled out his own weapon and pointed it at Seth.

If she took a shot right then, she could either aim for Brent or for Fabian.

If she took out Brent, Fabian could kill her brother.

If she took out Fabian, Brent could kill Seth. Provided, of course, that Fabian's fingers didn't spasm when he took her bullet—they could spasm and even as he died, he could shoot her brother.

I could lose them both.

Terror nearly choked her.

I can't fire. I can't do anything. She could do nothing but sit up there and watch and be absolutely, completely terrified.

This isn't me. I don't hide. I don't wait.

But she had no plan. Two men she loved were in terrible danger, and as she hesitated, they stepped under the porch and she lost any chance of a shot. *Dammit.* Harley whirled away from the window.

Forget the rifle. She'd go down with her small handgun and her knife. She could sneak up and attack. She could—

Beeping. Low, quiet beeping. The beeps had her freezing. *Why was the alarm sounding?* Seth had already turned off the beeping that had started when the SUV pulled onto the drive.

Are more of Fabian's men coming? Because she and Seth were already outnumbered. She'd texted Zion Raye before, when Seth first got the call from Brent, but she paused to fire off another SOS to him now.

Come in fast. No time. Fabian here.

She leaned over the monitors, trying to figure out why another alarm had been triggered. Then she saw the small figure on the boat out in the swamp. A boat that was edging closer and closer to the slumping dock. *Who in the hell...?*

The figure jumped from the boat. Tied it off at the edge of the dock. The moonlight fell onto the figure and showed her long hair, pulled up in a ponytail.

In that instant, Harley remembered...*A woman had made the nine-one-one call.*

As she watched that small figure on the screen, the woman pulled out a gun.

Right. Why not? Everyone has weapons tonight.

The woman took off down the dock, rushing toward the house.

Okay, that made...three threats. Fabian. Brent. And the woman.

Time to come up with a plan. Fast. Time to—

Boom. A gunshot blasted. Harley forgot about a plan. She ran for the door and yanked it open.

CHAPTER NINETEEN

*Step Nineteen: Everyone has a killer instinct.
Sometimes, we just like to pretend that we don't.*

Seth flinched when the gun exploded. He'd been walking down the hallway, heading to the old library, when the boom shook the house. For just a moment, he was sent hurtling back to his past. Back to that stupid, blood-soaked road as his mother turned toward him.

Boom.

Another blast. He whirled, expecting to see Ford slumped on the ground and wondering how in the hell he was ever gonna explain her brother's death to Harley.

But Ford was still standing. Wincing and tilting his head to the left, but standing. Behind him, Fabian had a gun up and aimed—the gun was actually damn close to Ford's left ear, so no wonder the man was flinching.

Those two blasts had probably nearly blown out Ford's ear drum.

While Ford was still standing, someone else was not.

Brent Marchello sprawled on the floor, with blood pooling beneath and around his still body. He'd taken Seth's gun and phone right before they went inside, and now Seth knew those items were beneath the agent, no doubt covered in his blood.

"Always hated dirty cops," Fabian said. "I mean, if they can be bought by one person, who is to say they won't easily trade their loyalty again down the line?"

Was Brent still alive? Or already dead? *He looks dead. I don't see him moving at all.*

"He's the one who put the hit on your girlfriend, by the way," Fabian added.

Seth thought he heard a squeak from upstairs. Like a door being opened or closed.

Please don't let anyone else have heard that sound.

Ford shook his head, blinking blearily. He'd definitely not heard the sound.

Fabian didn't look up toward the second level. He kept his eyes on Seth. "That bleeding agent on your floor? He's the one who took your ID, too. Not Andre. Brent took it right from your hotel room. By the way, do you know that he gave you an *empty* gun that night at my house? He was setting you up to get your ass killed. Lucky for you, I gave orders for no one to hurt you that night."

"Am I supposed to thank you right now?" What in the hell was even happening?

Fabian positioned his gun at the base of Ford's head once again. "A thank you would be an excellent start."

He needed to get them in the library. Because he was sure he'd just heard another faint creak from above. *Harley is moving up there.* Seth turned his back on Fabian, knowing he would either get a bullet blasted at him, or Fabian would follow him.

He was hoping the guy followed him. Seth was also very much hoping that Fabian wouldn't put a bullet in Ford's head.

Seth shoved open the doors to the old library. This room hadn't been updated yet. It smelled old and musty and the book-lined shelves were covered in dust. To the right, a big globe waited near a faded settee. The globe was actually a bar, with four spindly, wooden legs that shot down from the sphere to balance it. If you lifted up the top of that globe. you wouldn't find alcohol waiting inside.

You would find a loaded gun. Seth had been serious when he told Harley that he'd stashed weapons all over the house. If he could get close enough, and if he could distract Fabian, Seth would grab the weapon from inside the globe.

Until six months ago, the house had been owned by a distant relative. No one had actually *lived* in the place for years. It had just sat and waited. Gone darker and darker...

Until that relative died. Until the house went on the market.

Until I came home.

"Love what you've done with the place," Fabian drawled. "Cobwebs and yellowed books give the home a real glamorous touch."

The bastard *had* followed him inside. Good. Deliberately, Seth took a few more steps toward the globe before swinging around, as if to confront Fabian. "Do you think I give a shit about your opinion? You're just going to shoot me and add my blood to the floor. Another glamorous touch?" he mocked.

Fabian laughed, and he shoved Ford onto the settee. He kept his gun close to Ford, moving so that the gun was near Ford's temple.

That was really a whole lot of blood pouring down Ford's face. And his eyes seemed pretty glassy. Did the guy even know where he was? What was happening to him?

"You think I came here to kill you?" Fabian asked as his laughter faded.

Seth motioned toward the gun in Fabian's hand. "All signs would point to yes."

"I came here to offer you a deal."

What? "I'm listening." Like he had a choice to do anything but listen in that moment.

"Your girlfriend-slash-bodyguard abandoned you."

Seth stiffened.

"Brent told me all about how you left the bar without her. What happened? Did you go in for a chat with her big brother, and Harley had to pick an allegiance? You versus him?"

Ford's glassy stare darted around the library.

What did Ford reveal to him? Would Ford have sold out his sister?

Ford's stare slowly slid toward Seth. Not quite so glassy. At least, for a moment, it wasn't, and in that instant, Seth knew...*No.* Ford would never sell out Harley.

Just as Seth wouldn't. "She picked him," he replied with a shrug. "The Feds wanted to use me. I wanted to use them." Did he sound as if he didn't care? No clue. Hopefully, he did. Acting was extra hard when there was a dead agent in the foyer and a man with a gun just a few feet away. "Harley didn't like what she learned about me in that meeting. She kept thinking I was a good guy at heart. When she finally discovered I wasn't, she was done with me."

Fabian jabbed his gun into the side of Ford's head. "That's what he told me, too. Even after I had the bastard tortured for hours. Broke his leg. A couple of fingers. Beat the hell out of him...and he kept saying you'd been playing the Feds all along. That Harley had gotten on a plane and flown away from you."

I had the bastard tortured for hours. Seth swallowed. "I wanted to know who ordered the hit on my mother. Turns out, the Feds knew all along. They were lying to me."

"Who? Who did it?" Fabian demanded.

"My father."

Fabian burst into laughter. "The hell, he did." More laughter. "That the story they gave you?"

"Yes." A hiss.

"Then they lied. Or else, they were just clueless. As usual."

Fabian knows. He's not clueless.

With a shake of his head and that smug smile lingering on his lips, Fabian said, "That bastard loved one woman his whole life, and it was your mom. He didn't kill her. He didn't even know she was selling him out, not until much later."

Had Seth just heard another faint creak? A closer creak. Like the sound of someone on the stairs?

Fabian's eyes narrowed, and he started to glance back toward the doors—

"*Who ordered the hit on my mother?*" Seth thundered. "You know, don't you? *Tell me.*"

Fabian's gaze immediately flew back to Seth. "What part of this situation makes you feel like you get to give me any orders?" And the gun lifted from Ford's head. It pointed toward Seth.

Finally.

The library doors had been left open. The gun was away from Ford's head. Now, if Seth could just get a weapon of his own...

He took a step back, moving closer to the globe and lifting his hands in front of him, as if he was no threat. "Sorry. I tend to get a little emotional where my mother is concerned. That happens when you're a kid and you watch your mom get gunned down right in front of you."

Fabian's eyes darkened. "Never knew you were there."

"My dad made sure no one knew."

More laughter from Fabian. Bitter. Mocking. The gun rose another inch. Almost right on level with Seth's heart. "He did that a lot, didn't he? Kept his secrets. So many dirty secrets." An exhale. "You came here to find your mom's killer. You already know it was Justin Florent's dad. He's the one who pulled the trigger. But what you might not know is that Justin's family and mine have been linked for years."

Seth's stomach twisted. He'd just caught sight of Harley outside of those open library doors. *Don't look her way again. Don't.* "Linked?" he repeated.

"Justin's dad was an executioner for my family. You want to know who ordered the hit on your mom? It was *my* family. My mother, actually. She was tired of being just another one of your father's dirty secrets."

Seth's heart seemed to stop.

"And she thought if she could just get your mother out of the way, then maybe she'd have a chance. Your father met them both at the same time, years and years ago. At first, my mom thought he was going to marry her. Love *her*. But then your mom strolled into Eddie's life. Your mom—the one who wasn't tied to crime. A fucking debutante that could give him *respectability*. A perfect princess that he just had to claim." Disgust twisted his lips. "So he married her, and he kept my mom on the side like she was just some whore. She had me, I was his freaking first born, but you were the one he boasted about to the world. You were the one with the fancy schools and the perfect life."

Now Seth laughed. "You are so clueless."

"You had my life. Your mom had my mother's life! So—"

"So your mom took it away." His hands fisted.

Harley crept closer to the doors. She had her gun up. Aimed. Seth viewed her from the corner of his eye, knowing that if he showed too much attention to her, Fabian would immediately glance her way.

She's getting her shot lined up. When she is ready to fire, I need to get the hell out of the way. Because Fabian's gun was trained right on him.

Seth didn't want the guy's finger to get all twitchy when Harley's bullet thudded into him.

"She put the hit on your mom." Fabian took a sidestep away from Ford.

Ford hadn't moved at all. He just sagged on the settee, seeming to barely stay upright.

"Eddie was furious. He came charging down here after your mom died—I'll never forget his rage." Fabian swallowed. "But word reached him that day—just before I was sure he was going to murder my mom—he got a call and he learned that *your mother* was a lying bitch who'd been determined to take him down. If those bullets hadn't slammed into her, Big Eddie's world would have imploded. My mom saved him. *Saved him.*"

"Don't call my mother a bitch. Not ever." He didn't break eye contact with Fabian, even though he was aware of Harley inching forward. "My dad always said you had to kill people who betrayed you. Punish the betrayer. I guess the only reason he didn't follow through with your mother was because—"

"*She saved him!*" Fabian snarled once more. Spittle flew from his mouth.

That's DNA evidence, asshole. Way to leave your mark at the scene. But Seth wanted more. He wanted the bastard to dig his own grave completely. "My father didn't claim her after that so-called discovery. He didn't claim her or you. And when he died, he left everything to me. Not you."

"That's why I originally intended to kill you," Fabian told him. "Because you didn't deserve anything. Not a dime. *Nothing.*"

"I'm standing here." Seth spread out his arms. "Take a shot." His right hand touched the edge of the globe.

"No. You are the only family I have left."

Not what Seth had expected at all.

"My mother is dead. My uncles are gone. It's just *you*."

Lucky me.

"So I am gonna offer you a deal." Fabian nodded. "I'm gonna let you have a chance. You can prove your loyalty to me. We can work together. Build an empire. The way it should have always been. You owe the Feds nothing. We both owe Big Eddie *nothing*."

"I'm listening..." What the fuck else could he do? And why was Harley not *shooting?* He couldn't risk looking at her. *Could not.* "Just how am I supposed to prove my loyalty?"

"Simple. You kill the Fed." His gun lowered to press against Ford's head once again.

Fuck.

"You shoot him. You kill him. And your hands will be as bloody as mine. Two dead Feds. Two reunited brothers. A perfect ending, don't you think?"

***

She didn't have a shot.

Dammit, dammit, *dammit*.

First, the jackass Fabian had *finally* lifted the gun from her brother's head, but then he'd just aimed it at Seth. She'd been inching forward, hoping Seth would get out of the way—Harley had been terrified that she'd shoot Fabian, and he'd still manage to get off a shot at Seth. The same worry she'd had when the men had been outside the house.

And, then, just when she *thought* there was a chance to fire her weapon...

Fabian put the gun back to Ford's head. She couldn't risk her brother. There was no shot to take.

As she stood just beyond the library, trying to figure out what the hell to do, Harley heard what sounded like footsteps rushing through the house. Too fast.

She got in. The woman from the dock. Harley had known it would take the woman some time to get inside, but that time seemed to now be up.

Harley ducked down low, hiding behind a row of old boxes that had been shoved a few feet from the library's entrance. She reached her hiding spot just as she saw a redheaded woman come barreling through the foyer. The woman didn't even slow when her tennis shoes squished in the blood around Brent's still body. Harley had checked him for a pulse when she first found the body.

He's gone.

The woman never bothered to even glance his way. Her head *did* jerk to the left at the sound of voices coming from the library—Seth and Fabian were *loud.*. When her head jerked, Harley was able to get a partial look at the woman's face.

Shock had Harley almost falling on her ass.

***

"I'll be able to trust you fully," Fabian said.

"When I kill the Fed," Seth finished.

Ford bobbed his head up. Managed to look at Seth a moment before his head dipped forward again.

"Right," Fabian all put purred. "After you get rid of Ford, I'll be able to—"

Footsteps pounded. Fabian swung toward the sound with his gun raised.

"No!" Seth roared. Automatically, he lunged forward. *Don't shoot Harley. Don't!*

A woman barreled inside. She came to a shuddering stop, her red hair escaping from her ponytail to fly around her delicate features.

Red hair?

Seth's mouth hung open. *Who the hell is she?*

The woman smiled at him. "Hi." She had a gun held loosely in her right hand. Her head tilted toward Fabian. "Looks like I missed some action." Her head cocked and her eyes narrowed. "Who left the dead Fed in the foyer?"

"I did," Fabian replied easily. "But my dear brother is about to take out *this* Fed." His free hand clamped around Ford's shoulder. "So you really didn't miss much."

She grunted. "Took a little longer than I thought to get here by boat. But when we leave, I'll be able to navigate us out with no trouble."

Where is Harley? She'd been in the doorway one moment, and gone the next.

"Don't think you've met Mae yet, have you?" Fabian asked. "I believe I might have mentioned her to you before, though. She's the lovely lady who first tipped me off about Harley being your bodyguard."

Mae flashed him a grin. "Nice to meet you."

There was nothing nice about it. Seth took a step back. *I'm getting the fucking gun out of the globe.* "I thought...you said she was Justin's girlfriend."

Mae rolled her eyes. "That dumbass? Fabian thought he might be working some secret deals with the Feds—notably, with that dead asshole in the foyer. So I got close, I gathered what intel we needed, then I stabbed that grabby dick Justin fifteen times and left him to die in the cemetery." She shrugged. "That will teach him to put his hands on *me*."

She'd killed him? Seth shook his head. "You forgot the part where you set me up for murder."

Mae and Fabian shared a long look. "Did I?" Mae asked, all innocence. And suddenly, her eyes seemed extra large. Her face reflected a stunned surprise as if she just couldn't imagine doing such a thing. *Me? Set someone up for murder?*

His temples pounded. *I'm so sick of everyone pretending.* "Yeah, you did. Luckily, Harley was there to give me an alibi."

Mae glanced around. "But she's not here now, is she?" Mae waved her weapon toward Ford. "When I broke three of his fingers earlier, Ford assured me that Harley had flown away from you." Her lips twisted down in mock sympathy. "You just can't count on some people."

And some you could.

"Is he really going to kill the Fed?" Mae asked suddenly. "Or are we just going to stand here all night?"

"I don't have a weapon," Seth pointed out with a growl. "How the hell do you expect me to kill him? With my bare hands?"

Fabian inclined his head to Mae, as if sending a silent order. Smiling, she strolled toward Seth. Her right hand still gripped her gun. Her left...reached under her flowing top. When she lifted the top a few inches, he realized she had a second weapon tucked into the waistband of her jeans.

"Take the gun," she told him even as she lifted her right hand and pointed *her* weapon right at Seth's head.

He reached out and took the weapon from her waistband. The nozzle of the gun slid over the skin of her stomach, and she laughed. "That tickles."

His jaw tightened even more.

She kept aiming her gun at him. "Now turn, point it at the Fed, and shoot him."

He turned, he pointed the weapon at the Fed...but Seth didn't shoot.

***

I helped that woman! Harley stood to the side of the library, rage and fear twisting inside of her. She'd recognized the redhead—the woman she'd found at Fabian's house, being *choked* by Justin. Harley had helped her. And this was how the woman repaid that kindness?

By trying to kill my brother and my boyfriend?

Oh, hell, no.

Jeez. No wonder the woman hadn't wanted to contact the cops. She'd been working with Fabian!

Harley's nostrils flared. She didn't have any time to waste. She couldn't wait for the perfect moment. Couldn't just stand back any longer while she prayed Fabian would move his weapon away from Ford.

She had to attack. If she didn't, both Seth and Ford would die.

Not on my watch, they won't.

CHAPTER TWENTY

*Step Twenty: Getting shot hurts like a mother.
So don't get shot. Be the one who shoots.*

Seth stared over the barrel of his gun. Then he looked at a smirking Fabian. "You think I'm a damn idiot."

There was no immediate denial. But Fabian lost a little of his smirk.

"The woman is here because—" Seth began.

"Mae," she inserted. "My name is *Mae*."

"She's here to get you away from the scene." *Your getaway driver. Or boater. Or whatever the hell it was.* "When the authorities finally come, they'll find Brent's dead body. They'll find Ford's body. And they'll find me. Let me guess...after I shoot Ford, I'll somehow turn the gun on myself? Kill myself because I can't live with what I've done? Just too much freaking guilt to handle?"

"It is hard," Mae murmured. "When you realize you're as much of a monster as your father."

I'm not. At least, not yet. "There is no deal, Fabian. You don't want me to prove myself. You just want to torture *me*. Make me become as fucked-up as you are before I die. Then you and *Mae* will hop on the boat she was talking about, and you'll leave. That way, when the scene is searched, only Brent's SUV will be here. No one will ever know what you did. You'll be the fucking shadow that escapes."

"I'll be the stronger son," Fabian returned. "Just like I always was—"

"*Wrong!*" Seth thundered. "Because you weren't ever his son. That last damn night when he was with me...my father said I had to take over because there was no one else. That he'd been *lied to*. Betrayed yet again. I was the only blood he had left—he *told* me those words. I didn't understand at the time, but now I do. He realized that your mother *lied* to him all those years. He wasn't your father. Hell, maybe Justin Florent's dad was your real old man. Especially if he would go around killing so easily for your mom. *You are not my brother*. You are nothing to me—and—

"*Drop the guns!*" Harley screamed as she burst into the library.

Mae whirled toward her in shock, her weapon moving away from Seth.

Harley fired. Two rapid shots that slammed into Mae. Mae stumbled back and slumped into a heavy bookcase. Books rained down on her.

Fabian's face twisted with fury and hate, and his weapon jerked toward Harley. Seth knew that the bastard was going to squeeze his trigger—

Not happening. You will not hurt her. Seth fired. He squeezed over and over again, but only one bullet came out of the gun.

But then, one was all he needed. The bullet blasted into Fabian.

Ford threw his body forward, taking shelter on the floor, even as Fabian swayed. Fabian looked down at his chest, at the blood blossoming on him, and the gun fell from his fingers. His knees seemed to give way as he sank to the floor.

"Ford!" Harley cried.

"Okay," he growled back. "Just...have a fucking broken leg and fingers. *Sonofabitch, it has been a day.*" He rolled over, wincing. "*Someone get the cuffs off me!*"

Seth tossed the weapon that wasn't firing any longer. *You only gave me one bullet? What the fuck did you plan? For me to shoot Ford, and then, you were worried I might get bold and turn the weapon on you? So you wanted to make sure I was defenseless?* Screw that. He yanked up the top of the globe, grabbed the hidden gun, and stalked for Fabian.

Fabian was crouched behind the settee. His hands pressed over his chest. All the color had drained from his face.

"You aren't my brother," Seth told him.

Fabian's head lifted. "You...shot me." The bullet had plowed into his chest.

So much blood.

"I'm about to shoot you again." Seth gripped the gun too tightly. "This one has plenty of bullets." He raised the weapon—

"*Seth.*" Harley grabbed his arm. "Seth, you have everything on video. You wired the house. Detective Raye and the others will be here soon. *This is over.*"

His head turned toward her.

She stared at him...and smiled. Her dimple flashed. Her eyes lit up. She stared at him...*Like I'm something good.*

"You did it, Seth! You got him to confess."

He wanted to shoot the SOB again.

"It's over. You're free. No more deals. No more secrets. Me and you—that's what's waiting. *Me and you.*"

Mae moaned.

Harley's gaze darted toward the woman, then back to Seth. "I need to see about her. Don't shoot, okay? You don't have to kill him."

The bastard could already be dying.

"Harley, get me out of these cuffs!" Ford snarled.

"You should have been able to get yourself out of them," she snarled right back. "How could you not have a key on you?" She didn't let go of Seth. *"Me and you,"* she said once more.

He nodded.

Only then did she let go. Her feet scampered over the floor. He looked over his shoulder to see her rushing toward Mae. The redhead was still alive, but damn bloody.

"She...shouldn't...be here..."

His gaze slid back to Fabian.

Fabian had fallen onto his back. One hand pressed to his chest. The other...

The tricky SOB was reaching for the gun he'd dropped a few moments before.

Seth moved forward. His foot crushed down on Fabian's wrist, stopping him from grabbing the weapon and breaking some bones in the process. "Sure, she should be here." He leaned down. "She's my bodyguard, where the hell else would she be?"

***

Dozens of vehicles filled the drive in front of the old house. Ambulances, police cruisers, unmarked FBI vehicles. Seth stood outside, watching the chaos, and feeling oddly numb.

It's over.

Fabian had already been taken away in one of the ambulances, under an armed guard. He'd been soaked in blood and unconscious at the time.

Maybe he'll live. Maybe he'll die. Seth should feel something about that, shouldn't he? Something other than the numbness.

"Is he your brother?" Ford stepped beside him. Or, limped beside him.

Seth raked a glance over him. "Shouldn't you be getting into the back of an ambulance?" At least the guy was out of his cuffs.

"My case. My scene. I don't leave until everything is tied up." Gruff. "And I'm already in a shitload of pain, not like it's gonna get any worse."

"You didn't tell Fabian and Mae that Harley was with me." Seth's gaze slid over to where Harley was in a deep conversation with Detective Zion Raye.

"Of course, I didn't."

"Even though you *knew* she was with me."

"Of course, I did." He huffed out a breath. "That's my sister, I wasn't gonna betray her. I live and die for her."

He couldn't take his gaze off Harley. "Me, too." *I live and die for her.*

"You'd better. If you don't, you'll have me *and* my four brothers on your ass." Ford slapped a hand on Seth's shoulder. Then shuddered. "*Freaking broken fingers...*"

"Fabian isn't my brother." Or at least... "I don't think he is."

Ford released Seth's shoulder. "Your father really say that stuff at the end? About being betrayed and you being his only blood?"

"Yes." He just hadn't understood. Until now.

"Blood doesn't matter. I can get a DNA test run for you, if you want, to see if Fabian is related to you, but...*blood doesn't matter.*"

So said the man with four brothers who also happened to be heroes, just like he was.

Seth kept his eyes on Harley.

She looks at me like I'm a hero. Did she know...the only reason he hadn't fired a second bullet straight into Fabian's head...was because of her?

"You aren't your father. You aren't Fabian. You're the man who my sister loves. You get confused about yourself again, just remember that—it's the part that matters."

Seth forced himself to look at Ford once more. "I love her."

"Yeah, figured as much when your fool-ass walked out of the bar without her. Knew right then and there I'd have to be welcoming you into the family one day soon." Ford offered his hand toward Seth. "Just don't squeeze too hard, okay? *Broken fingers.*"

Gingerly, Seth curled his fingers around Ford's. "Are all the brothers like you?"

"You mean incredibly charming, intelligent, and daring?"

Harley's soft laughter teased Seth's ears.

He let go of Ford as she approached. The swirling lights showed her dimple.

"I think he means..." Harley laughed again. "Are all the brothers assholes?"

"Ever notice," Ford whispered, "that she can sometimes say the word 'asshole' like it's an endearment? When she does that, she's just swearing with love."

Seth swallowed the lump that had risen in his throat. Suddenly, he didn't feel quite so numb any longer. *Harley is here.* "I've noticed it a time or two."

"Thought you might have." Ford took a step forward. Then stopped. His stare swept over Seth. "We're gonna frame this just right in the press. We'll make it clear you were never involved in any of your father's illegal activities. Going forward, there will be no more undercover work. No more cons. You're free."

Harley gave her brother a hug, one that had Ford grunting. "Ribs," he gasped. "Ribs!"

"Get in an ambulance," she groused back, then squeezed a little more. "And I love you."

"You, too, sis. You, too." He let go. Limped for an ambulance.

Harley sidled closer to Seth. His hands had fisted. The better not to reach out and grab her.

"I'm sorry," she told him, tilting back her head to stare up at him.

"For what?"

"For taking so long in the house. I was afraid to make the shot when you were standing outside, then even more terrified when I saw you in the library. I couldn't stand the thought that you or Ford might be hurt—killed—and I froze." Her lips pressed together, but he thought he'd seen them tremble, just a bit.

"You don't need to be sorry." Not ever. "You came in with guns blazing, sweetheart."

"Gun, as in single." The wind tossed her hair over her cheek. "At the end, I had to act. I thought...if I screamed, I could get Fabian and Mae to turn toward me, to focus their weapons on *me* when I rushed in the library. I knew I'd be able to shoot at least one of them, and I figured if the other shot me, at least that would give you a chance to fire and—"

He yanked her into his arms. *That* had been her plan? Screw that! "You were willing to die for me?"

"For you and my brother. Absolutely." Her arms curled around him. "Because I love you both."

She took his breath away. *And she gave me my life back.* "Baby, do not ever, *ever* risk yourself like that again."

She pulled away, just enough to look up at him. "Promise me you won't ever engage in some life or death con again...and the risk won't be necessary."

"I don't want a con."

"What do you want?"

He was staring at her. "You."

Her dimple came, peeking at him.

"I only want you," Seth told her. She was it for him. "Forever."

Harley rose onto her toes. Her lips feathered over his. "I think I can make that happen…"

EPILOGUE

How To Marry My Daughter (From General Chason Adaire)

Step One: Meet the family...You'd better not show any fear, son.

We can smell fear like sharks detect blood in the water.

"So...you're the man who got Fabian Butler locked away for the rest of his life." General Chason Adaire swept a considering glance over Seth as he stood in front of a massive fireplace.

"I had some help on that case," Seth replied. "Couldn't have done it without Harley and Ford." Speaking of Harley...*where are you, baby?* They were at her father's place, a cabin up in Montana, and this was his first time to meet her whole family.

He was sweating freaking bullets. Harley had been with him a moment before, then she'd gone bustling out of the room.

Just as the general arrived.

Chason grunted at his response. "The way Harley tells it, Ford spent the whole time being cuffed. You were the one pulling the trigger on Fabian." He moved to stand directly in front of

Seth. "Got Fabian and that wannabe assassin of his—Mae Deveraux—you got them both locked away."

Seth and Chason were now standing eye-to-eye.

"You *did* pull the trigger, didn't you?" Chason pressed. "You shot Fabian?"

"Yes."

"Missed his heart. Shame that." Chason pursed his lips. "Heard you had the chance to shoot him again. Why didn't you?"

"Because..." Seth stopped.

Chason raised his bushy brows. "Nothing to say? What? Did you forget? You don't know why you hesitated?"

He hadn't forgotten a thing. "I didn't do it because Harley was there."

"What the hell does that have to do with anything?"

"Harley thinks I'm better than I am." He swallowed. "She makes me want to—"

Chason's brow furrowed. "Jeez, don't tell me the woman makes you want to be a better person or some other sappy crap. Fucking hell."

Seth locked his jaw. "I will be better, for her."

Chason ducked his head in a slight nod. A sigh slid from him. "Hell, son, if it makes you feel better, I knew I was a goner, too, back in the day—right when Megan started making me want to be better, too." Another sigh, but this one sounded long-suffering. "You have no idea the dumb shit I did to make that woman smile."

What?

Chason pointed at Seth. "Didn't let a crime boss live, though. Can't say that, but, hey, at least Fabian will be in a maximum-security prison for the rest of his days. We'll call that a win." His lips pursed. "You gonna marry my daughter?"

"If she'll have me."

"*I will.*" Harley's voice. From behind him.

Seth whirled toward her. The whole room seemed to light up when she smiled.

"Once you formally ask and all," Harley added. "Something grandly romantic."

Oh, shit. Now he had to try and be *romantic.* No problem. Maybe. He could do it. For her, he could do anything.

"I think I like him, Harley," her father said as Seth tried to figure out a proposal that would fit the "grandly romantic" definition. "He's not nearly as much of an asshole as Ford claimed."

What? Hold on. Ford had said—

The general laughed. "Just kidding, son. Welcome to the family."

Seth jerked his head back toward the general. The man was offering Seth his hand.

Seth took it in a firm shake.

Chason leaned toward him. "Two down," he said. "You got me and Ford on your side. Good luck with the others..."

The others?

"Seth." Harley cleared her throat. "These are the rest of my brothers."

Once more, he turned to look at his Harley. Four big bruisers crowded in the doorway behind her. They all glared at him.

She was still flashing her dimple. *She is the most beautiful thing I've ever seen.* "I don't need luck," Seth heard himself say to the general. "I have Harley." She was better than luck any day of the week.

Then he walked forward, and, right in front of her family...

He kissed her.

THE END

A NOTE FROM THE AUTHOR

Thank you so very much for taking the time to read HOW TO CON A CRIME BOSS. I've had such a good time writing the "How To" books in my Wilde Ways world. Harley was a take-no-prisoners heroine, and I loved pairing her up with a hero who'd come from his own tortured past.

If you'd like to stay updated on my releases and sales, please join my newsletter list.

https://cynthiaeden.com/newsletter/

Again, thank you for reading HOW TO CON A CRIME BOSS.

Best,
Cynthia Eden
cynthiaeden.com

ABOUT THE AUTHOR

Cynthia Eden is a *New York Times*, *USA Today*, *Digital Book World*, and *IndieReader* best-seller.

Cynthia writes sexy tales of contemporary romance, romantic suspense, and paranormal romance. Since she began writing full-time in 2005, Cynthia has written over one hundred novels and novellas.

Cynthia lives along the Alabama Gulf Coast. She loves romance novels, horror movies, and chocolate.

For More Information

- *cynthiaeden.com*
- *facebook.com/cynthiaedenfanpage*

HER OTHER WORKS

Wilde Ways: Gone Rogue

- How To Protect A Princess (Book 1)
- How To Heal A Heartbreak (Book 2)
- How To Con A Crime Boss (Book 3)

Ice Breaker Cold Case Romance

- Frozen In Ice (Book 1)
- Falling For The Ice Queen (Book 2)
- Ice Cold Saint (Book 3)
- Touched By Ice (Book 4)
- Trapped In Ice (Book 5)
- Forged From Ice (Book 6)

Phoenix Fury

- Hot Enough To Burn (Book 1)
- Slow Burn (Book 2)
- Burn It Down (Book 3)

Trouble For Hire

- No Escape From War (Book 1)
- Don't Play With Odin (Book 2)
- Jinx, You're It (Book 3)
- Remember Ramsey (Book 4)

Death and Moonlight Mystery

- Step Into My Web (Book 1)
- Save Me From The Dark (Book 2)

Wilde Ways

- Protecting Piper (Book 1)
- Guarding Gwen (Book 2)
- Before Ben (Book 3)
- The Heart You Break (Book 4)
- Fighting For Her (Book 5)
- Ghost Of A Chance (Book 6)
- Crossing The Line (Book 7)
- Counting On Cole (Book 8)
- Chase After Me (Book 9)
- Say I Do (Book 10)
- Roman Will Fall (Book 11)
- The One Who Got Away (Book 12)
- Pretend You Want Me (Book 13)
- Cross My Heart (Book 14)
- The Bodyguard Next Door (Book 15)
- Ex Marks The Perfect Spot (Book 16)
- The Thief Who Loved Me (Book 17)

Dark Sins

- Don't Trust A Killer (Book 1)
- Don't Love A Liar (Book 2)

Lazarus Rising

- Never Let Go (Book One)
- Keep Me Close (Book Two)
- Stay With Me (Book Three)
- Run To Me (Book Four)
- Lie Close To Me (Book Five)
- Hold On Tight (Book Six)

Dark Obsession Series

- Watch Me (Book 1)
- Want Me (Book 2)

- Need Me (Book 3)
- Beware Of Me (Book 4)
- Only For Me (Books 1 to 4)

Mine Series

- Mine To Take (Book 1)
- Mine To Keep (Book 2)
- Mine To Hold (Book 3)
- Mine To Crave (Book 4)
- Mine To Have (Book 5)
- Mine To Protect (Book 6)
- Mine Box Set Volume 1 (Books 1-3)
- Mine Box Set Volume 2 (Books 4-6)

Bad Things

- The Devil In Disguise (Book 1)
- On The Prowl (Book 2)
- Undead Or Alive (Book 3)
- Broken Angel (Book 4)
- Heart Of Stone (Book 5)
- Tempted By Fate (Book 6)
- Wicked And Wild (Book 7)
- Saint Or Sinner (Book 8)
- Bad Things Volume One (Books 1 to 3)
- Bad Things Volume Two (Books 4 to 6)
- Bad Things Deluxe Box Set (Books 1 to 6)

Bite Series

- Forbidden Bite (Bite Book 1)
- Mating Bite (Bite Book 2)

Blood and Moonlight Series

- Bite The Dust (Book 1)

- Better Off Undead (Book 2)
- Bitter Blood (Book 3)
- Blood and Moonlight (The Complete Series)

Purgatory Series

- The Wolf Within (Book 1)
- Marked By The Vampire (Book 2)
- Charming The Beast (Book 3)
- Deal with the Devil (Book 4)
- The Beasts Inside (Books 1 to 4)

Bound Series

- Bound By Blood (Book 1)
- Bound In Darkness (Book 2)
- Bound In Sin (Book 3)
- Bound By The Night (Book 4)
- Bound in Death (Book 5)
- Forever Bound (Books 1 to 4)

Stand-Alone Romantic Suspense

- It's A Wonderful Werewolf
- Never Cry Werewolf
- Immortal Danger
- Deck The Halls
- Come Back To Me
- Put A Spell On Me
- Never Gonna Happen
- One Hot Holiday
- Slay All Day
- Midnight Bite
- Secret Admirer
- Christmas With A Spy
- Femme Fatale

- Until Death
- Sinful Secrets
- First Taste of Darkness
- A Vampire's Christmas Carol